30/5/14

21 JUN '14
19 JUL '14
16 AUG '14
15/10/16

X ALT

D0513780

C015677169

FULL CIRCLE

Further Titles by Connie Monk

* *available from Severn House*

FULL CIRCLE

Connie Monk

This first world edition published 2013
in Great Britain and 2014 in the USA by
SEVERN HOUSE PUBLISHERS LTD of
19 Cedar Road, Sutton, Surrey, England, SM2 5DA.

British Library Cataloguing in Publication Data

Monk, Connie
  Full circle : love and friendship in the 1950's.
  1. Women accountants–Fiction. 2. Female friendship–
  Fiction. 3. Triangles (Interpersonal relations)–Fiction.
  I. Title
  823.9´14-dc23

ISBN-13: 978-0-7278-8345-2 (cased)

All Severn House titles are printed on acid-free paper.

Severn House Publishers support the Forest Stewardship Council™ [FSC™],
the leading international forest certification organisation. All our titles that
are printed on FSC certified paper carry the FSC logo.

Typeset by Palimpsest Book Production Ltd.,
Falkirk, Stirlingshire, Scotland.
Printed and bound in Great Britain by
TJ International, Padstow, Cornwall.

One

Whatever Louisa had expected when she read the letter from the firm of solicitors regarding the death of her aunt Violet Harding, it certainly hadn't been this. 'All that I possess I leave to my niece, Louisa Ann Harding.'

'But I didn't even know her.' She spoke her thoughts aloud. 'I only met her once and that was years ago, before I even started school. Are you sure she didn't make a more up-to-date will?'

'Perfectly certain. I didn't know your aunt personally – she usually dealt with Mr Hayward, our senior partner – but, unfortunately, he is indisposed. Of course, there will be things to attend to before her affairs are finalized and you are in possession. There is the house in Lexleigh—'

'House? You mean the landlord will hold me to giving notice? Surely her death must automatically terminate any agreement.' Louisa took it for granted that her spinster aunt must have lived in rented property, for what sort of work could she have done to earn her the money for anything else?

'There is no landlord. We hold the deeds of the property here and have done since she became the owner in nineteen thirty-one, twenty-six years ago. See, I have all the papers relating to Miss Harding here.'

'Do you know how she died? Was she ill a long time?' Then, speaking out of character but knowing it was the only way to make him understand, 'You see, she was estranged from my father – her brother. They'd had nothing to do with each other for years.'

'Ah, I see. So you aren't aware of the accident. Miss Harding was returning from a trip to London when she was knocked down by a fast travelling car. Her death was instantaneous, I believe. The young driver is in trouble.'

'Was she alone or was anyone else hurt?'

'Quite alone. She lived alone too, so I understand.'

'How dreadful that she had no one to leave her things to except a niece who was only four when she last saw her. I can't even remember her clearly.'

Earlier in the week the letter from Hayward, Knight and Gibbins had arrived, having been sent to the one-time family home in Reading and re-directed to her parents' new address in north Cornwall before being put in a second envelope and posted on to her. She hadn't thought then of her aunt's brief visit so many years ago. Now, sitting in this dreary office facing the junior solicitor, she remembered the few hours of a sunny afternoon in June, 1931. She seemed to hear the echo of raised voices as she approached the house from the garden where she had been playing and clearly remembered the tight, knotted feeling in her tummy as she heard the unusual sound of her father's voice raised in anger. Her parents had never quarrelled; in fact, neither had they ever actually laughed aloud, but to the four-year-old she had been at that time they had represented calm and stability. The appearance of this uninvited visitor, however, made strangers of them.

As she had turned from the closed door, meaning to retreat to her secret hiding place in the garden, her father had come out, slamming the door behind him and seeming not to see her as he'd brushed past her on his way back to work. Then the door had opened again and her mother had called her.

'Come here, Louisa. This is your father's sister, your aunt Violet. She has an hour or two to wait until she goes for her train and I shall be out this afternoon. You will have to look after her. Now I'm going up to get ready so I'll say goodbye, Violet.'

'And you won't wish me well?'

'I wish you what you deserve.'

'You and Victor are happy; surely you can understand?'

All these years later Louisa remembered the cold expression on her mother's face as she answered, 'You ask me to condone your wickedness? Yes, Victor and I are happy; we are also decently joined in wedlock. You are no sister of his if you continue on the road you are making for yourself.' And with that she had turned away and started up the stairs to get ready to go out.

Not understanding her mother's crossly spoken words, Louisa had felt ashamed. How could they treat this lady so rudely? If *she* had behaved like that to a visitor she would have been sent to her room in disgrace. So she had smiled at this new-found aunt and held out her hand to draw her into the garden.

As the afternoon progressed she had wondered again and again how her parents could have been so nasty to someone who was such fun. They had played wheelbarrows, and when she had demonstrated how she could turn somersaults her aunt had done just the same. That she was a proper grown-up lady was hard to believe, especially when she had performed a perfect cartwheel displaying the prettiest, laciest knickers Louisa had ever seen.

Yet despite being sure she would never forget those few hours of fun, as time went by the memory had receded further into the back of her mind. Only when the letter had come from the firm of solicitors had she realized how many years it had been since she'd spared a thought to the woman whose name was never mentioned in her parents' home.

'I take it you don't know Lexleigh?' the solicitor was saying. 'It's a small village some fifteen or so miles from Gloucester. There is a railway halt and as you come through the gate from the platform turn left. You'll see the village street. Walk straight on and you'll come to the house – a walk of less than half a mile. The Retreat; it's on the right-hand side of the road facing a short terrace of cottages.'

'I shan't keep the house. My work is in Reading, so of course I shall put it on the market. But I must go and see what's involved. I don't know the district at all – can you advise me on an estate agent and, I suppose, house clearance people?'

She might have been surprised if she could have read his mind, for it was seldom his work brought him a client so attractive. Louisa Harding was a good-looking woman, her tailored skirt and jacket classical, her make-up immaculate, her hair well cut in the fashionable pageboy bob. Little did he guess that her faultlessly groomed appearance was a ploy to cover up her lack of confidence. The only child of parents who had been in their forties when they had married and with pregnancy no part of their plans for the future, she had definitely been a 'mistake'. Nevertheless, her upbringing had been kind, if cheerless, with rules not made to be broken. At school she had been looked on as something of an oddity: clever and hard-working, but withdrawn. Only one of her classmates had broken through her barrier of reserve and that had been Jessica Wilmott, who had lived with her grandparents. Jessica had known without being told that Louisa could never invite a playmate to the house – she had known it because her own circumstances had been the same. And as they'd progressed to senior school and their peers talked and giggled about crushes on film stars, their lives had been very different. Saturdays had been spent on their bicycles with a packet of sandwiches and two coppers for a bottle of lemonade while they made plans for their future. Childish dreams carried them to far-flung places and, indeed, as the years had passed Jessica had carved a life away from Reading. Both girls had been hard-working and ambitious, and had gained their school certificates. At that point Louisa's father had insisted she should leave school and find work locally, whereas Jessica had been allowed to stay on and matriculate so that she could go to university. A degree had led her to a teaching post, but those early plans couldn't be forgotten. It was five years since she had made the decision of a lifetime and emigrated. In Australia she was living the adventure she had dreamed of. But the friendship remained just as important with half a world between them as it had been when they'd cycled the lanes of Berkshire.

Now, as the young solicitor wrote down the names of two estate agents and a house clearance firm, Louisa's thoughts took a journey of their own. This evening, as soon as she got home to Reading, she would write to Jessica and tell her the news; in her mind the sentences were already forming.

'I believe you'll get all the help you need from these people.' The words cut across her straying thoughts. 'If I give you the key to The Retreat perhaps you'll put it in the post to me when you get back to Reading or, better still, I'll put my name on a label and tie it on and you can put it through the letterbox here if you have time on your way to the station.'

'You've been very helpful. I'll go and have a look at the house and whoever I decide to contact I'll let you know.'

'I'll look forward to hearing from you. I'm confident you'll have no trouble in selling the property.'

And so they parted. Dennis Huntley watched from his window as, on her ridiculously high heels, she walked effortlessly and fast in the direction of the railway station. Once away from the building she forgot the man who had given her such life-changing news. 'All I possess I leave to my niece, Louisa Ann Harding.' All Violet Harding had possessed wasn't a mortgage, wasn't an overdraft; it was a house, a motorcar and a surprising amount of money in the bank. But how? Surely if she'd done anything really outstanding, even though the family had fallen out with her, someone would have been interested enough to mention it.

Louisa was the only person to alight at Lexleigh Halt. The train hissed and puffed as though it objected to being slowed to a shuddering standstill in a cloud of steam. The moment she slammed the door closed it started forward again, leaving her alone on the platform. There had been something unreal about the whole day, but it was in those first seconds since arriving in Lexleigh that her change in circumstances came home to her. Instinctively she straightened her already straight shoulders, raised her chin, breathed the lingering sooty smell from the departing train in deeply and felt an unfamiliar sense of release. But release from what? She'd been a free agent for years, leaving home with no objection from her parents as soon as she'd earned enough to pay for a bedsit near where she worked. From there she had moved to a comfortable flat in a converted house in a good residential road. Here she was, a qualified accountant, thirty years of age and capable of earning a comfortable living, so where was the logic in this sudden excitement? The house would probably be a country cottage with no facilities, and the car years old and something she would have to pay to have removed. Aunt Violet was her father's younger sister by almost ten years and he was seventy-five years old. But that could never have been a forty-year-old woman who had turned cartwheels on the lawn.

Her thoughts moving on those lines, she left the railway halt and started along the road, passing one or two cottages (yes, that would be the sort of place she had inherited) and then a few shops. It couldn't be much further, so she crossed to the right-hand side of the road ready to look for the name on a gate. She could see a terrace of cottages on the left side but on the right was only one solid, detached building backing on to farmland. It must be further on than that.

But as she came level with the gate she saw on it the words 'The Retreat'.

Any stranger watching her might have assumed she knew exactly where she was going, as she seemed to look neither right nor left as she opened the gate. But in fact she had noticed the movement of the curtains in the middle cottage opposite and knew her arrival was causing interest as she took the key out of her handbag and walked to the front door. She would have liked to have stood outside and looked at the house, but her natural show of assurance wouldn't allow her to let anyone see her hesitate. So, just as if this was what she did every day of the week, she opened the front door and went inside.

It was already nearly four o'clock and at the end of March the days were short. Louisa stood in the hallway just inside the front door of the house that was hers, surprising herself that she desperately wanted to bring alive her memories of her aunt. But how could she when she was so far removed from the young child who had believed she would never forget the magic of the few hours they had been together? It was all so long ago that it was like looking at a life unconnected with the woman she had become. When had the will been written? Surely years ago; nothing had changed in Violet's life in recent times, as far as she was aware. But how sad; how could such a vibrant woman have had no one closer than a niece she'd seen only once, more than a quarter of a century ago?

From room to room she went, increasingly surprised by what she saw. The sitting room was well furnished and comfortable, the kitchen obviously refurbished much more recently than the house had been built. Upstairs the bathroom told the same story. Perhaps Aunt Violet had won money on the football pools, for this house had been brought up to date with small regard to cost. Two of the three bedrooms weren't fully furnished, but there was nothing inferior about the rugs or curtains. On opening a wardrobe Louisa found clothes that jogged her memory as she recalled those pretty knickers that had been given an airing as her aunt had turned her cartwheels. She wished she could remember her better, but all she knew was that she had been like someone out of a book, not quite real and different from all her mother's friends. And the garments hanging in the wardrobe weren't for a woman of her mother's age; indeed, they were what she would wear herself. All that I possess I leave to my niece, Louisa Ann Harding. Could she really have been in her sixties?

The third bedroom looked out across the fields at the back of the house and here the bed was made up. This is where Violet must have slept the night before she was killed. Louisa sat on the edge of the bed and found herself taking the night-dress from its case, as if that would give her a clue to the woman who must have hung on to the memory of that magic afternoon. It was chiffon – delicate black chiffon with the lingering aroma of perfume. An inner voice warned her that she must watch the time; she was only here to inspect the state of the house and meant to catch the train back to the main line in Gloucester at quarter past six. Yes, this was a good room; she forced herself to see it as it might impress a perspective purchaser. It would fall to her to arrange for the furniture to be taken to an auction house so she must get some idea of what would be involved. Without a backward glance she left the bedroom and went back down the stairs. Allowing herself no time for daydreaming, it was Miss Louisa Harding, chartered accountant, who glanced around the 'lived-in' kitchen, the small workroom furnished with a table, three chairs, a bookcase and a treadle sewing machine. Violet must have had a well-paid job for her to maintain a house like this. If only it weren't so far from Reading it would make a lovely retreat for weekends . . . The first stab of temptation. But, always sensible and practical, she trod it down. How still it was here, still and silent; the very atmosphere gave her a feeling of unreality. Then something happened, something she couldn't explain even to herself. It was as if, just for a moment, she felt Violet's presence close to her. Still there was no clear picture of her, but she was conscious just as she had been on that long ago afternoon of what at four years old she had thought of as magic. What she wasn't prepared for was a strange sensation that in this one-eyed village, as she thought of it, she could break free. But that was nonsense; she hadn't worked all these years to be pulled off track by the sentimental memories of a four-year-old. Think of the salary she earned; think of the security of being qualified to do the job she had chosen. Why had she chosen it? No, that was a question she couldn't answer, for in truth she had drifted into it, having taken a job as a junior clerk in a firm of accountants where it hadn't been in her nature to remain at everyone's beck and call, making the tea and coffee, running errands, stamping the mail and taking it to the post office on the way home. She had been determined to climb the ladder. But where had it got her? Where could it ever get her? Was she to spend her life in that office with nothing better to see out of the window than a wall? Violet's happy laugh echoed down the years.

Soon she would have to start walking back to the station. Or ought she to stay here for the weekend, sleep in Violet's bed and while she was in Gloucester on Monday morning go to one of the estate agents the solicitor had recommended? Yes, that's what she would do. She would phone the office on Monday and explain, saying she would be back the next day. She could try to get the house clearance people to come on Monday afternoon, she decided, not anticipating any stumbling blocks. Just one day, that's all she needed. So instead of going into that relaxing sitting room to start making a list of the furniture to be sold, she turned back into the workroom, again drawn to the window. The long view, the expanse of winter-pale sky, the distant sound of a cow lowing and the croaking of rooks high in nearby elm trees made this a different world from the hubbub of town.

It was a moment that would stay with her through the years, whatever the outcome of her sudden decision, a decision that took her by surprise and left her absolutely certain that what she was about to do was right. She wished she could tell Violet.

But perhaps she knew; perhaps she had planned it when she wrote her will.

Hunting in the bureau, Louisa found a writing pad and envelopes then, drawing a chair to the table, she took her fountain pen from her bag and started to write.

With the envelope sealed and addressed, she took a book of stamps from her handbag and with habitual meticulous precision attached one to the top right-hand corner. There! It was done! The voice of conscience whispered that she was crazy. Her working environment was depressingly dull but it was safe and her future secure month after month, year after year.

She started to laugh, 'Aunt Violet,' the words tumbling out and mingling with laughter, 'next thing you'll have me turning cartwheels. And why not? Just look at it out there, the big clear winter sky, the stillness, no Saturday afternoon shoppers pushing along the crowded pavement in Broad Street looking as though they carried the cares of the world.' She stopped speaking her thoughts aloud, but they still filled her mind. She'd show this male-dominated business world that she could work independently. For surely at the back of her discontent was the certainty that for her there would be no offer of a partnership in the firm, an established accountancy business where the partners named on the letter-headed paper were all male. Her qualifications were as high as any but she was a woman in a man's world.

Perhaps so far out of town there wouldn't be an evening collection from the post box she had noticed as she walked through the village but, even if her letter had to sit there until the next day, Sunday, or even the whole weekend, her decision was made, and never in her life had she experienced such a feeling of freedom. Was that the message Aunt Violet was sending her with her legacy?

Locking the front door behind her and standing back to survey the house, she saw it in a new light from when she'd arrived not much more than an hour before. In her contract she had to give three months' notice so it would be late June before she could move. But there would be weekends; for now that this was where life was taking her it would be worth spending Saturday afternoon travelling here and Sunday evening returning. Three months in which to set the course for her future. After the end of June there would be no monthly salary cheque but she had always been prudent and over the last five years had managed to save. Add to that the money she was inheriting and she ought to be able to live and pay her household expenses as she built up a clientele. She saw no problems and if, somewhere deep in her mind, was the acceptance that her decision was foolhardy, she chose to ignore the warning voice. The Louisa Harding who had lived such a narrow, dull life and worked so hard for her qualifications would never leap before she looked. And that was what made what she intended to do all the more exciting and challenging. Her parents would never understand; in fact, that her plan had come about because she was moving into Violet's home would make them prophesy doom. She chuckled, remembering her aunt. In truth, she couldn't imagine her face; the memory of her went no further than what she was wearing – clothes so different from those of the women she was used to seeing. What was clear was more important than appearance: it was the spirit that told of a joy in living. And she would find that same joy; in fact, as she'd walked through the house she had felt it building in her even before she understood the message it was conveying.

So deep in her own thoughts was she that she opened the gate and stepped on to the narrow pavement hardly aware of what she did. The young girl walking past tried to avoid the collision but it was too late.

'I'm so sorry.' Louisa put out a hand to steady her as she almost lost her balance. 'I was miles away. I didn't hurt you, did I?' What an enchantingly lovely girl she was, with her honey-brown hair framing a face of perfect symmetry. When she replied with a smile that lit her wide, dark blue eyes, a dimple appeared in each cheek.

'No, I'm OK. I saw you earlier on when my husband and I were driving up to the farm. You were just opening the front door to go in. Are you from an estate agent or are you thinking of buying the house? I do hope you are. It would be so much nicer for Dad to have someone there, someone young and cheerful.'

'Your father? Is he a neighbour?'

'My husband's father, Mr Carter. He owns Ridgeway Farm. They grow fruit and veg, not cows and things. The house you've just come from used to belong to it – one of the managers lived there, I think. But Dad got rid of it and the land that goes with it.'

'Did you know the lady he sold it to?'

'No, only that Leo said it was a woman on her own. It's Dad I worry about because Leo and I live miles away. I love it here; perhaps that's because it was where Leo was brought up. It's one of those places where everyone knows everyone. Do you come from Gloucester, or are you from an estate agent nearer?'

They were both going in the same direction so they had automatically started to walk together.

'No, I'm from Reading, but I've decided to move here. It'll be a while before I can actually move in, and anyway, I have to give three months' notice at work. This is it, this is my notice.' She waved the envelope in front of them. 'Decision made. I'm not giving myself the chance to have second thoughts.' It surprised her to find herself talking so freely to the pretty stranger; it must be something to do with her new-found freedom.

'That's wonderful. When you meet Dad you'll love him. It's so sad for him now that he's alone. Leo's mum died quite suddenly very soon after we were married and they'd been together for ages. Leo is thirty-eight and his elder brother David is nearly forty so that shows you what a long time. When we arrived this afternoon Dad was so near to crying that he could hardly talk. I wish we were nearer but Leo works in the family business in Birmingham and it's too far from here. We can't keep coming every weekend when I get huge. I'm having a baby, you see. Do I show? Could you tell?' She asked the question hopefully. What a child she seemed. Looking at her, Louisa would be amazed if she had yet reached twenty. It was hard to imagine she had a husband not far off forty. Then, leaping from one thing to the next, the girl chattered on: 'You don't wear a ring; I noticed when you came charging out of the gate, but you're older than I am and must have had lots of experience. And it's so good to have a woman to talk to. There was no one of my age in the boring office where I worked before I was married.'

What had happened to reserved, conventional Louisa? Perhaps her confidence had been given a jolt by her companion's remark, giving her credit for having experience. For the truth was that at thirty years old she had never even had a boyfriend. Walking at the younger girl's side, her five-foot-six-inch body made taller by the four-inch heels of her russet-coloured court shoes so right with her scarf and leather handbag, she was unaware of the elegant image she created. There was nothing new in the way she wore her tailored clothes, and partly it was her classically austere attire combined with her solitary lifestyle that had frightened off many when she'd been younger. Now, at thirty, even her work colleagues looked on her as frigid and prim. A clever, humourless woman destined for spinsterhood was their unspoken opinion – with a rider that it was a good body wasted.

Her young companion's easy chatter was a new experience. In ordinary circumstances she would have had no time for someone who gave an initial impression of being empty-headed and naïve. But today's circumstances were anything but ordinary.

'If you live so far away I suppose you haven't any friends here?' Louisa tried to sound more interested than she really was, for in truth it was as if she stood outside herself, heard herself speak, but her heart and mind weren't quite with her.

'No, but usually I'm with Leo and soon there'll be the baby. I've left him to talk to his dad now. I thought Dad would like to have him to himself, and anyway I needed some exercise – we'd been in the car for what seemed like hours. I don't really care for car journeys, although Leo is an excellent driver,' she added in case her new friend got the wrong impression. 'Now tell me about you. Do you work – well, you must do, I suppose, if you're not married? And these days lots of married women work anyway. With a baby coming, of course, I don't. But I'm lucky: Leo is in the family business with David, and I suppose it's because of being older that David likes to think he's King of the Castle. Not that Leo cares too much. He's an engineer, and lots of the things they make for use on the farm are his design. Sometimes he decides not to go in to the works – Leo, I mean, not his brother. David gets very boot-faced, but that's not fair because Leo always does a lot of work when he stays at home. What he would really like is to be using the implements he designs. But, you know, I think to David they are just a means to make money; he has his eye on the running of the factory – profits and losses are his interest – and I don't think he would notice if they made bicycles instead of farm stuff. They're not a bit alike, Leo and David. And, do you know, although they're brothers and both in the business, I'm sure they don't even like each other much. And I just *know* that David and Lily, his wife, think that when Leo married me he stooped and picked up nothing.'

'It's what Leo thinks that matters,' Louisa said, feeling an unexpected stab of sympathy for her outspoken young companion.

'Yes, of course,' Bella answered, her confidence back in place. 'And right from the start I could tell that his parents liked me. It was so sad, his mum dying like that. David can't be *all* bad, I suppose; he was really cut up at her funeral. Leo said they'd always been very close, Mum and David. Leo and Dad are good pals, although since Mum died I can tell that Leo can't get as close to him. Poor Dad, it's as if there's a wall of misery holding everyone away.'

'If your husband would rather be using the machines he designs, doesn't he consider coming to work on the farm here?' Louisa instilled more interest into her voice than she felt. The truth was that, from what she had heard of the two brothers so far, she had a natural sympathy with David rather than Leo. What was the matter with the man? It sounded to her as if he was using the family business for an easy ride.

Bella chuckled as she answered. 'I expect Leo and David are more alike than they seem: if he came home to the farm he and Dad would both want to be King of the Castle. They are ever so fond of each other – not that Leo ever says so, but you can always tell, can't you? He's been away from home for far too long to go back to not having his own place. He couldn't be a farmer's boy to his father. He got a degree in engineering and then there was his time in the army during the war, although he wouldn't have been called up on account of growing food being so vital during the war. I expect what he ought to have done was to strike out on his own when he was demobbed, but somehow he went into the family business.'

'Farmers have a pretty tough life and, from what one hears, there isn't any great wealth to be made from a small farm.'

'All one needs – don't you think? – is to make enough to live on. Leo knows much more about the things they actually *make* than David does – or Dad either – but on paper Dad is top of the tree although, except for the Annual General Meeting, he only comes up to the factory once in a while and doesn't actually *do* anything, so Leo says. Have you ever heard of Carters? In the farming world they are quite a big name. They make farm implements, things like muck spreaders, potato diggers, cultivators, mowers – that sort of thing, not huge machines. I'm getting to know quite a lot – I feel I ought to as it's a family business. Dad went into it just like his own father, but in the beginning the things they made were much simpler; farming must have been achingly hard work. But I was about to tell you how Dad came to work away from the family business: he married Leo's mum and stayed here on the farm. It had been in her family for simply years. But, like I said, he is officially the chairman of Carters' now that he's head of the clan. He's not really keen on the business side of it, though, not like David is.' Then, with a chuckle, 'Dad and Leo are so alike. They both believe that life is for enjoying. That's what Leo says.' And if that's what the perfect Leo says, then it must be right, her tone implied.

By Louisa's standards he became less appealing by the minute, but her expression gave away none of her thoughts.

They had reached the post box. 'Oh, good,' Louisa said as she dropped her letter in, 'there's a Saturday collection at five o'clock. They'll get that on Monday morning. I am taking a day's leave and I have things to organize in Gloucester.'

'What do you do?' Bella seemed genuinely interested. 'Are

you a shorthand typist? No, I bet you're someone's personal secretary.'

'I'm an accountant. I check figures for annual audit.'

'Goodness!' Clearly her young friend was impressed. 'It sounds awfully important. I thought those sort of jobs were for men. You must have taken exams and all that. Goodness.' Then, on a brighter and more confident note, 'But it still keeps you cooped up. So you're going to give it all up and be free.'

'Yes and no. I'm going to leave the firm I've always worked for. I shall still do the same work once I can get established here working for myself. It's not really dull work – it's challenging.'

'But the people in the village are quite ordinary; they wouldn't have enough money to need someone to check their figures. Are you sure you're doing the right thing giving up your job? Maybe the place has thrown fairy dust in your eyes. But that won't pay the bills.'

Louisa looked at her afresh: a lovely girl, with the innocent candour that made her vulnerable, yes, but also with an unexpected streak of common sense.

'I think fairy dust was what I needed. But right now what I need is some shopping. Can you wait while I go into that shop opposite? There's nothing in the house; I must buy enough for the weekend.'

'Are you allowed to do that? You've only been to look at it.'

'It'll be mine when all the paperwork is done. I promise you, no one is going to prevent me sleeping there. By the time I've worked my notice I shall be in honest possession.'

Soon they turned back towards home, saying very little as they walked. But the silence was easy. Two women, poles apart in lifestyle and ambition but, on that late afternoon, content to accept the difference and perhaps each draw something from the other. Still, Louisa told herself, we're hardly likely to see each other very often, if at all. At the gate of The Retreat they parted company and it was only as Louisa went back into the house that she realized that neither of them had enquired the other's name. Already her thoughts were running ahead of her; she was imagining herself becoming established in her profession, the little workroom becoming her office with its window facing the large empty space of field-like garden.

'I've had a lovely time,' Bella told Leo when she got back to the farm and found him with the bonnet of the car open, checking the water in the radiator. 'Did you know, Leo, that the house at the end of the lane is sold? Well, it's as good as sold. A nice woman is moving in. We walked to the village together.' There was a ring of pride in her voice as she went on, 'She was on her way to post a letter quitting her job. She said she was taking some holiday and had things to arrange in Gloucester. But guess what she does for a living – no, you'll never guess. She is an accountant, something to do with auditing; properly qualified – exams and all that. A woman! Have you ever heard of that before? By the time she's worked her notice the house will be properly hers.'

'Damn it,' Leo said, screwing on the radiator cap. 'Where is she staying, Bella? In the village somewhere?'

'No, at the house. Just for the weekend, or maybe just tonight, I'm not sure.'

'But she has no business to stay at the house until there's completion on the sale.'

'She's a very smart sort of person; she won't make a mess or hurt anything, I'm sure. Just think how good it'll be for Dad to have someone nice close by. Where is he? I must go and tell him the good news.'

'No, don't do that. I've been trying to persuade him he ought to buy the house back and get a manager here. As it is, even with the two chaps who work here, he is always tied to the place. A break away might cheer him up. Leave it with me, Bella. He doesn't seem against the idea so I'll try and persuade him to talk to the agent who's dealing with the sale. If this woman has already put down a deposit it might be possible to pay her out. He can't be tied here by himself in the house, not in his depressed state, and it would be good for him to have a manager living there again.'

She could see the logic in having a manager once again, but it was such a shame when she had got on so well with the nice woman she'd met. But if that's what Leo wanted then she wouldn't say anything to his father. Watching him checking the engine, she thought, as she had a thousand times, how much she loved him, and she sent up a silent thank you for the way her life had worked out. Thinking back to her birthday on New Year's Eve – such a perfect evening, dinner at the sort of hotel she'd never been to before, wine, champagne . . . perhaps she'd even been a little bit tiddly but she had been walking on air when he'd taken her back to his flat. Together they'd stood at the open window and let in the year that was to see her life change. When he'd kissed her she'd felt weak with love and longing. And in the first hour of 1957 she had become truly his.

Her hero had been proved not to have feet of clay, for three weeks later when she had told him she was worried because she was a week late he'd wasted no time in getting a licence so that they could be married immediately. No three weeks to wait while the banns were read, simply a visit to the local registry office where an office clerk and a cleaner came in to act as witnesses. Any dreams she had had of a white wedding melted, but no bride could have been happier or more proud. The following day they had driven to Lexleigh and he had introduced her to his parents. Such darlings, both of them; so lovely, in fact, that she had forgotten what Leo had said about not saying anything straight away about the baby and before she could stop herself she had told them everything. Dear Mum, she had been so excited. How dreadfully sad it was that she wouldn't be there to be a granny.

Louisa had arrived at the house seeing it through the eyes of someone sizing it up for sale. But she looked at her surroundings differently now. This would be her home, her very own home. It wasn't something rented, it was *hers*. If she wanted to paint the ceilings midnight blue dotted with golden stars no one could prevent her doing so – not that she did want to.

Now that her letter of resignation was in the post she set about waking her home from its slumbers. She found the mains water tap under the sink in the kitchen and turned it on; next came the electricity, and by the end of the afternoon in the dusk of March she'd flooded the place with light. But even on a day of such importance she was ever practical and, having gone from room to room switching on the lights, she made a second trip upstairs to turn them off. One thing lacking was warmth, but at any rate in the sitting room that was soon rectified by the electric fire standing in the grate, attempting to give the impression it was heated by burning coal. With the immersion heater preparing the water for a bath, she unpacked her shopping and made herself an uninspiring meal of tinned soup followed by scrambled eggs on toast.

By that time the last of daylight had gone and when she went to close the curtains, the new moon was riding high. She switched out the light to better see the sky. She was a practical woman who'd never let herself waste time daydreaming, but gazing out across the overgrown garden to the farmland beyond, raising her glance to the crescent moon and the first hint of a few stars in the darkening sky, she felt that this must surely be an omen.

Later, she stepped into the steaming bath, the room filled with the perfume of Violet's expensive bath salts – something Louisa never used at home, but they expressed as clearly as anything the step she was taking from her old life to her new. Another thing completely out of character was for her to lie in the bath while the water cooled and the steam condensed and trickled down the tiled walls. She wouldn't do it again, she told herself. After she let the water away she would open the window wide, but just for the moment she was enveloped in luxury that had never been part of her life.

Next, wrapped in a bathrobe which she found hanging on the back of the door, she went into Violet's bedroom and with no feeling of guilt opened the drawers, telling herself there must be warm pyjamas in there somewhere. But there were no such things. Never had she handled such exquisite under-wear: French knickers, cami-knickers, bras, slips, dozens of pairs of silk or nylon stockings, some a shade Louisa thought of as natural, but some black just as some of the suspender belts and bras were black. It was all a mystery to Louisa, who had always dressed as smartly as finances allowed, but never possessed garments like the ones she was discovering as she went from drawer to drawer. This was the first night of the rest of her life and it should be celebrated by wearing something utterly different from anything she had bought herself. '*All* that I possess I leave to my niece, Louisa Ann Harding.' The words echoed, adding to the feeling of unreality. On a hook on the back of the bedroom door was a black silk negligee, so she selected a black nightgown of silk so fine that as she dropped it over her head the material seemed to caress her skin. It was a shame to cover it with the negligee, but the chill of the evening demanded it and, anyway, she thought as she slipped her arms into the sleeves and tied the sash around her slim waist, it had been *hers*, *she* must have worn it and now it's mine. Perhaps Violet had been a model, or an actress. But even if she'd been born an afterthought in the family she could no longer have been young. Whatever high-salaried work she had had, surely when she got home she would have wanted something casual and comfortable. I wish I'd known you, Violet; not just as a memory through the eyes of a small child, but known you and talked to you – laughed with you like we did that afternoon.

It was evident that comfort had been a priority in the house, for even in the sitting room with its mock coals, as in each room in the house, there was an electric radiator. So before Louisa went downstairs she turned on the one in the bedroom, imagining the comfort Violet must have been used to. Often enough, Louisa spent her Saturday evenings in front of the electric fire in her apartment in Reading, sometimes watching her newly acquired television but more often reading. So what would she do with the rest of this evening? There was plenty of reading material in the bookcase, but her mind was much too active to want to lose herself in a world of fiction. With a slight feeling of guilt she opened the bureau. It seemed wrong to be looking through her aunt's personal papers, as if she were prying into her secret life. Ought she to take the bank statements to the solicitor? Would he need them for probate? This was her first experience of dealing with death. Glancing at the figures she was amazed, but more than amazed she was puzzled. Her own salary was good and she had a professional qualification, but her own account never showed figures like these. With the reading lamp shining down on the open bureau she drew up a chair and was about to immerse herself in what she was discovering when she heard something that brought her to her feet, seemingly frozen to the spot.

Someone had opened the front door. Her usually sensible mind flew in all directions. Could it be the police? She had no right to be here – the house wasn't hers until the solicitor had settled Violet's affairs. No, don't panic, the police wouldn't have a key; it must be someone from one of the cottages across the lane, someone who kept an eye on the place if it was left empty. Louisa forced herself to stand very straight as the sitting-room door was thrown open and at the same time, before he'd even entered the room, the intruder yelled, 'What in Christ's name do you think you're doing? Close that bur—' The sentence hung in the air, half finished. 'Oh, God! Vi.' In a hushed tone full of fear, 'Vi.'

Instinctively Louisa pulled herself very straight, holding his gaze defiantly. 'I might ask you the same question. Who are you and how is it you have a key to the house?' Her tone was frigid, yet even as she spoke she believed she knew the answer. There was something in the slump of his shoulders and the way his hand shook as he pushed his fingers through his iron-grey hair that hinted to her that he had been closer to her aunt than a mere neighbour. 'You must surely know that my aunt isn't here. There was an accident—'

'Your aunt? You're Louisa? Looking at you I can see *her*, a lifetime ago. Of course I had a key.' He met her gaze, and seemed to be weighing up the situation. 'No word from any of her family for more than a quarter of a century, and now I suppose you're one of the vultures.'

'Of course I'm not. If you and Aunt Violet were friends, were close, she would be disgusted with such a remark. I know there was a family rift; what it was about I've no idea and I didn't want to know. I hadn't heard of her since I was four years old, not until I found I was her heir.'

'Louisa,' he said softly, lowering himself into an armchair by the hearth. 'She never forgot you. I remember when she came back from holding out an olive branch to your parents – dear God, how she cried.' He closed his eyes as if speaking about it had transported him back. 'But she told me about you; I remember her exact words. She said, "If only we could have had a child, that's what she would have been like. If only . . . if only." But we both knew that for us a life together was impossible. I had a wife and sons – a God-fearing, truly good woman and dear sons who needed a father. Why am I telling you all this?' He seemed to be looking right through her.

'Because no one has ever told me anything, and we owe it to her that I understand.' Louisa needed to hear more.

'Your parents – and the rest of her family – wouldn't try to understand. To them there could be no excuse for love except within marriage. It was marriage that was important, not love, not a meeting of spirits.'

'Go on,' she prompted softly, sitting on the arm of his chair.

'So we took what we could.' There was a long pause and when he spoke again he might have been speaking his thoughts aloud as he looked back through the years. 'I remember teaching her to ride. She was a natural. Natural, yes, that's what she was, in every way. She held nothing back. She cared not a jot for what people thought of her. The hours, the days we spent together were the only thing that mattered to me – to either of us. There's a family business the other side of Birmingham; I invented calls of duty taking me away for days at a time so that we could be together. She was living in Birmingham in the beginning. That's where we met. Day or night, we found joy in each other.' As he talked he lay back in the chair with his eyes closed. Emotion got the better of him; she saw his mouth quiver and his voice was tight as he went on. 'She was my life. From the first day we met, we knew that . . .' His battle was lost, his words died. Louisa found herself putting her arm around his shaking shoulders as he wept. For him the relief of releasing so much bottled-up misery was enormous. After a minute or two he became calmer and went on: 'Alice was a good woman.' (Alice? She must be his wife, Louisa concluded, but she didn't interrupt him to ask.) 'She could have kept the farm; it was hers more than mine. She was the worker, not me. I never gave a damn about it after I met Violet. She was all I wanted, all I could ever want. It was the same for her.'

For a moment or two neither spoke; the only sound in the

room was of his occasional muffled gulps as he gradually
regained control.

'But you kept faith with your marriage?' Louisa prompted
after a moment.

'Kept faith? When affection turns to resentment? Is that
keeping faith? I tried to believe Alice didn't know what had
happened, why it was that Violet moved into this house. She
used to come to the farm sometimes and I tried to pretend
everyone saw her as a family friend. Alice never accused me. I
thought she was too wrapped up in the farm to even notice.
I had that stable block built on the far side of the land here
and bought Tilda for her, a gentle creature. Alice made believe
she thought it was a good idea when I said I was bringing
Brutus down from the farm, said the space would be useful
for equipment that got left outside. I didn't care what they did
with the space; I didn't care about anything on the farm. I
taught Violet to ride, and it was her suggestion that Leo had
a pony.' Leo? Wasn't that what the pretty girl had called her
husband? So the farm her visitor talked about must be the one
the house backed on to. It all began to fall into place in Louisa's
mind. He was talking again: 'The three of us used to spend
hours riding together – as if we were a family. But of course
there was gossip. My comings and goings were noted by the
people in the cottages opposite. Word got around. That was
evident from the way the women cold-shouldered Violet. Yet
Alice said nothing. I believed – I made myself believe – that
she accepted her as a neighbour and friend. I was a fool, a
coward and a fool. I tried to give the impression Violet was
no more to me than any other woman. May God forgive me.
She didn't care about the gossip; she had the courage of a lion.'
Still he lay back in the chair with his eyes closed. Louisa felt
he'd forgotten she was there and was talking to himself. Another
silence, then: 'Now that she's gone, both of them gone, I can
see what I should have done. Perhaps not while the boys were
still too young to understand. I should have broken my vows
and taken her away, my blessed Violet. Married or not, we
would have been proud to be seen as living together. And
Alice? Would she have been any more hurt than she was? For
years she ran the home, she oversaw what crops were grown.

I let her get on with it. For all the use I was I might as well not have been there, and all the time she must have known I didn't love her. I loved Violet – and so I shall till the day I die. It killed Alice; it was what caused her death as surely as that fast car caused Violet's. That night when we heard about Violet's accident the whole lie we'd lived blew up in our faces. Nothing can ever wipe out the things we said; I had to hurt her, as if that would take away the hell of losing Violet. I came over here; all I wanted was to find something of Violet's spirit here where we had known real – *real* – joy. Hours later when I got home I found Alice dead on the bedroom floor. A stroke, that's what the doctor said. But the doctor hadn't been there to know what had gone before. All her venom was aimed at Violet, but it was me she should have hated.'

Watching him, Louisa knew he was haunted by the horror of his memories. She wasn't sure exactly what had happened on that fateful night, but she had no doubt the ghosts gave him no peace. An hour or so ago, she'd known nothing of his existence, except what the pretty girl had said that afternoon. But clearly the pretty girl knew only half the story.

He opened his tear-reddened eyes. 'There's drink in that cupboard,' he told her. 'Let me pour us something.'

Five minutes later they were sitting facing each other across the hearth, she with a cigarette and he puffing a pipe.

'You've done a lot for me this evening,' she said, speaking quietly as if she were simply voicing the thought that had just come to her. 'I wanted to remember her, to feel I knew her. There's no logic' – and this from Louisa, for whom logic had been her guiding star – 'it's as if the magic of those few hours when I was with her had been waiting to be nudged back to life. How could I have stopped remembering?'

Ignoring the question, or perhaps he hadn't been listening, he said, 'When you turned round from the bureau it was as if the years between hadn't happened. You are so like she was when we were both young.' Then, going back to what he had been saying earlier, 'It was she who persuaded me – begged me, in fact – not to leave Alice and the boys. She said it would come between us, that my conscience would plague me and that she couldn't bear the thought of me losing my sons. Was she right? I swear it would never have come between us, but it would have cast a cloud. That's why she came to live here. I'd been going up to the works as often as I could – not that I did anything useful there and neither was I interested. A few stolen days, perhaps once a month. We wanted more than that. So I gave her this house and she used to visit the farm. How sordid it sounds. But it wasn't, I swear it wasn't. What we found was something rare. After more than thirty years it was as complete, as *right* as it had been in the beginning.'

When he finally left to walk back to the farm he hesitated for a moment by the front door.

'If I've helped you remember her, you have helped me to find comfort in the memory. I came because I saw lights on here. I thought . . . Don't know what I thought. Then I met you and you have given me – peace? Acceptance? No, it's not that easy. But this evening I have come nearer to Violet than I've been able to over these last weeks. Seeing you here, so like her and in memory so dear to her – the child we could never have – has brought a kind of comfort.' Then in a more hopeful tone: 'I shan't listen to Leo and his suggestion that I get a manager and make my home with them. I shall stay at the farm. I've a couple of good men working there; the place doesn't need a manager. I don't do much, haven't for years. That pretty child is having a baby – no doubt she told you –' He said it affectionately and with the closest thing to a smile that Louisa had seen.

'She certainly did. A sweet girl.'

'Pure gold. But such a child.' The note of hope was lost. 'Alice was pure gold, although she never had the looks of beautiful Bella. But looks aren't the most important thing. Leo is so much older than her. He has a good brain but a restless spirit. It worries me. It's not goodness that holds a man, nor yet beauty; it's something that defies description.'

'She adores him.'

'No doubt about that. Please God he doesn't meet someone who is more than a pretty face and a sweet nature – that and the mother of his child.'

'You don't mean that. Would you have been happier had you not met Violet?'

'I can't imagine my life without her.'

After he'd gone Louisa went back to the electric fire and lit another cigarette. How far away her immaculately tidy, functional and characterless flat seemed. Already after just a few hours the spell that was Violet was reaching out to her. For three months she would be working in Reading, but there were weekends when she would be here. With that reassuringly in mind, she at last climbed the stairs, took off Violet's silk robe, looked at her unfamiliar reflection in the glamorous black nightdress and then climbed into Violet's bed.

But working five and a half days of every week she found a trip to Lexleigh each weekend wasn't possible. That's what she told herself, but the real reason was less straightforward. Leaving the firm where she had worked for fourteen years in one capacity or another, leaving the town that held all of her past, held no regrets. On the contrary, it was as if a door to freedom had been opened to her. And that's the way she wanted it to remain. When she next arrived in Lexleigh it must be to begin her new life, and for that she was prepared to wait until she could close the door on all that had made up her thirty years. She was like a chrysalis about to burst from its shell and become a butterfly.

Two

Harold saw that the light was still on in the sitting room when he got home. He was very fond of Bella, dear sweet child as he thought of her, but after the emotional evening he had spent in the house so full of memories of Violet he felt he couldn't face her chatter. So, closing the front door as loudly as he could to be sure to attract Leo and her to the fact he was home, he called out to them as he crossed the hall to the stairs.

'I've been meeting our new neighbour. I'll go on up to bed now. Sleep well, you two.'

'Oh, Dad, do come and chat. What did you think of her? Nice, isn't she? I met her when I went for a walk.' Bella opened the sitting-room door.

'She seemed very pleasant.' How pleased he was with his cheerful voice. 'I didn't know there was anyone there – you didn't say. I called there when I saw a light on – thought someone must have broken in. We had a nice evening. Now, my dear, I'm going to hit the hay.'

She crossed the unlit hall and raised her face to his. 'Now we know you're home OK we'll come up soon. Night night, Dad, God bless.' In the dark her kiss landed on his chin then, as he started up the stairs, she went back to Leo. 'There, silly, you said not to tell him. But it's done him a world of good to meet someone new. And she's really ever so nice. It's a pity she's not moving in straight away – she has to give three months' notice at work.'

'Lucky her. I wish I could say the same. By this time tomorrow we'll be back in that concrete jungle again. Coming here as often as I have these last few weeks makes me realize just how much I detest being stuck in that ruddy factory. How about living a gypsy life, carrying our home behind the car, moving where the spirit guides us, meeting new people?' It was a pipedream, not a serious question.

'Oh, Leo, you are funny,' she chuckled, 'a real old dreamer.

And anyway, real life is much better than dashing from pillar to post not knowing what you're looking for. We have a really comfy flat and soon we'll start collecting up the things we need for a baby.'

'I know. Lots of poor devils have little chance of getting their own homes. Oh, I know all that. Coming here, sniffing the country air instead of the hateful smoke of factory chimneys always unsettles me.' Little did she guess the effort it cost him to smile at her and ruffle her honey-brown wavy hair. 'The flat may be what you call cosy, but it's not going to be suitable for much longer.'

'I know. Can't you just imagine Mrs Pyke's face – you know, the haughty one from flat three – if we left a pram in the entrance hall,' she chuckled.

'Don't know why I bought the wretched place. No one there would know the meaning of the word "fun". We'll have to start looking.'

She nodded, wriggling closer to him as she sat on the arm of his chair. 'I don't mind where we live so long as I'm with you,' she said, sliding from her perch to lie back on his lap. 'Dad's gone on up, so shall we go to bed?'

'Now there's an invitation.'

'Leo Carter, I love you so much that sometimes I'm frightened. If I hadn't got you there'd be nothing.'

Raising his eyebrows in the quizzical way she adored, he moved his hand on the slight bump of which she was so proud. 'Nothing?' he teased, while, uninvited, the thought came to him of just how young she still was.

'I'm ready for us to go to bed, aren't you?' she whispered, nuzzling her face against his neck.

'Put like that, no man could resist.'

'It's my very favourite time, darling Leo, when we snuggle down together. Bed is the best place of all – with the door shut and the covers over us it's our own world. Don't you think that, when we cuddle down each night?'

'At this moment my thoughts aren't on cuddling down.'

He heard that familiar, contented chuckle and for a moment felt ashamed of his instinctive feeling of irritation. Surely he ought to be thankful that she was always willing when he wanted to make love; sweet, generous Bella was always there for him. And if a silent voice whispered to him that being there for him wasn't the same as understanding and sharing what drove him, he pushed the thought away and drew her closer. Utterly content, she had no inkling of the workings of his mind.

Once upstairs they got ready for bed but when she raised her nightgown to slip it over her head she found it taken out of her hands.

'You don't need that,' he told her, drawing her close.

'But we shall be cold.' Although that was what she said, leaning against him she could feel the warmth of his body as, still holding her close, he walked her backwards and gently pushed her down on the bed. 'It would be warmer under the covers.'

'No. I'll make you warm.'

She wanted to remind him that she was gazing straight up at the light and it wasn't nearly as romantic as when the light was out and there was nothing but themselves in their world. Darkness added a sense of mystery and, lying straight on top of the satin eiderdown, she couldn't relax. She was always thrilled to know he wanted to make love to her and she really did wish she could get as excited about it as he did. Sometimes, just when she was loving the feeling of his warm body on hers she closed her eyes and gave herself up to the strangest sensation that pushed everything else out of her mind, as if she reached a goal she's been straining towards. Usually, though, all she wanted was to know that she was the one who heightened her beloved Leo's passion and who held him close when he reached his climax.

'Let's turn the light off, Leo, darling. It's so much more romantic in the dark – and it's shining in my eyes.' She thought he was going to do as she said as he moved a little away from her, but instead he dropped to kneel on the floor, gently forcing her legs further apart as he rested his head on her and she felt the moist warmth of his mouth as his tongue caressed her. She wished he wouldn't. Why did he want to do that? She felt uncomfortable, as if he were intruding on something too personal to share. This wasn't making love. He'd never done this before and she did wish he'd stop so that they could settle into bed and do it properly. But perhaps this was part of being married. It wasn't that she didn't want them to know each other as if they were one person, really belonging – of course she did – but while he was down there on his knees she felt like a 'thing', not a person. Pushing herself on her elbows she sat up and then reached out so that she held his shoulders. Surely that would tell him she wanted him to come close.

'Come back. Let's love properly. Keep the light on if you want to. I'll shut my eyes.'

She might as well have dowsed him with cold water. Getting up, he turned his back and reached for the light switch, then crossed the dark room to draw back the curtains and open the window while she got into bed, satisfied now that she could look forward to what would come next. When he got in by her side and she wriggled close she was surprised and hurt to find that his earlier passion had faded. She had failed him.

'Leo, it was just that you were so far away down there on your knees and I was getting so cold.' She drew his hand to where a minute or so ago his mouth had been, pressing it tight against her as she moved her hips and arched her back. She knew that she had repaired the damage of her previous rejection. 'I want to feel us so close we are one person. Please love me, Leo, please.'

That night she had no desire to strive for any goal except to find her own reward in knowing that in her he had found his own fulfilment. A few minutes later as she settled comfortably for sleep she had no doubt that he did the same. But how could he when he knew there was something fundamentally important lacking? He was ashamed of the anger that filled him as he imagined the years ahead. He was ashamed of the thought that he had been a fool not to have been careful she didn't get pregnant. His memory took him back to the evening of her birthday when he had taken her out to dinner. She had been as excited as a child at her first party, but a combination of champagne and wine had led her to make obvious what he had already known: he was the centre of her universe. He'd enjoyed the admiring glances of other diners, for surely she was the loveliest creature he had ever seen, her figure agile, her wavy hair such an unusual honey-brown colour with a tinge of gold in the sunlight and her features delicately perfect. Fringed with abnormally long lashes her dark blue eyes had begged him to love her. It would have taken a man with a stronger will than his to listen to the inner voice reminding him that in experience she was a child, a love-struck child with the body of a woman. He had taken her back to his flat and together they had listened to the hooters sounding as the nearby church clock struck midnight. The start of a New Year: 1957. He had known she was slightly drunk, for sober she would have held on to her reserve. Instead, with blatant lack of finesse, she had wordlessly played the temptress and on that night – no doubt thanks to her alcohol-produced lack of inhibitions – she had held nothing back. But the occasion had never been repeated. Was that the real Bella? Or had that been simply the result of birthday excitement, dining in the best restaurant in town, drinking her first champagne? Was the devoted, gentle girl who would always be there for him, not as a duty but because her joy came from making him happy, all he was ever to know? He vowed he would never hurt her; she was as good as she was beautiful and she would be his lifelong companion. Truly he loved her, but not in the way he had supposed a man would feel for his wife. And the thought came to him, *Not as Dad had for Violet.* He didn't ask himself why he could think of what had been between his father and Violet without resentment; it had been something he had always accepted and understood, although it had been something no one mentioned. David had never liked her, he mused, looking back down the years, but he never went out with them or had any fun like I did. She was something special; I used to think so even when I was a kid. And Mum never seemed bothered. Poor old Mum, she never seemed to look further than what the farm was producing, that and the home. Perhaps men were different from women, he told himself. He was no inexperienced youth and he'd had women friends, but no thought of marriage. He should never have let himself take what Bella had so blatantly offered during that first hour of the year; for him it had meant no more than a passing whim whilst to her it had been the experience that had changed her life – changed both their lives as it had turned out. But without the coming child, would he have found it in his heart to cast Bella aside? She would be a good wife to him, loyal and caring; she would be a perfect mother to their children. So what was wrong? Why didn't he look to the future with enthusiasm?

Turning over, he was determined to sleep, but his mind moved on to his father. It bothered him to think of him living alone in the farmhouse with just Eva Johnson coming across from her cottage every day to 'give the place a tidy through' as she put it, making sure that when she went home she left him a meal that, at the most, only needed warming in the oven. No wonder the poor chap looked so peaky. He'd have another talk to him about getting more help on the land. If he'd been down to The Retreat talking to the woman who said she was buying it perhaps he had come to an arrangement with her that she wouldn't go ahead. Then they could put a manager in to oversee the growing of the crops and take the poor old lad back to live with them. Bella would keep him cheerful; he'd enjoy having a pretty girl making a fuss of him.

Then his mind jumped back to Bella. She deserved a husband who really adored her, a young chap with a steady job who would look for nothing more than an unchanging routine, who would make love to her in a warm bed a couple of times a week and be as satisfied as she was herself. Poor kid. Even being part of a family makes her happy. She's had no proper life at all, evacuated when she was so young that she can't remember much about her parents, both killed early in the war. What a rotten life for her. Evacuated until the end of the war and then put in an orphanage.

Turning over to face her, he put his arm protectively across her. Bella was safe with him now. As he had many times before, he promised himself that he would be the best husband he could possibly be. She deserved nothing less. And, as he also had so often, he silently vowed that he would make her happy always.

As Louisa worked out her three months' notice and the solicitors dealt with probate, for her the time seemed to drag.

Moving away from her flat was so different from moving into it. She remembered how proud she had been seven years previously when she left her bedsit and rented her first real home. Now she saw it differently. The furniture wasn't her own; the curtains weren't of her choosing and neither were the rugs. Soon she would be in her own home and even though everything there had been provided by the aunt she could hardly remember, the thought pleased her and gave her a sense of belonging. The only thing that surprised and disappointed her was that the garden was a shambles, but in the life she envisaged ahead of her she would have plenty of time to work on it.

At last the day came when, with her portmanteau collected by the carrier from the railway station, she locked her front door, returned the key to the agent and then walked briskly to the station. This was the beginning of a new life; no longer would her days be ruled by the clock. She had always accepted the town she had grown up in, the sound of the biscuit factory hooter at the beginning and end of the working day, the vinegary smell from the much smaller factory where sauce was made, the swish of the trolley buses which had replaced the old tramcars whose tracks had been just the width to trap her bicycle wheel when she'd been a child. In her last week she'd become aware of all the sights and sounds and smells she had lived amongst and hardly noticed.

But as the train shuddered into life and pulled away from the station, she had no feeling of nostalgia. Ought she to be scared of what the future held? Perhaps she would find no one wanted to entrust their accounts to a woman! Well, if that were the case she would do something else. Her life had been orderly and unchanging, just as she'd taken for granted it would continue. Now, instead of being frightened of the uncertainty of what lay ahead, it brought a challenge that was the most exciting thing that had ever happened. It was up to her to make a place for herself in Lexleigh, just as it was up to her to become recognised in her profession.

She had closed the door on The Retreat on a windy Monday morning at the end of March; she turned the key in the lock and took her first step into her own home on the first day of

July. Her portmanteau wouldn't be delivered until the following day so all she had to unpack from the weekend bag were the necessities for one night, food for the evening and toiletries. All this was now officially hers. Tomorrow she would look in all the drawers and cupboards, not prying into someone else's life but knowing that she owned every stick and stone of it. And tomorrow, too, she would walk up to the farm and tell Mr Carter that she was living here now. Perhaps she was being fanciful, she told herself, but because he and Violet had been so close it made her feel that already she had fitted into a slot here.

So next morning that's what she did, seeing Ridgeway farmhouse for the first time.

A middle-aged man came across the yard to meet her as she approached, touching the peak of his battered trilby hat as he spoke.

''Morning, ma'm,' he said, seeming to scrutinize her as he came nearer. 'Can I be of any assistance?'

'Good morning. Yes, please, you can if you can tell me where I can find Mr Carter. Would he be in the house or in the fields somewhere?'

'You're a week too late. His son took him off to have a break with him and his wife. Offhand I can't tell you his address, but if you like to bang on the door of the cottage, the one with the well in the front garden, my missus has got it written down.'

'No, never mind. I've just moved into The Retreat.'

'Well, I'm damned. But I might have guessed. One look at you and I might have guessed.'

'Mr Carter said I looked like my aunt, but you can never see resemblances yourself, can you?'

'You'll know him quite well, I suppose, after all the years they . . .' the sentence trailed into silence.

'No, not that well.' Today Louisa might have left her old life behind her but her new-found freedom didn't stretch to discussing with this stranger the evening she had met Harold Carter. But, hearing the tone of her reply as curt, she added, 'I've met Bella. Do they come often?'

'They did, in the early days after it happened . . .'

'After Mrs Carter died so suddenly, yes, Bella told me about that. She said they tried to get here at the weekends. But of course that left him alone all through the week. So they've taken him back with them. And you're looking after things here?'

'Ay. You could say that, I suppose. They've been trying to carry him off with them every time they came, but he couldn't be persuaded. What the difference was this time I can't tell you but he went off like an obedient child. I dare say he realized that Bella's time was getting closer and feared they wouldn't keep getting here so often. To be honest, it makes no difference to the work whether he's here or there.' He thrust the prongs of his fork into the ground, seeming to indicate he was settling for a chat. 'He and I are much of an age and when he married and came here to his wife's family's place, her dad was really the guv'nor, although his old father was still alive too at that time. Crippled with arthritis the old man was, so not much use on the land. Both of us new to producing veg to the scale we do here, his father-in-law took the two of us in hand; fine man, he was. Pity Mrs Carter hadn't been born a boy – she would have been just such a one. But Harold Carter, he blew hot and cold, if you understand my meaning. Picked the job up quick as you like and for a while seemed to have his heart in it right enough, but he never was the staying kind. Now me, I wouldn't do anything else. Best job in the world, if you ask me. But after a few years, with the old man (and granddad too) gone and him left in charge, that's when he took fright, if you ask me. Looked ahead and saw the rest of his life never changing, season after season, crop after crop each year – ah, that's when he got fidgety. I couldn't help feeling sorry for him, even if I couldn't understand. Takes all sorts, I suppose, but just look around; can you tell me of a better way to earn a crust?'

'I'm not qualified to answer that,' Louisa told him with a laugh. 'This is the first time I've ever been on a farm of any sort. But I expect Mr Carter must have been glad to know he could go away now and leave you to look after things here.'

'More than forty-one years I've been here – since just after him who's guv'nor now got wed. Him and Miss Alice as I thought of her in those days were happy enough and no couple was more proud of their kids than they were when the boys were born. David, he came first, and eighteen months later there was young Leo. Never a sight or sound of David here at the farm these days; not since his mother passed away. She always spoke about him with such pride – the way he runs that factory place where they make the tools and implements.' Then with a laugh that held more affection than humour, 'Good thing the firm doesn't rely on Leo. Full of fun, always was and, like they say, a leopard doesn't change its spots. Anyway, when Leo said he wanted to take his dad with them I told him he could leave things just as they were here. Me and the boss get along well but, between you and me, his heart isn't in farming. Funny, Leo is like him all over again – restless, flighty I might say; will-o'-the-wisp, that's what Eva, my missus calls him. Says it with affection, mind you. I dare say she sizes him up right – she's usually pretty cute about things, but to my mind he's a chap who might settle down real happy here. Queer how it is with people, you know. A string of real red-lips girls he's had over the years, none of them for more than a few months. Then he marries a sweet little soul like Bella. And I bet you another thing: it would be the same if he settled down to take his place as guv'nor here. I bet working on the land he'd *find* himself, if you get my meaning, 'cos I'm damned that he has in that factory place.'

Nothing he'd said had needed an answer from Louisa, but she'd nodded occasionally to let him know she was listening. It seemed he might continue for the rest of the afternoon if she didn't stop him, so she said, 'I've not met Leo, but Bella told me he would rather be using the implements than designing them. I must go; I've a lot of sorting out to do. I'm sorry Mr Carter isn't here, but when he's had a break I expect he'll be back. I've enjoyed our talk, Mr—?'

'Mr Nothing. I'm Ted Johnson. Just Ted.'

She held out her hand as she said, 'And I'm Louisa Harding. Do you know, after working where everyone was mister or miss, I like the thought of Christian names.'

Before he took the hand she offered him he wiped his own on his trousers, although it was doubtful if it was any the cleaner for it.

'If there are any little jobs you're stuck for or anything you want moved in the house, give me a shout. Either young Geoff – he's taken the truck to collect a bit we wanted for the 'tato digger – yes, either Geoff or me'll slip down and see to things for you.'

Louisa realized as she walked back down the lane that she had come to find Harold because despite her eagerness for the future she had needed a friend to talk to. She felt she had found one in Ted Johnson, and imagined the rest of the village would be as welcoming.

It didn't take long for her to realize her mistake. But despite the way she knew she was being stared at with unsmiling interest, her bubble of optimism didn't burst. Had she had more time to dwell on the villagers' unfriendly curiosity she might have been cast down, but time was one thing she couldn't afford. During her first week she changed the position of the furniture, ordered another wardrobe for one of the spare bedrooms and hung her clothes away in it, for those inherited from Violet filled the rails already there. When she walked to the grocer's, wearing a dress which she might have chosen for herself but had been her aunt's, purchased the previous summer, she was aware of the head-turning of three women who stood talking as she approached. As she passed, one of them said in a loud whisper obviously intended to be heard, 'Thought it was a ghost,' to which another replied in the same vein, '*Her* trouble was that she was frightened to let herself be her age, frightened of losing her fancy man.'

Louisa gave no sign of hearing, let alone understanding the comments, as with her head high and shoulders straight she walked on along the road.

I don't care, she told herself. I wouldn't have anything in common with a lot of village gossipers. Anyway, what business is it of theirs what Aunt Violet did? Just think of Harold Carter, he loved her – and he knew her, which is more than people like that ever did. Even so, the comments had made their mark and taken away some of her joy in the freedom of the summer morning.

But the village was only one part of Louisa's life through the next weeks. She typed out an article which she took to the offices of the *Weekly Western Gazette* announcing that she had moved into the area and intended to work on a freelance basis. She knew it was a forlorn hope that they would find the space but her idea was that if it could be printed on the same page as her advertisement saying where she could be contacted it might bring her first clients. Fate was with her. There may have been other female accountants in town, but none of them were setting up in business for themselves and the idea appealed to the editor. The upshot was that at the end of the week when the paper was published it carried her article and, at the editor's suggestion, a photograph of her. Local businesses didn't keep her telephone ringing, but by the week following the publication of the paper she was contacted by the owner of a pharmacy wanting her to audit his books; whether it was her photograph or her qualifications that had made him decide to entrust his work to a woman could only be guessed at. Her new life was evolving on the lines she intended.

She had realized that transport would be essential and during her final three months in Reading she had taken driving lessons and had passed her test just before she moved. So one of the first things she had to do was have the ownership of Violet's one-year-old car transferred to her name. With some pride she arranged insurance and then she was free to take the vehicle on the road alone. She was probably as nervous as any new driver would have been, but Louisa had learnt long ago not to show her feelings so, walking with confidence she was far from feeling, she opened the double gates leading on to the track to the farm, then, praying she would do everything right and thankful that the car started straight away, reversed out and set off to explore the surrounding country. A stop at a garage to have the tank filled, then two hours driving to nowhere in particular and she returned home with new confidence.

That dingy office in Reading might have been on another planet. Miss Louisa Harding had the world at her fingertips.

In the first month she had one or two enquiries from the advertisement in the weekly paper. She drove into Gloucester in answer to one, and to a nearby village to respond to another.

In each case she was given the work and by the end of August the little room she had earmarked as an office had come into its own. Louisa realized it would be some time before she earned as much as she had when she'd been employed in a busy accountancy firm but, thanks to half-remembered Violet, she wasn't worried.

Letters continued to pass between Jess and her, Jess regaling her with descriptions of where she and Matt, her husband of some eighteen months, had been camping and the doings of her everyday life. In the past Louisa had always been aware of how dull her replies were. But all that had changed now, again thanks to Violet. She took photographs of each room in the house, one of the car, and even the garden, although what was intended to be lawn was no more than a rough patch of grass, dandelions and moss (which fortunately didn't show up in the photo). For five years now Jess had been in Australia, but they still felt as close as they had through the years of their childhood.

On an unusually hot day towards the end of August, Louisa was thinking about her friend as she knelt on her weedy would-be lawn digging out the dandelions. If the two of them had been doing the job together it would have turned a chore into fun. There was no logic in it, yet imagining the two of them together brought home to Louisa how alone she was. Jess was happily married; remembering all they had shared as they were growing up wouldn't give her the empty, lonely feeling that suddenly cast a cloud on Louisa's afternoon. Sitting back on her heels she gazed at the house, unable to push away images of Violet and Harold. They had known real, consuming love, love that had lasted more than thirty years and would never fade from that poor man's mind. What did it matter that the family had cast her out? What if the villagers had looked on her as a scarlet woman? Surely if you found someone who was a soul mate, someone who gave you love like theirs, what would anything or anyone else matter?

She raised her face to the sun, then she unbuttoned her thin, sleeveless blouse. She was working behind the house and the field beyond the wire fence was empty so it felt natural to pull the garment off and return to her gardening, feeling the summer heat like a caress. But her thoughts were restless, from Jess and Matt in their marriage, to Harold and Violet in a love that defied the world, to the delicate and glamorous lingerie she had inherited. A few minutes teasing out the dandelions while her thoughts carried her into the lives of others, then again she put down her fork and turned to the sun. Hardly conscious of what she did, she let her hands move on the smooth satin of her bra. Her mood changed. Was this what her life would always be like, dreaming, imagining, thinking of people who had each other, who had the love she yearned for? Oh, God, make it happen for me too, she pleaded silently, let me find someone to love and someone to love me, a companion – more than that, someone who will make a proper woman of me. Look at me, thirty years old – women are married and have children years younger than I am and I've found no one. It must be so wonderful . . . Oh, God, what's the matter with me? In the middle of the day is it natural to feel like this? Not enough to think about, that's the trouble. But this is all I want to think about. All by myself; no one to see me . . . While her mind raced on she had forgotten her weeding and, carrying her blouse, gone back into the house, quite unnecessarily locking the back door behind her as she went in. Then like a thief in the night she went up the stairs into her bedroom, where the rays of the sun warmed the counterpane invitingly. With a feeling of relief she closed the door. No one could see her; nothing could stop her. She kicked off her sandals and with her eyes closed and her imagination running ahead of her, hurried towards what was leading her.

She felt a sense of shame for what she was doing, yet stronger than shame was the need that drove her. Only afterwards, lying naked and alone while the sun streamed down on her, was she assailed by a feeling of emptiness followed by self-disgust. Three o'clock in the afternoon, an afternoon which had started with her happily working on the uncared-for plot, determined to transform it into a garden, and look at her! Getting off the bed she picked up the garments she had torn off so unceremoniously and left on the floor, and went to the bathroom. A tepid bath and then some repairs to the damage to her make-up and

she would go back to the patch she was determined to transform into a lawn worthy of the name.

Her mission completed, she was halfway down the stairs
when there was knock on the front door. She knew no one
except the tradespeople. Who would come calling? She felt
that what she had been doing must be plain to the world.
With her head held high it was no-nonsense Miss Harding,
career woman as capable as any male, who opened the door
to her visitor.

'Good afternoon?' Her tone questioned why this stranger
was at her door.

'I hope you don't mind me popping by like this, but I know
you don't grow veg and we've got so many runners. Oh, sorry,
I ought to tell you who I am. My Ted has been in a couple
of times, making sure you were OK.'

'Mrs Johnson? Won't you come in?'

'Seems a shame to be inside on a day like this. Can't we
sit a minute on that old bench? Could do with a coat of paint,
couldn't it? I'll give Ted a hint about it when I get home.
And I'm Eva. I bundled up some runners for you. Grow like
weeds, don't they? When they start to get old and the seeds
are big I'll give you some to dry off to plant out next year if
you like, Miss Harding. Your aunt, she wasn't keen on the
garden.' Then, as if she realized it sounded like a criticism,
'Well, we can't all like the same things or it'd be a dull old
world.'

'I'd like to plant some next year, and perhaps some salad
stuff. We used to have a vegetable garden when I was a child.
Raw peas, they were my downfall. It really is kind of you to
bring these for me. I love them and they never seem as good
from the shop.'

'Can't be, can they? These were only picked half an hour
ago. Cook them for your supper and have a knob of butter
on them. You're getting on OK here in the village, are you?
You don't find it dull after a town like Reading?'

'Not a bit. I've been working and then there is plenty to
sort out in the garden.'

'I read about you in the *Western*. Fancy you doing work like
that.' She chuckled as she added, 'I said to Ted, well I never.

I always pictured men in black suits with pinstripe trousers and half-moon glasses doing work like that. And look at you, a pretty young lady smart as paint.'

Louisa found Eva Johnson an easy companion, even though they were two such different personalities, and the minutes slipped by. It wasn't until she was leaving that Louisa casually mentioned Harold.

'When are they bringing Mr Carter home, have you heard?'

'No,' Eva answered with a worried frown. 'I had a letter from Bella a week or so ago. She says they are glad to have him where they can keep an eye on him, so forgetful he's been getting. It won't be young Leo who keeps an eye on him, be sure of that, fond as he always has been of his dad. But little Bella, she's a treasure if ever there was one. She's as fond of the guv'nor as if he were her own father and we can all rest easy as long as she is taking care of him. Well, I must scoot – my Ted looks in for a cuppa and a slice of cake round about four o'clock. That keeps him going until supper. Now, mind you remember – anything you want you just come up and bang on my door; the middle one of the cottages, the one with the well. And I'll have a word with Ted, see if he hasn't got a bit of that green paint left from when he did our back door. He'll soon spruce that bench up for you.'

And spruce it up he did, arriving with his tin of paint two days after Eva's visit. For Louisa it was a heart-warming experience to have people 'watching that she was all right' as Ted put it when she thanked him.

'The guv'nor would like to know we were keeping an eye on you, you being Miss Harding's niece. You know, I wouldn't wonder if Leo keeps him till after the nipper is born. Can't be more than a few weeks now and Bella needs to have someone at hand if the baby gives notice of coming while Leo's at that factory. They haven't been this last month or so. It wouldn't be right to leave her on her own and she was never keen on car journeys. Still, one of these days they'll turn up, all four of them I shouldn't wonder; the proud parents will want us all to see the bairn.'

After he'd left her Louisa shut herself in her office and spent the rest of the day on the accounts of a garden centre a few miles distant. She had the ability to shut everything else out of her mind when she was working and the hours slipped by until, when she finally closed the ledger and looked at her watch, she found she had missed tea. In fact, it was already nearly eight o'clock. Two poached eggs on toast and a cup of strong coffee, then a cigarette and a second cup and it was quarter to nine. She'd watch the nine o'clock news and then have a bath and go to bed with a book. As she made her plans she chuckled aloud: what had the solitude of this place done to her that she could look forward to an early night with a book? The news over, in her usual way she plumped up the cushions on the sofa and made sure she was leaving the room tidy (as she always did, nothing to do with her changed way of life), then she ran the water for her bath. Tonight would see the end of Violet's delicately scented bath salts and such was the change wrought on Louisa that she made a mental note to buy more the next time she was in Gloucester.

The bedroom window faced the empty field so, knowing she couldn't be overlooked, she happily drew back the curtains and opened the window before getting into bed and settling down to read. The warm bath had been relaxing but, despite the glowing reviews that had prompted her to buy the book, she found it disappointingly dull and before many minutes her eyelids were getting heavy and her concentration drifting. There was no conscious moment when she gave up the battle and turned off the light; the literary critics must know more about it than she did and she was determined to carry on until she discovered whatever it was that had impressed them so favourably. But by the time she reached page ten her eyes were closed, the book fallen from her hand and the light still on.

She had been in a deep sleep for about ten minutes when she was woken by someone touching her.

'What . . .!' Shock and fright left her speechless. Then, as she collected her wits and recognized who it was, 'Get out! Don't touch me.' She was at a disadvantage, only regaining consciousness as Harold Carter knelt above her as she lay.

'You've come back! They took me away. I knew you'd be here when I came home. Vi, Vi . . . Thank God. I've found you.' He was beside himself, kneeling astride her prone body and getting increasingly excited as he slid the straps of her nightdress from her shoulder and then pushed the bedcovers down as far as his own body would allow so that his hands moved from her shoulders to just beneath the covers so that he could touch her breasts. With every ounce of her strength she tried to free herself but he was anchoring her with his full weight. 'Together again, my love, my blessed love. Say something, Vi. I've been so frightened. Tried to get home to you but they watch me; they never let me free. Home again. Prayed I'd find you here. You're so warm, real, alive. They lied to me – they said you'd gone. I wanted to die.' He talked incessantly, seeming unaware that beneath his weight she was struggling to get free. His face was only inches from hers as, with his knees imprisoning her, he pulled her towards him. She could feel his hot breath and then his mouth on hers, moving as though he were eating her, then his tongue probing.

'Get off me, blast you,' she tried to say but it was hard to breathe, let alone shout. 'Take your hands off me!'

'Not that game,' he panted, and she imagined she heard laughter in his voice as if he was remembering times when Violet's playful mock-refusal had excited his passion and possibly hers too. 'Tomorrow, that game, and all the others, eh? Can't play games tonight, my angel, not tonight. Say something – say you've missed me. Tell me you were looking for me.'

Louisa heard the change in his voice and suspected reality was coming through the mist of his troubled mind. But she was too revolted by what he was doing to feel pity for him.

'Get off me now!' and, pulling her hands free, she again tried to force him away from her.

When he'd followed the beam of light shining from her window and hurried to the house, instinct had made him creep up the stairs. But with the sight of her lying asleep every other thought had gone from him. The young woman lying in the bed was the Violet he had fallen in love with so many years ago, so for him those years had ceased to exist. He had felt young, strong – joy and relief had pushed the last shadow of reason away. For him it had been as if the only thing that had kept him from the glory he and his beloved Violet had known was that he had been taken away, taken away and watched to make sure he couldn't get back to her. Now, as Louisa struggled beneath him, his mind started to clear. Still confused, his paramount emotion was loss, almost immediately swallowed up by misery as a sob broke in his throat. Then the whole scene changed.

He hadn't closed the bedroom door and neither he nor Louisa had heard the second intruder mounting the stairs two at a time. Taken completely by surprise, he found himself lifted off her as if he'd been a rag doll.

'For Christ's sake, Dad, what the hell do you think you're doing?'

'I thought . . . I thought . . .'

'Well, you thought wrong. I told you I wouldn't be out for long.'

Louisa's mind jumped back to the day she had met Bella and heard the wonders of the perfect Leo. Surely, though, she had said how close he was to his father. Well, this certainly wasn't *her* idea of care and affection. And how dare he come marching into her bedroom as if he owned the place, treating her as though she didn't exist. She heard the sound of Harold crying – not tears of anguish, but the almost silent weeping of helplessness. If she were dressed she would get up and try to comfort him, for with the advent of this arrogant intruder her initial anger towards poor, confused Harold had melted away.

'Come along, it's no use sitting there snivelling. The car's outside.' Then, as he ushered his father towards the door, he turned briefly to Louisa with the parting words, 'I'll get him home and make sure the door is locked and bolted. You'd better do the same when we've gone. He'll be about the place tomorrow, so you should keep the bolt across.'

'I shall speak to the locksmith first thing in the morning and enquire about new locks.' It was most certainly Miss Louisa Harding who replied with not an ounce of emotion in her voice. Then, more kindly, 'Goodnight, Mr Carter.'

Harold turned to look at her, and now that the struggle to throw him off her was over she was aware of how he'd altered since she'd last seen him. He looked lost.

For a moment he resisted being pushed out of the door as

he turned to her, shaking his head helplessly. 'Louisa,' he murmured. 'I remember now. I'm sorry, so sorry.'

'Try not to think about it,' she answered. Then, with a conspiratorial smile, 'Let's both forget all about it.'

'I thought—'

'For goodness' sake, do come on. Eva Johnson wants to get home but she won't go until she knows you're safely indoors.'

She listened as they went down the stairs, then she heard the front door slam, the click of the latch on the gate, the slam of two doors on the car and then the motor, growing quieter. And here she lay in Violet's bed, Violet who had loved him sufficiently to lose her family for him. Did Violet know what his misery was doing to him? And, if she did, couldn't she find a way to bring him comfort and let him know she loved him still? Louisa had never given much thought to death or the emptiness of separation, but on that night it was brought very close. Surely there must be more to a relationship – a loving, united relationship – than something physical? Surely when two caring people talked and laughed together that must be a joining of spirits as surely as any bodily union? She didn't know. How could she when she had never experienced that sort of love?

Less than an hour before, she had been too sleepy to concentrate on her book. But what had happened between then and now had left her wide awake. Her fury at Harold had gone, swept away by the sight of his desolation and grief. Her thoughts moved to his son. She remembered Bella's adoration of her so-perfect husband again and tried to connect all that she'd heard about him with the man who had bundled his father away with no consideration for the older man's confusion. Perfect husband be damned, she thought, he's a big-headed pig and, if it hadn't been that I didn't want to make things even harder for his poor, muddled father, I would have enjoyed telling him so. I bet if I walk over to the farm tomorrow Mr Carter won't so much as remember what happened just now.

But in the morning events took another turn. It was too early to make her planned visit to the farm so just before ten o'clock she decided to have an hour working on the garden's transformation. She was a determined novice and only time would tell her whether the herbaceous plants she had put in would make healthy roots, but so far they hadn't had time to give up the ghost and, at least in front of the house, the garden began to look cared for. Pushing a wheelbarrow bearing her tools she was just emerging from the shed when she heard the garden gate slam shut. Oh, no, not Harold Carter again! That was her immediate reaction, but it died even as it was born. The man coming towards her was a stranger, and yet there was something vaguely familiar about him.

Three

'Violet Harding's niece? But, yes, I can see that you are.'

'That's right, Louisa Harding. Are you a neighbour?' Her smile was welcoming as, leaving her wheelbarrow, she came towards him with her hand outstretched. Surely he couldn't be from the village; even in a crowded town he would have stood out. Perhaps six foot tall, dark brown hair of the kind that wasn't quite straight and yet neither was it wavy; it stayed happily as it had been combed without the aid of any hair-dressing favoured by so many men. His moustache was well trimmed; his dark eyes seemed to tell her that he found life a very pleasant affair. But more than any of that, there was something in his bearing, his general appearance, which would have set him apart even without the obvious advantage of his good looks. Louisa had never been a regular cinemagoer but, looking at her handsome visitor, her mind took a leap and arrived at Errol Flynn. His answer to her question took her by surprise.

'Yes and no,' he said, taking her hand in a firm grasp. 'I'm Leo Carter—'

'Leo? But then who took Mr Carter home last night?'

'It's last night I wanted to speak to you about,' he said, not answering her question. 'I'm sorry about Dad. Are you desperately keen to garden or can we talk for a few minutes?'

'The garden can wait. But I'd been told Mr Carter was staying with you and Bella, so I naturally assumed that was who took him home.'

'That was David, my brother. He collected my father from our place yesterday evening and brought him back to the farm. I ought not to have let him come. David stayed the night at the farm and phoned me indecently early this morning. I should have realized that being back here would unsettle my father, but he'd seemed so much better that I honestly thought his mind had adjusted to all that had happened.'

'Come inside. I see my opposite neighbour has found her casement window needs her attention.'

Leo Carter laughed, turning to wave a greeting towards the woman opposite who was making pretence of rectifying a fault in the latch of her window. Now, pretending not to notice him, she quickly closed it and moved behind the curtain.

'Nothing changes,' Leo said with a chuckle. 'Yes, let's go indoors. I'll give her half an hour and there won't be a person on the High Street who hasn't heard that I've come a'calling.' Then, more seriously, 'Will you mind?'

'Not in the least, if they have nothing better to think about.'

She had left the front door propped open and as they reached it he looked back at the middle cottage of the three on the opposite side of the lane and gave a cheery wave.

'You've not changed things much in here,' he observed as she led the way to the sitting room. 'No wonder the old boy thought he'd stepped back in time last night. I always liked coming here when I was a kid. She was a pretty special person, your Aunt Violet.'

'I wish I'd known her properly. I remember her just as a bright light in my early childhood. She was shunned by my family.'

'And by you, too? Bright lights have a way of holding your attention? Or did your views coincide with those of your family?'

She felt she ought to have been annoyed by his hint of criticism. Why should she explain herself to this stranger? Whatever the reason, that was exactly what she found herself wanting to do.

'Apparently she didn't hold your silence against you,' he said, the movement of his handsome head indicating that he was referring to the home he'd quickly realized Louisa had inherited.

'I feel ashamed to think that while I was concentrating on myself, she remembered me.'

'Don't waste time on regrets for something that can't be altered. Violet Harding was a woman of intense understanding and compassion. If she'd felt any bitterness on account of your neglect you would hardly be entertaining me this morning in what used to be her home.' Then, with a smile that could only be described as mischievously flirtatious, 'So let's just enjoy where Fate has brought us on this lovely Sunday morning.' Taking a cigarette case from his jacket pocket, he opened it and offered it to her. 'Only one thing is missing: a good strong cup of coffee.' Then, with a smile that started in his eyes and must have helped him to get his own way all through life, 'No milk, thank you, and no sugar.'

The Miss Harding her colleagues had been sure was treading the path to spinsterhood nudged her and whispered silently that he was a conceited bore. But she was caught up in the unexpected delight of his manner.

'An excellent idea.' She couldn't have held back her smile even if she'd wanted to. 'I'll accept that cigarette when I've made it. It won't take long.'

'Better, I'll come and give my manly advice. Don't you find men are at their best in an advisory capacity?'

'I'd be the last to know. I'm not in the habit of seeking advice.' She was enjoying herself. 'If you're coming with me you might as well be useful. You'll find cups and saucers in—'

'I know exactly where they are. This kitchen has always seemed special. When I was on school holiday this was often my place of escape.'

'Escape from what?' For he certainly didn't strike her as the type to hide away out of fear.

He chuckled, following the journey his memories were taking him back through the years. 'A variety of things, depending on the season. My *bête noire* was following the digger and picking up the potatoes. The coffee smells good. Where shall we go? Indoors or out?'

'Out, on a morning like this. Why didn't Bella come with you to see me? Or is she keeping Mr Carter company?'

'She was still in bed when I left home this morning. Having had a call from Big Brother, I was up with the larks. David spent last night at the farm to make sure Dad stayed in his own bed like a good lad, but he had to be back home and on the golf course by half past nine; that's his sacred ritual for Sunday morning. A man of habit is Brother David, so I promised to get up here by eight o'clock. A social visit from him to Bella and me is rare, but he said he had to pass the door yesterday so he looked in. Dad behaved perfectly, not a sign that his mind is getting muddled. How is it that people have a new cunning when the situation demands? Anyway, he and David talked about the business – I left them to it. I have enough Monday to Friday without a second helping at the weekend. Then David informed me he was taking Dad home to the farm. He said Bella and I were making a fuss about nothing, and all the old boy needed was to be back in his own surroundings. And like a fool I wanted to believe him. Of course, I hadn't bargained for someone to be living in Violet's house yet.'

'Well, I'm afraid he will have to get used to it,' Louisa told him with a sharp edge to her voice.

By that time she had erected a small garden table by the newly painted seat while he followed, carrying the tray.

'He will,' Leo answered. 'Bella will see to that. She is incredibly good to him. I believe she genuinely cares about him.' Then, as if he'd just become aware of where the conversation had brought them, 'And so she should. He's a damned nice guy. When I was younger I used to look up to him and want to be just like him. Rotten the tricks life can play on a man.'

'Or a man on a woman,' replied staid Miss Harding, who managed for a moment to gain the upper hand and spare a thought for the unknown Alice Carter.

'Ah, that too.' Then, with a change of tone as if he wanted to steer them away from a topic he'd rather avoid, 'Good coffee. Now we can have that cigarette and enjoy the glorious Sunday morning sleepiness of the countryside. You like it here?'

'*Like* isn't quite the word. I feel as if I'm a different person – at least most of the time. The country had little to do with my past, but I certainly have no wish to go back to all I left behind. What you were saying just now about retreating here during the school holidays rather than helping on the farm – that surprised me. Bella had given me the impression that your heart was in the land and not in the industrial world.'

'My heart? It's certainly not in that wretched factory where I spend so much of my time. But working on the farm? Oh, no. *Being* on the farm, *living* there, that's one thing, but actually getting up at the crack of dawn, working in all weathers, that's quite another. You know, there are plenty of men who think there can be no better life.'

He surprised her more by the minute. She had been brought up to expect that strangers no more than skimmed the surface of conversation and yet here they were digging deep and getting to know one another without the peripheral niceties of new acquaintances.

'I learnt a lesson from Aunt Violet, or rather from Aunt Violet's will,' she told him. 'When I came to see the solicitor I had no expectations that a spinster aunt would have anything but perhaps a few pounds in the bank – or even a few debts to be paid. When the solicitor put me in the picture I meant to sell the house. Then I came here – do you remember about Saul on the road to Damascus? It was like that, as if I suddenly saw my future clearly, as if I had found a new freedom, a new appreciation. I don't mean I was like Saul in a religious sense.'

'Are you sure?' His words surprised her. 'I'm not some Holy Jo, but if life gives you anything to hang on to surely it's to be found in the country. In any benighted town the only thing one knows of the change in the seasons is that it's warmer or colder, or that the shop windows have their lights on earlier. It's the country that is meaningful.'

Louisa looked at him with more interest, surprised by the sincerity of his sudden outburst and even more surprised that a man of such obvious self-confidence should be embarrassed by his show of honesty. She thought of Bella and her adoration of him.

'Bella put it well,' she said. 'When she knew I had decided to leave my job and start a new life here, she was frightened for me. She told me the place had thrown fairy dust in my eyes.'

'And had it?'

'After just a few summer weeks I can't answer that. If we meet again in six months ask me then and I'll give you my answer.' Then, changing the subject and with a feeling of guilt that she was harbouring Bella's adored husband when he ought to be at the farm reassuring himself that his father was fit to be left: 'It's a pity you couldn't bring Bella with you. She must be getting near to having the baby? I remember how proud she was about it but I forget when it's due.'

'In a few weeks' time, I believe. If that business hadn't happened last night I think my father would have been able to be left on his own. The Johnsons have lived in one of the farm cottages almost forever and they would have kept an eye on him. Of course, I hadn't realized this house was now lived in. He saw the lights . . . and forgot everything else.'

'Surely you don't think he'll do it again? Why didn't you take his key away from him?' The new and liberated Louisa was overtaken by her previous self, who was permanently at the ready not far below the surface. 'I'm not prepared to lock myself in here in case your father has a memory lapse.'

'Indeed.' He nodded in agreement. 'As things are, I intend to take him home with me again.' But, despite his words, was she imagining it or did she see a glint of amusement in his eyes? Either way, the tone of their conversation seemed to her to change. They spoke politely enough but their words added up to nothing of importance, nothing to remember afterwards. It was five minutes later, when he was midway through explaining to her the rotation of vegetable crops at a farm such as Ridgeway, that he suddenly broke off mid-sentence and turned to her, his expression telling her that his interest hadn't been on what they were talking about but something far more important.

'I must get going. I'll finish your lesson at a later date.'

'Yes, of course, you mustn't leave Bella too long.' But did he even notice the cold over-politeness in her tone? Her underlying lack of confidence had got the upper hand, making her ready to believe he had stayed to talk more out of kindness to a lonely woman than because he had been interested in anything she said.

'What? No, it's not that! It must be this house, as you say. From nowhere I just had my own road to Damascus experience. I know exactly what has to be done. I must get back to the house and phone Bella to tell her to pack a couple of cases, then I'll make sure the Johnsons will hang on to Dad for the day.' He sounded eager to put into action whatever it was he had been thinking about while he'd been talking to her. 'I'll collect Bella and bring her to Ridgeway. She's good with my father – having her around will help him settle.' Then, with a smile that only minutes ago would have fooled her into believing he was sharing a secret: 'I can work things so that I can use the house at the farm as a base. A lot of my time is spent out, talking with agents and all that sort of thing. Play my cards right and I need only look in at that Birmingham hell-hole once or so a week.' Like a mischievous child who has thought up some prank, she continued, 'Now what could be better than to live at the farm but not be roped in to *work* on the land? Miss Louisa Harding, Louisa – it suits you, a delightful name – talking to you has made me see clearly what I should have done ages ago.'

'Not moved away from your parents' house?'

He laughed, seemingly not noticing her intentional criticism. 'Put like that it sounds a slight on my manhood,' he agreed, not in the least offended. 'But now that my mother isn't there the house needs a woman, and Bella will fit the bill admirably. Dad dotes on her; he always had an eye for a pretty girl. The two of them will fall in with the plan, of that I'm sure.' He seemed to be imagining their pleasure when they heard what he'd decided. 'And except for the occasional day or so I shall be free of those wretched workshops.'

For Louisa, his remarks cast a shadow over the pleasure of his visit. Why should she care that the idea of moving back to Lexleigh appealed to him for reasons she considered selfish? For her, work had always been an important responsibility and she had neither time nor respect for anyone who looked on it as anything less. As they had sat together talking over their coffee and cigarettes she had felt completely comfortable – she had even fooled herself into believing that they had made the base of friendship. Now she felt she saw him more clearly. But why should it matter to her that he had shown himself to have feet of clay? She thought of Bella, so trusting, so adoring, and told herself that it was on Bella's account she was angry.

'Aren't you taking it for granted that Bella will want to move when, by now, she must be booked in at a hospital or nursing home ready for the baby's arrival? Is it fair to expect her to move?'

Again, that impish smile which unfailingly won hearts and got him his own way. 'Once the first impact has sunk in she will believe she put the idea in my head. Don't worry about Bella. And, as for my father, he'll delight in it. I must be off. Thanks for the coffee and the chat. Let's do it again, shall we?'

Ignoring the suggestion, her parting shot was, 'Don't forget to take away your father's key to this house. I can't have him rushing over here every time he sees the lights on.'

'I'll have a word with Bella. She may be able to get him to part with it. No use me asking him for it – he'd probably think I had some ulterior motive for wanting it!'

Louisa's expression told him just what she thought of such a suggestion. Yet she hated herself for not being able to laugh the situation away. She felt gauche, unworldly. But no matter how she felt, his thoughts had already moved on. 'May I tell Bella she can call on you?'

'Bella won't need to be told. Of course, I look forward to seeing her again.'

For a second he looked at her without speaking before he answered, 'Really? That's kind. She's a good girl.' He hesitated, as if he was considering expounding on the comment, and perhaps he would have, had she not cut in.

'That's a disgracefully arrogant way of speaking about your wife.' Why should she feel so angry? She hardly knew the girl, and if she were honest with herself she would acknowledge that she had found her tedious, her conversation revolving as it had around her perfect Leo. 'Tell her I shall be pleased to see her, but I imagine her time will be very full with a house to run and a father-in-law to watch.'

'I anticipate being there most days. I shan't keep her on a lead. You may wish you hadn't said you'd be pleased to see her at any time.' And surely his eye half closed in a quick and intimate wink as he added, 'I'll water down the invitation, don't worry.'

'I always mean what I say. Now I must get on with the work I'd promised myself I'd do trying to turn this into something like a garden.' She heard her words as rude and unattractive. He must be laughing at her, seeing her as socially inept; she wanted him gone.

'Then the invitation shall be passed to her verbatim. Until next time . . .' He held out his hand and she felt hers taken in a firm grasp. And then he was gone.

Somehow the garden had lost its appeal, the wheelbarrow standing empty waiting to be filled with weeds from the 'would-be' lawn. She carried the tray indoors and rinsed the cups, dried them and put them away, as if that way she could wipe out the last hour. It was ridiculous to let it upset her, but she found it impossible to go back outside and re-kindle the delight she had felt first thing that morning as she'd collected her tools. Through the weeks she had been at Lexleigh, the Miss Louisa Harding of old had almost faded out of existence. Her place had been taken by a new Louisa, a competent young woman with a ready smile and self-assurance which already had brought her work enough to build on. Her strength had always come from work and it was that to which she automatically turned on that Sunday morning. The wheelbarrow stood untouched as the hours went by. She made a sandwich and coffee for lunch and took it back into her workroom, priding herself that she had put the morning's visitor out of her mind. But, of course, had that been true, the thought wouldn't even have entered her head.

Her invitation for Bella to visit had been made in a moment of annoyance at Leo's assumption that he could organize his young wife's life without consulting her. In truth, she expected there would be far too much for her to do to come calling until her more pressing arrangements had been sorted out. So when at nearly nine o'clock on that same Sunday evening there was a knock at the front door, her first thought was that Harold Carter had escaped again. If a mood can be heard in the sound of footsteps, then whoever was waiting for the door to be opened must have felt unwelcome, a sentiment reinforced at the first sight of Louisa's expression.

'Leo told me you said I could come, but I'll come tomorrow instead if you like.'

Louisa immediately felt guilty. 'No, no need. I couldn't think who it could be; I thought you'd be much too busy to get away so soon.'

'Leo said he and Dad would be OK. They can talk farm

talk – they usually do from what I've heard, but it's so much
better now they're actually here.'

Ushering Bella inside, Louisa was surprised to find herself
pleased that the girl had come so soon. There was no logic in
it; they could have nothing in common. That was her first
thought, but hard on its heels came another. Yes, they had in
common that they were both women. Hadn't she experienced
more than enough herself of being made aware that in the
business world men were superior? Wasn't that why she had
been angry this morning on Bella's behalf?

'Isn't it wonderful that Leo has decided to bring Dad home
and us to stay with him? Driving here today he explained to me
how your aunt used to be very friendly with his parents; he said
that this house used to belong to the farm. Did you know that?
Dad sold it to your aunt and, like I said, she was very friendly
with them. It must have been so hard for him losing them both
and having this place standing empty all those weeks.'

'I expect it was,' Louisa answered, making sure her voice
was casual. Clearly the perfect Leo hadn't related how his father
had had to be dragged off her the previous night. 'How about
a drink? I think I have sherry or gin either with tonic or
orange.'

'Gosh, that sounds nice. I've not had gin and orange since
New Year's Eve when Leo took me out and I think I got a
bit tiddly.' She chuckled as she looked back on that night, the
night that had changed her life. 'Haven't I got huge since you
saw me last?' She cradled her swollen tummy lovingly. 'Less
than two months to go.'

'I suppose you were booked into a maternity nursing home
or the hospital? You'll have to start all over again.'

But Bella seemed not a bit worried as with a laugh she said,
'That's Leo for you. He'll drive me into town tomorrow and
we'll go to the maternity place; I looked it up in the telephone
book. Leo says that when I tell them I've only just arrived
they'll book me in without any trouble. I just hope he's home
when the baby starts because it's quite a long drive and I
wouldn't like Dad to have to take me. He's got so confused,
sometimes it's quite frightening. Mrs Johnson suggested I see
the local doctor and arrange with the same midwife that quite

a few women in the village have had. Then the baby could be born at Ridgeway; I like the thought of that.' She sipped her drink, looking a picture of contentment. 'This is a nice drink; you've put a lot of orange in it to make sure I don't get tiddly. Pregnant ladies mustn't. I was saying about Dad, wasn't I? Leo told me when we were driving here about him calling on you last night.'

'He told you?'

'Oh, but you mustn't worry – he wouldn't dream of talking about it to anyone else. You can see how it is with Dad, though. He saw the light and I suppose forgot that your aunt had been run over. He must have been so glad to think he had an old friend to talk to. Don't you think sometimes how sad it must be to have no one around you sharing your memories, no one of the same age? I really don't want to live to be a hundred, do you?'

'I don't know. If I were ninety-nine and healthy, I think I might.'

'But all your friends would have gone.' Bella seemed genuinely concerned.

'I've never had many friends.'

'Snap! Neither have I. It really depends on your background, don't you think? My parents were killed in the war and I went to an orphanage. We were all in the same boat, but no one made special friends like you would if you had a home to invite them to. Like you did here, when you sent the message by Leo. I'm glad you've met him. Now you know why I fell in love with him. Would you think it an awful cheek if I called you by your Christian name?'

'I hadn't realized that you didn't. I call you Bella.'

'I can't. I don't know it. Leo referred to you as Miss Harding and I haven't called you that either.'

'I'm Louisa.'

'Louisa. That's a lovely name. It's a real responsibility to have to think of a name for a child. It would be easier if you could look into the future and know if it was to be clever or sporty or lazy or full of life and energy. Leo isn't lazy, you know, although David thinks he is. He never likes sitting around doing nothing. But it doesn't suit him to go every day to the

works, even though quite often he has to go out and meet
clients.' She chuckled and Louisa knew that she was imagining
her beloved Leo making the most of wining or dining a client.
'At Ridgeway there's plenty of space so he can take over a
spare room and have his drawing desk and stool brought over
from the works.'

'Surely he can't keep designing new implements. A plough
is a plough, a potato digger a potato digger.'

'You'd be surprised at the clever things he draws: better
fittings to attach to the tractor, small tools too. I'm sure the
success of Carters' is mainly due to *him*.'

Never had Louisa heard such hero-worship. She hoped Bella
would soon suggest it was time for her to go home. The
obvious thing would be to say she was tired and had promised
herself an early night but, even as the thought tempted her, it
was immediately crushed by another – that this childlike soon-
to-be-mother hadn't an unkind thought in her head. At the
first sign that Louisa was bored she would have stood up ready
to leave, feeling hurt and embarrassed; to do that to her was
impossible. So Bella chattered on, satisfied with no more than
the occasional comment from Louisa to prove she was awake
and listening.

That was the first of many visits through the next days,
some no more than a quick enquiry to see if Louisa was
needing anything from the village shop or, better still, if they
could walk there together; sometimes with time to spare and
an offer to help in the garden, polish the car, dry the dishes
or share any job Louisa was doing. If Bella found out her new
friend was about to drive into town to collect or return work
there was nothing she liked better than to go with her. Of
course, that meant phoning the house first to make sure Leo
would keep an eye on his father.

About four weeks before the date the baby was expected,
Bella arrived just as Louisa was disconnecting the garden hose
from the kitchen tap.

'You look shattered,' was Louisa's greeting, a tactless one to
a girl who was already feeling clumsy and unattractive. 'You'll
find a cold drink in the fridge. Sort yourself out while I put
the hose away.'

'I expect it's because I've been hurrying. Leo's driven to Oxford to see an agent of Carters'. Usually I'm stuck when Leo is away but this afternoon Mrs Johnson has come in to give the kitchen a thorough "scrub-up" as she calls it and she suggested I come out if I wanted to. While she's there Dad will be fine. She chats away to him and he forgets to be scared. I'm sure that's what's wrong with him. He's such a dear and I know he can't help being like he is, but this morning wherever I went he followed. He knows he's muddled and he's frightened. Well, we all would be, wouldn't we, if we knew we weren't thinking straight. This lemonade is gorgeous. It's so sticky hot today. Shall I pour a glass for you?'

'No. I'm just going to put the hose away and then have a very quick tub. I was hedge cutting before I watered. From the look of the sky I think I wasted my time, it's getting very black – and, hark, isn't that distant thunder?'

'Oh, I do hope we shan't get a storm. I can't bear thunderstorms; they make me feel really ill – and it's no good telling me there's nothing to be frightened of because it's not that sort of fright. They're so – so sort of . . . against nature.' Bella clamped her bottom lip with her top teeth and cradled her 'bump' as if she were protecting it from some evil spirit.

'That's one thing they're *not*,' Louisa replied. 'They're nature at its mightiest. I'll just go and put this hose away.'

The wind had been gaining force while she'd been watering, but she wasn't prepared for the sudden gust that slammed the door of the shed wide open and sent the branches of the trees into a frenzied dance. In the same second the rain started, large drops bouncing on the tarmac of the lane, then lightning and a clap of thunder getting nearer. She hung the wound hose on its hook in the shed and, despite the wind, closed and locked the door before running back across the slightly improved grass to the back door of the house.

'It's getting closer; you must stay here until the rain stops. Mrs Johnson will have to stay at the farm too. It started so suddenly but already it's bucketing down and the wind has blown up from nowhere.'

'I hate thunderstorms,' Bella mumbled, keeping her eyes closed as though what she couldn't see wasn't really happening.

Louisa had never had any patience with people who gave way to mindless fear and surely that was exactly what Bella was doing. But there was something about the girl that touched her.

'The storm may not come to much,' she said, making sure her voice was encouragingly reassuring, 'but the wind and rain soaks you in a minute. Look at me – I'm a drowned rat just running from the shed.'

'Leo's driving all the way from Oxford. You can hardly see the lane even. I wish he was here. Oh!' She gave a sharp cry, then gripped the back of the kitchen chair. 'Oh!'

Louisa surprised herself. The Miss Harding of old was trying to gain the upper hand and insist the girl was behaving stupidly, but Louisa trod her down. Nature wasn't helping though, as at that same second the lightning seemed to light up the room and the crack of thunder was almost immediate. Bella's breathing was loud and fast, her mouth open as if she had to gasp for air.

'Come on, Bella, we'll go in the other room. I won't leave you down here on your own – my bath can wait.'

'I'm so frightened. I haven't felt the baby move for hours. Is something wrong? This morning, two or three times I had an odd feeling, like the pain you get with a period but much worse, but each time it soon went and I felt OK again. When you were outside it came again, much worse; I could hardly think. I shouted for you but the wind was too loud. Then it went away and there was just the storm. Oh, Lou, it's starting to come back, getting stronger, oh, oh,' she panted, 'oh, oh.' She couldn't find the breath to speak, but somehow she managed to say what sounded like, 'Something must be wrong.' She opened her eyes wide, eyes that were full of fear. 'It can't be born yet . . . it's . . . too soon.' She gripped the back of the kitchen chair so hard that her knuckles were white. Nothing about her was normal, even the way she stood with her feet wide apart as she bent forward.

Louisa was out of her depth. She knew nothing about pregnancy, although through the last two or three weeks, when a day hadn't gone by without a visit from Bella, she had been regaled with descriptions of the unborn child's energy, the way it twisted and kicked; she had had the 'bump' forced on her to feel how it was moving. Today it was still and Bella was feeling pains that must surely mean only one thing. She was about to miscarry.

'I think we ought to get the nurse, or at any rate talk to her.' Louisa made sure her voice sounded calm. 'She may be able to reassure you. I'll get her number. What's her name?'

'Wilkins. She doesn't live in Lexleigh; she's in Ledbridge. It's easing again. Perhaps it won't come back.' And clearly it was losing its grip, for Bella's breathing was lighter, even though the fear hadn't gone. 'Mustn't lose my baby. Perhaps it's my punishment?'

'Rubbish. The nurse may say that when you get to the last month or so, this sort of thing can happen. The trouble is, neither of us know what you have to expect.' As Louisa spoke she ran her finger down the Ws looking for a Wilkins in Ledbridge. There it was: 21, George Street. She picked up the receiver and dialled '0' for the operator. The line was dead. She tried again, standing with her back to panting Bella and keeping her movements unruffled. As if orchestrated for the moment, a huge gust of wind brought a bough crashing to the ground from a tall elm by the garage, followed by a slate from the roof shattering on the ground by the kitchen window. She could hear Bella whimpering, something that might have irritated her in normal circumstances, but there was nothing normal about the afternoon. It had grown so dark that to read the telephone directory she had had to switch on the light and now, as if everything was contriving to add to the horror of the afternoon, the power was lost.

'Lou, something's happening. I haven't weed myself, but something's happened. I'm all wet and it's on the lino too. What's happening, Lou? I'm so scared!'

Louisa was also scared, for in that moment she knew they had no choice but to face together what lie ahead. She forced her voice to sound calm and confident, even though her heart was hammering.

'I've heard somewhere that you carry a lot of water when you're pregnant. When the baby is coming, the water breaks. The phone isn't working, Bella, but together we'll manage.

First thing is to get you upstairs and get your clothes off, at least from the waist downwards. I'll help you. You and me together, there's nothing we can't do.'

Bella was transformed. Her baby was coming; she didn't care how much it hurt as long as it was well. Fear had gone from her expression; she breathed deeply and appeared not to notice a loud crack of thunder.

'I don't mind the pains,' she breathed as another contraction gripped her, 'I don't mind anything if only the baby is born and well. I've prayed so hard it would be healthy. I mustn't fail. I've got to trust. It's no use praying and then not trusting. Let's say a prayer—'

'We shall both be doing that in our heads, but not down here. The Lord helps those who help themselves. When the pain loses its grip we must get you up to the bedroom. I'll go up there first and strip the covers off, and find all the towels I can.' And without waiting for an answer she ran up the stairs to the sparsely furnished spare bedroom and started pulling the covers off the bed. She had no waterproof sheet – all she could do was put towels over the mattress, but even as she brought a pile of them from the bathroom cupboard she told herself nothing she did could save it. But right now that was unimportant. Taking a quick look around the bedroom as she made for the door, she felt the whole scene was unreal. She hardly realized how, in the last few minutes, her fear had given way to confident determination. Bella's part in the proceedings was obvious, although neither of them had any clear idea of what was involved. As for her, at this stage her mind was blank, but she trusted her own ability enough to be sure that, presented with any challenge, she would be capable of overcoming it.

Back in the kitchen she saw there was something different about Bella. With one hand she still gripped the back of the chair while the other hand moved as if to hold the gap between her widely straddled legs.

'What do I do? Help me, help me Lou, something's happening. I can't get up the stairs.'

'Then we'll manage down here.' Her voice had to reassure Bella, so she made sure it sounded as if she were in control of the situation. 'You'll have to lie on the floor, but hang on while I get some cushions from the other room.' It didn't take more than a few seconds to grab the loose cushions then rush back upstairs for the pile of towels, but when she came back she found Bella half squatting, her legs wide apart, not even aware of how loudly she was grunting as, gripping the edge of the table with both hands, she was pushing with all her might.

Help me! Please, God, help me.

She held Bella under her arms and tried to take her weight as she guided her towards where she had laid the cushions on the lino-covered floor. Guiltily she acknowledged the thought that on this floor the mess could be scrubbed up, whereas had she been able to get Bella upstairs and on to her stripped bed the mattress would have been ruined. But there was nothing in her manner to hint at the way her mind was working.

'I've got your weight.' She heard her own voice as irritatingly cheerful. 'Just let yourself drop on to the floor. Your head and shoulders can be on the cushions and I'll put towels down to take away some of the hardness of the floor.'

'Ooooohhh,' Bella breathed, doing as she was told but now with her hand once again between her legs as if she expected the baby to drop into it. Once on the floor she instinctively bent her legs and parted her knees as if she wanted to give the baby space. She seemed not to notice as Louisa gently wriggled her soiled skirt and knickers off her and cast them aside.

'Now we're ready.' Ready? Even as Louisa said it in that same over-confident voice, she knew that in truth she was anything but ready. But if she let herself go down that avenue she would be no use at all.

The minutes passed in a series of grunts and suppressed yelps but no progress. Once again Louisa tried the telephone, knowing it couldn't possibly be mended and yet half expecting a miracle. She had never felt so helpless as she did as she replaced the receiver and looked at Bella. How could she ever have believed her to be no more than an empty-headed girl? Just look at her now, fighting to bring her baby into the world on a cold kitchen floor and fighting, too, not to give way to what must have been terror. Was she still haunted by the fear that something was wrong to have stilled the movement she had become accustomed to? Whatever was in her mind, she was determined to be strong – so determined that a trickle of blood stained her chin from where she had clamped her teeth on to her bottom lip rather than scream. She had said she wanted them to pray and never in her life had Louisa prayed so hard for anything as she did in those moments, knowing herself to be totally inadequate for the task before her.

As if in answer to their silent pleas for help, through the unrelenting noise of the wind and storm she heard a car stop outside, then the slam of the garden gate. She ran to open the front door, sure that by some miracle help had come. But the person hurrying up the path was Leo under the shelter of a golf umbrella.

'Mrs Johnson said Bella was here. I'll take her back in the car or she'll get drenched.'

'A blessing you've come.' Louisa's voice sounded different, the words tumbling out almost too quickly for him to understand. 'The baby is being born. My phone isn't working. Go and fetch the midwife, Mrs Wilkins, twenty-one, George Street, Ledbridge. Hurry. Hurry! The baby's coming.'

'But it can't be. She has another month or so.'

'Just go! Twenty-one, George Street. Bring her quickly.'

For a moment he hesitated, not used to obeying commands. Despite the situation Louisa found herself enjoying being the one to despatch him so unceremoniously; she felt he deserved it for the way he had referred to Bella on his last visit. Then, as he turned back towards the car she closed her front door and promptly forgot him. He couldn't collect Nurse Wilkins and be back in less than three-quarters of an hour. She had always heard that babies took hours to get themselves into the world and the thought that experienced help would soon be here restored her flagging confidence.

But coming back to the kitchen she could see immediately that this confinement wasn't running to pattern. Sweat was standing out on Bella's face as she fought her battle, pushing with all her might, blood from her bitten lip trickling down her chin. She took no notice of Louisa; she knew nothing except the agony of her torn body and the knowledge that at the end of her struggle she would have brought her baby into the world. Everything was aimed towards that moment. Louisa knelt in front of her, aware of her own inadequacy. She held her hands to touch Bella's and felt them taken in her grip, glad to feel the girl's nails digging into her palms.

In those moments the acquaintance she had borne with patience altered. For them nothing could be the same as it had; a bond was formed in that hour that nothing could break.

By the time Leo and the nurse arrived a baby girl was swaddled in a cashmere shawl which had belonged to Violet. When the nurse weighed her she tipped the scales at exactly five pounds but, although she was so tiny, she was beautiful, as beautiful as might be expected of a child of Bella and Leo. As for Bella, she gave herself up to the nurse's ministrations, almost too tired to know what was happening, only conscious that she had never known such happiness. Louisa had concentrated on tidying her from the waist upwards, taking off her bra and blouse and replacing them with the top of a pair of her own sensible pyjamas, washing her face then combing her sweat-dampened hair. The stained towels had been taken away and replaced with clean ones, then a cover put over her as though the floor were a normal bed. The nurse had a busy hour ahead of her and wanted Leo and Louisa out of the way.

'The storm is more or less over,' Leo said as she led the way into the sitting room, 'so as soon as the nurse finishes whatever she has to do I'll run her home and come back to collect Bella and the infant. I owe you a debt of gratitude; I didn't realize you included midwifery in your qualifications.'

'I know nothing about babies.'

He laughed as he answered, 'You may not have this morning, but by this afternoon you can add "child delivery" to your credentials.'

'This one delivered herself. And never look on Bella as a – as a –' She floundered, uncertain exactly what impression he had given when he mentioned his young wife, but clearly remembering her anger at his tone, 'an innocent child you consider beneath you. She isn't. She is braver than *you* or me either. You can't imagine what she went through, and with

no anaesthetic. All I did was try and look as if I was confident
everything would be all right. In truth, I had never been so
frightened in my life.'

Leo paused, and Louisa thought she saw a momentary flicker
of something in his eyes. 'I think we should wet the infant's
head, don't you? Have you anything in that cupboard we can
drink?' Then, his dark eyes shining with merriment: 'I say, this
is my second visit. The first I ask for coffee and this time it's
alcohol. What will it be next time?'

'Clearly you know where to find the drinks and I shan't
need to tell you where the glasses are. I'll have gin and tonic;
it'll have to be without lemon or ice – we can't go in the
kitchen until the nurse says so. And you take what you want.'
Despite herself, she was starting to feel relaxed. She watched
as he went to the cupboard and poured the same for both of
them. 'Thanks. Now we'll drink to Bella. She's a remarkable
girl. She's come in here most days, but this afternoon I saw a
side to her I would never have imagined. Such strength of
character. But you must know that better than I do. Have you
two decided on a name if it was a girl?'

'I'd not thought about it. She said something about if it
turned out to be a girl it ought to be named after my mother.
Dad would like that. Alice. I don't really care, but it's not a
name that conjures up a picture of beauty. Still, perhaps it's
safe. If she turns out to be plain it's no use lumbering her with
a glamorous name.' He passed her a cigarette and as he was
lighting it suddenly gave her that mischievous smile she remembered from their first meeting. 'Tell you what, she shall be
Alicia. If she's pretty that's OK, but if she's no beauty we'll
drop the fancy end. How's that?'

'Of course she'll be beautiful. But both names are very nice.'
She heard her reply as being prim and humourless. Why
couldn't she have answered him in the same light-hearted way
he'd spoken? However, he seemed not to have noticed. 'The
thunder may have passed, but hark at that rain,' she said,
changing the subject. 'You ought to forget the idea of taking
them home tonight. When I've finished this drink I'll re-make
the bed in the spare room for Bella. Then we'll have to conjure
up something for Alicia.'

It sounded easy, but the truth was that the tiny creature had neither clothes nor a crib. For months Bella had been making preparations and everything had been brought to Ridgeway and put in the nursery bedroom, despite the baby not being due for another month. That must be for tomorrow, supposing the nurse gave permission for Bella to be moved so soon. When she'd booked to go to Britley Maternity Home for the birth she had been told it was usual to expect to be there for at least a fortnight.

With the bed re-made Louisa looked around the room as if she expected something resembling a crib to appear. Then inspir-ation came. By combining the contents of the two drawers in the dressing table she removed one of them and laid it on the bed while she worked out the next stage.

Deep in thought, she was surprised by Leo's voice. 'I can't sit down there like a dummy. I've come to help.'

'You've come at the right time. Go to my bedroom, Aunt Violet's old room, and fetch the little armchair. If we stand it by the side of the bed in here we can rest this drawer across the arms. It'll be quite safe and we can make a snug bed for Alicia's first night. She has no clothes, poor mite.'

'When I've brought the chair, I'll drive home and collect up a bundle of stuff. Bella had everything in a case ready to take to the nursing home.'

'Splendid. Make sure she has put in safety pins for the nappies; I won't have any big enough.' Then she was struck by another thought. 'Leo, would you rather I got my own room ready? This is a special night – your first as a father. You ought to all be together.'

'A kind offer, Louisa, but nursery living isn't my scene. I'd be less than useless. And next thing my father would arrive to join in the fun. No, I'll bring the things and go back to my parent-watching duties.'

She knew he was right but his reply left her feeling angry and disappointed. Bella deserved better.

At the sound of the front door slamming, then his car starting, Nurse Wilkins emerged from the kitchen.

'Has he gone? Has he forgotten he'd promised to see me home?' She spoke in a whisper and looked relieved to be reassured that he would soon be back. 'I'm thankful he hasn't insisted on taking her back home. She really ought not to be moved for a day or two. But you know what young people are like – think they know best even if they come to regret it. Sweet little soul, not a word of self-pity. Gritted her teeth and clenched her fists when I did the stitching. I'll be back in the morning to get her washed and sorted out. And the babe, she's bathed and had a cuddle with her mum, but there was nothing for it but to give that shawl a turn-about and wrap her up in it again. You say he's gone for her things – I'll see she's sorted before I go. She's had a go at the breast, but of course there's no nourishment yet-a-while. Still, she got the hang of it, bless her.' Ethel Wilkins happily talked on, albeit in hushed tones, requiring no answer. And that was probably as well, for Louisa was smarting under her reference to 'young people' as if, like the nurse, she no longer came under that category. Did she look older than her thirty years? After all, 'young' Leo was pushing forty – not such a spring chicken.

Twenty minutes and a cup of tea for the nurse later, the car returned. The house suddenly seemed to be alive with action: Leo carried a sleeping Bella up the stairs and into the bed, where she opened her eyes. Was she dreaming or was this happening? Where was he putting her?

'. . . you've seen Alice?' she whispered – or did she imagine she had said it? Her mind wasn't quite her own yet.

'Alicia,' he corrected. 'I'll bring her up in a minute. See the crib Louisa has made for her? She'll be right by the side of your bed.'

Bella might not have been thinking clearly, but she smiled as her heavy lids closed and she drifted back to sleep. She felt safe; her world was perfect.

Downstairs, the nurse prepared Alicia for her first night. Tiny vest, nappy securely pinned on, flannelette nightgown pulled down before she was cocooned in a shawl.

'There we are, Daddy,' she said in the voice she kept for new fathers and small children. 'Now you go and lay her in that bed Miss Harding has got ready for her.' Duty done, she looked around her at the once again restored kitchen (thanks to Louisa's labour) and in a tone that conveyed satisfaction with her contribution to the last few hours, said, 'Then I think it's all fair and square down here so I'll be ready to get on my way. Miss Harding has been doing all the cleaning up. What with that and the rush the little one came into the world in, my job's been an easy one – that I must admit. Now just lay her in her cot on her back and drape that thin blanket over the top. Off you go now.'

As Louisa carried the bucket and floor mop out to the washroom and the nurse took off her apron and rolled it away in her workbag, they heard the tread of Leo carrying the baby up the stairs. Secretly Nurse Wilkins considered him a rum sort of father – a rum sort of husband, too, for he had made no attempt to see his poor wife lying there on that hard floor. Well, if he was no use with the struggles of childbirth he was better out of the way, but he could at least have made pretence of wanting to share those first moments with the poor girl.

And Louisa? She imagined him carrying his bundle into the spare room and laying it on the blanket she had folded in the wooden drawer. She felt confused, excited and frightened; and yet there was no logic in the nameless emotion. It must be because the day had been like no other. She made herself think of Bella, brave, strong-minded and yet, surely, this night should have held something that Louisa was sure was missing for her.

Bella didn't stir when Leo came into the room; exhaustion and relief were taking their toll. He felt a moment's shame that he was thankful she didn't stir before he dumped his bundle in the makeshift crib, his mind elsewhere, meaning to creep away quietly.

What happened next was outside his control and took him by surprise.

Four

It wasn't to the sleeping figure in the bed that Leo turned, but to the baby. If he had laid her down gently she probably wouldn't have stirred. Nurse Wilkins had pushed the bundle into his arms and, having delivered her to the makeshift bed, he started to move away, his mission accomplished. But something pulled him back and made him bend over the tiny form. From her shoulders downward she was tightly wrapped, only her face visible. Rarely, if ever, had he felt such a rush of tenderness as he did for the tiny creature. His daughter, his flesh and blood, so small and vulnerable, dependent on him to love and care for her. Very tenderly he moved his finger down her cheek, silently mouthing the word, 'Alicia'. She opened her eyes, seeming to gaze up at him even though, in reality, at no more than a few hours old she hadn't even learnt to focus. As he watched her his vision misted, not with tears that would escape for the world to see, but something he shared just with her. Only a minute before, he had dumped her unceremoniously in the drawer; now he picked her up tenderly and held her so that he could reach to lay his face against hers. Instinct told her to nuzzle against him, to open her mouth.

'What, not got her in that bed yet?' In a stage whisper the nurse's voice cut across his emotions, leaving him feeling exposed. 'Goodness me, this won't do. Now, don't you wake your poor wife. After what she's been through today she needs a good sleep. Nature will make her ready for you by morning. Now, give me this bundle. Come along, my pretty, into bed you go.'

Like an obedient child, Leo handed the bundle over. 'I'll wait for you downstairs and run you home as soon as you're ready.'

And so the day of Alicia's birth came to a close. The day had been orchestrated by a storm that would find the locals talking about it the next day and remembering it long after;

but by late evening the air was clear and the clouds had rolled away leaving a cloudless, starry sky. The only evidence of what had gone before was a few old and brittle branches in the lanes and one tree uprooted and fallen across the road on the far side of the village. With the coming of evening all was calm. Nature had sent a reminder of its power and a reassurance that after the storm calm would always follow.

Despite Bella's ethereal beauty there was a quality of true grit about her. The morning after Alicia's birth, when Leo drove to fetch her home to the farm, she refused his offer to carry her to the car, holding up the nightdress and dressing gown she had borrowed so that the hem wouldn't get dirty from the muddy pathway as she led the procession to the parked vehicle.

'The nurse is coming to Ridgeway to see Alice and me – no, it's not going to be Alice. Leo likes Alicia. Pretty, isn't it? She said I must stay in bed until either she or the doctor tells me I can get dressed. But think how silly that is. I want to be getting on with living, especially now that the baby is here to be introduced to the world.'

She looked from Leo to Louisa, trying to influence them into agreeing with her.

'I don't know anything about babies,' Louisa said, unable to crush a feeling of relief that for a few days her life would be her own again. Her views on Bella may have changed through the weeks and no longer did she find her chatter empty, but even so, she had always been a loner and the promise of time on her own appealed to her. Then she imagined the fear Bella had been determined to fight the previous day as she had struggled to give birth to the baby Leo carried with tenderness, and felt mean and unfair.

Leo remained silent. Still cradling the baby, he opened the door on the passenger side and, once Bella was seated, passed the bundle into her arms. Bella had eyes for nothing and no one except the day-old miracle.

'I can't thank you enough for what you did yesterday,' Leo said as he made sure the door was safely closed, 'and for keeping them overnight.'

'I've never experienced anything so humbling. Bella is a remarkable girl.' Then, before he had a chance to enlarge on what she'd said: 'Don't hang around. She ought to be home and in bed – that was the nurse's instruction.'

'Ah,' he answered, raising his eyebrows and with that mischievous twinkle in his eyes. 'The good nurse – she who shall be obeyed.'

Despite all her good intentions not to let his mood influence her, Louisa laughed.

'Certainly she deserves nothing less. What she must have thought when she arrived to find her patient bedded down on the kitchen floor I can't imagine. But she took it in her stride. Don't hang around here talking, Bella ought to be home and resting. Off you go.' She dismissed him before opening the passenger door a couple of inches and saying to Bella, who was gazing at the baby as though she couldn't believe there could be a miracle so beautiful, 'In a day or two I'll walk up and see you, if I may, Bella.'

A minute later the car was making its way up the track to the farmhouse and Louisa collected her weeding tools. After yesterday's storm even the deeply rooted dandelions ought to give themselves up. Satisfied that the action was over, Gladys Holmes, from the end of the three terraced cottages opposite, moved away from the window. 'Like looking back in time,' she muttered to herself. 'Just like his father, that one. And as for the Harding woman, spitting image of her aunt, she is. Well, we shall see. It wouldn't surprise me if—' But even to herself she didn't finish the sentence. Good, plodding Alice was a far cry from that pretty child Leo's burnt his hands on . . . and serves him right. He'd always been a rascal and that was *his* affair, but little Bella was nought but a child and deserved better than she'd ever find with a ne'er-do-well like Leo Carter.

If she could have looked into the confusion of Louisa's thoughts as she stabbed and yanked at the weeds it would have done nothing to set her mind at rest. For Louisa was angry with herself. There was an arrogant self-assurance in Leo's manner that annoyed her. That was what she tried to make herself believe, but the truth was not so straightforward. Yes, she disliked that, but even more she felt uncomfortably suspicious that he was laughing at her, seeing her as a humourless spinster who tried to keep up with his natural and good-natured flow of lightweight chatter. He was just the sort of man she most disliked, but he was Bella's adored husband and for that reason she must make herself polite to him – coolly polite.

It was mid-morning the next day when there was a knock at her front door.

'Damn,' she muttered, getting up from her worktable and marking how far she had added the sales figures from the ledger of an old-fashioned bespoke tailor's establishment where she was preparing his forms for income tax. Closing the workroom door behind her she hurried across the hall to see who could possibly be calling on her.

'The top of the morning to you,' Leo greeted her. 'I set off for a walk and then I saw your gate ajar and was tempted in.'

'I thought you were supposed to be working from home. Surely you haven't taken a day off already?'

'Indeed I have not. If there is thinking to be done, then where better than walking the country lanes?' The smile on his face was reflected in his tone of voice as he added, 'My mind turned to my previous visits here and I sensed I could smell coffee brewing. Would I be right, or was it wishful thinking?'

She seemed powerless to refuse him, or even to stop her face from breaking into a smile. He was indolent; he played at work because he felt safe in the family business while his elder brother shouldered the responsibility. He didn't appear to take even his marriage or parenthood seriously. He saw life as a game. These were some of the things she was telling herself as she led the way to the kitchen. He was the sort of man for whom she had neither time nor respect. So why did she fill the globe-shaped bowl of the coffee maker with water?

'We need the coffee beans ground. The grinder is—'

'I know where the coffee grinder is. It's just inside the larder door. Oh, but I say, you've got rid of the old one. This is very state of the art.'

'It still needs all your elbow grease, so if you want coffee you have to earn it.'

He spooned the beans into the funnel and started to turn the handle.

'This is nice. You don't exactly welcome me with open arms and yet I feel so at home here.'

'If you've been used to coming here most of your life you are hardly likely to feel a stranger.' Perhaps that sounded more welcoming than she intended, so she added, 'I look on Bella as a friend so naturally I wouldn't turn her husband away.'

'That's my girl. The beans are ready; shall I put all of them in the top of the machine?'

'Yes. I measured them out before you ground them. They won't take long. I usually let the water boil up twice.'

'A lady after my own heart; there's nothing worse than a feeble cup of coffee. Ciggy?'

'Let's wait until we take the coffee outside. It's too good a morning to waste indoors.'

'Wasn't that what you were doing when I interrupted your labours? I seem to remember hearing your workroom door shut before you bid me enter.'

What was there about him that gave her this feeling that he was laughing at her – *at* her, not *with* her? 'That's different,' she snapped, 'I wasn't wasting my time, I was working. Just as I shall be again when we have had our coffee and you've gone on your way. Do you take sugar? I can't remember.' In fact, she could remember perfectly well that he wanted neither milk nor sugar. 'No? Then we won't bother to take it out with us.' To her own ears she sounded crabby, unwelcoming. But he appeared to be completely unaware of it, which did nothing to improve her humour.

A few minutes later it was impossible not to relax outside in the warm sunshine, sipping strong black coffee and inhaling the vaguely scented smoke from the cigarette he had passed her.

'I've never smoked these before,' she said, looking at the cigarette she held between her fingers, 'the oval shape makes it feel odd to hold.'

'You don't like them? *Passing Cloud*. I bought my first packet when I was still at school and felt frightfully sophisticated.' He laughed, remembering. 'I considered them more glamorous than the ordinary ones Dad smoked.'

'And are you still striving to give the impression of sophis-
tication?' She made sure her tone held a note of mockery, even
though as happened so often with him, she was interested in
his answer.

'No. That sort of thing dies with adolescence. It's all part
of growing up. You must have found that yourself.'

'I honestly don't think I gave it any thought. I only had one
goal and that was – still is, for that matter – to be as well qualified as my male peers and, if I'm truthful, to overtake them.'

He was looking at her thoughtfully, trying to imagine this
groomed and confident woman being young and gauche.

'Now, there's a wasted youth for you! I shall never believe
you had nothing more exciting to dream about than other
people's finances.'

She frowned, annoyed with herself that she had led the
conversation into a trap.

'To be honest,' she answered, speaking the truth, 'I wasn't
interested in a client's finances except that my work involved
the figures and I was, I *am*, vitally interested in accuracy. Right
is right and there is no other way.'

For once he studied her seriously. 'You are a remarkable
woman, Louisa Harding. I understand what you mean. I knew
it without your having to spell it out to me. Just to look at
you: not a hair would dare to escape out of place, as immaculate at home on your own as you would be in town with a
client.' The brief moment of seriousness had been overtaken
by the merriment that danced in his eyes.

She was annoyed. Was being fastidious in her appearance
something to turn her into a figure of fun?

'And you?' she retorted, none too politely. 'Work may not
be important to you but clearly you are pernickety about your
appearance. So why should you expect me to be different?'

'Don't be cross,' he smiled disarmingly, 'you know I was
pulling your leg.' And again he had wrong-footed her, sending
her confidence on a downward spiral.

'How are your family, Bella and Alicia?' she asked.

Immediately his manner changed. There was warmth in his
expression, and she felt she had intruded into happiness she
had no right to see.

'She is so beautiful,' he said softly. 'I've never felt so – so
– I don't know what it is. It's not just love; it's not as simple
as that.'

'Yes, she is truly beautiful. And, Leo, she must have been
frightened to death but she was so brave, so incredibly brave.'

'Bella? Yes, you said, and I'm sure she was. She's a good
lass. You know, I envy her. Nature gives her a claim on Alicia
that I'm outside of. This morning I went into her room and
she was holding Alicia. I was jealous. I'm ashamed to say it,
but it's the truth. The baby was at her breast, lying there in
her arms and gazing up at her with a sort of unblinking stare.
You could almost feel the bond binding them together and I
was on the outside.'

'But that's imagination, Leo. The love Bella feels for Alicia
is natural, but it won't take anything from what she feels for
you. If ever a young wife adores her husband, then it's Bella.'

He frowned, puzzled. 'I didn't mean that. Never mind. I
can't expect you to understand how I felt when I can't even
understand it myself. The night she was born, when I carried
her up to the bed you'd made for her, it was the oddest, most
overwhelming sensation I've ever known. A feeling so pure,
so – so humbling.'

'She's a lucky little girl. I wonder whether all new fathers
feel like that?' She thought of her own father and felt sure they
didn't. In the last minute or two she believed Leo had let her
see a side of his nature he usually kept hidden behind his
banter. Later she would think about it or, perhaps more accurately, she would try to push it to the bottom of her mind.
For she was certain his words hadn't been spoken lightly and
she knew instinctively he wasn't a man to share his emotions
easily. Then she conjured up the image of Bella holding the
baby to her breast, Bella who adored him and deserved more
from him than he gave. 'It's time I went back to my world of
figures and you got walking and dreaming up some new agricultural masterpiece. Give my love to Bella and tell her I'll
look in tomorrow, if that's OK.'

'Yes, m'am, message received. If there's to be no, "May I
get you another cup?" I shall leave you to your labours.' He
stood up to leave and then hesitated. 'Louisa, you didn't mind

me dropping in like this? I enjoy talking to you, you're – oh, I don't know – you're *sound*. Is that crazy? It is meant as a compliment, I promise you.'

'I'm not looking for compliments. If you want to call in, of course you may. But, if I'm up to my eyes in work you mustn't mind if I send you packing.'

His smile told her he was pleased with her answer.

As summer gave way to autumn they followed the rules: every few days he would stroll up the garden path and, on her instruction, rather than knock at the front door he would walk round to the back door and go straight into the kitchen. If she was busy, true to her word, she would 'send him packing'. Otherwise, they would exchange views on things they'd read in the morning paper, often but not always seeing things from the same angle. Louisa's life had been insular, but that wasn't borne out in her interests. Like so many loners she read widely, was interested in the arts and loved music, even though she had never learnt to play an instrument. And to her surprise, fun-loving Leo was very similar, so there was never any shortage of topics for them to unravel and rebuild. Louisa found herself increasingly enjoying her time with him, but while she grew closer to Leo and, she was sure, he grew closer to her, she was mindful of the fact that he was Bella's husband, and never considered his attentions as anything more than those of a friend.

Bella was a natural homemaker and was in her element at Ridgeway Farm. If she needed advice she asked Eva Johnson, who enjoyed teaching 'the pretty child who had stolen young Leo's heart after all his years of philandering'. Eva had never had a daughter and her two sons had moved far away up north, so she liked to think of herself as taking the place of the mother poor Bella had lost so long ago. Altogether it was a happy situation and with every passing day Bella gained more respect for the way she filled her role. As for Harold, as his mind became more vacant he found a new contentment. To have Leo, always his favourite, actually living at home again made him feel secure. But more than that there was Bella with the baby, a new joy to fill his days.

To be well groomed was second nature to Harold. Each

morning when he arrived at the breakfast table he was shaved, his tie the correct shade to go with his shirt and a clean white handkerchief just protruding from the breast pocket of his jacket. Yet despite that, there was one morning in October when he wore one brown shoe and one black. When Leo pointed it out to him he was mortified, especially as Bella was within earshot. What sort of an old fool would she think him? But Bella, with more consideration of other people's feelings than her husband, gave no hint that she had been listening to what was said, purposely making a noise running water and clattering plates as she prepared to bring the dish of food to the table. The shoes were forgotten and Harold might have been left wearing odd ones all day but for the fact that as Leo went to get ready before setting out for a meeting with an old client she followed him upstairs.

'Before you go, don't forget to help Dad with his shoes,' she whispered quite unnecessarily as Harold was downstairs leaning over Alicia's pram, chattering to her and trying to be the one to have her first smile.

'You can do that,' Leo answered, puzzled by the request.

'No, please, you help him. He didn't know I heard so let him think no one noticed except you. He'd be embarrassed.'

Leo put his finger under her chin and tipped her face towards his. 'You really are a very nice person, Bella Carter.'

Did she imagine it or did the colour really rush to her face as she stood quite still with her lips parted? Of course, he read the invitation and accepted it. His mind was running away with him. Ever since he had brought her home with a one-day-old baby she and Alicia had shared the room next to his. She had said that with three-hourly feeds she would worry that he was being disturbed. So did she imagine he slept contentedly all night? How could she feel Alicia's sweet mouth pulling at her breast and not be aroused, as aroused as he was as he lay there imagining?

She moved slightly away from him but he pulled her close, his hand moving under her jumper to hold the firm fullness of her swollen breast.

'Careful, darling Leo. It's nearly time for baby's feed; you mustn't do that to me or it'll leak.'

He withdrew his hand, his sudden ardour banished by her matter-of-fact tone. To fondle her full breast, to imagine the blood-warm milk trickling on to his fingers had brought him almost to the point of losing control, yet her voice had the effect of dousing him with cold water again. Letting go of her he turned away, but she appeared to think he was simply seeing the wisdom of her warning.

'You will remember to help Dad?' she whispered.

'Of course.'

'Thanks. What time are you meeting . . . whoever it is?'

'Not for ages. But I shall go as soon as I'm ready. I prefer to be early.'

In fact, he needn't have left home for another hour, something that had been in his mind as he had made such an ineffectual effort to excite Bella.

Breakfast only just over and a day waiting to be lived, he knew this was no time to give in to the way his thoughts were turning. All he really needed was for her to let him know that her imagination had carried her on a journey similar to his. But this was Bella, sweet, affectionate but with a mind that never strayed away from the routine of her day. Not for a second would she have suspected that his caress had been more than an affirmation of pleasure that she had followed him to the bedroom that, until Alicia's birth, they had shared.

'I'd better go down,' she said. 'I told Dad not to pick Alicia up, but you know how he loves to hold her when I pass her to him. He's really much better here, isn't he? And he even understands now that it's Louisa at The Retreat when we go there, not their old friend. You know what I was thinking, Leo? I was thinking that when I go into the village this morning I would take him and we'd call and see Louisa on the way. If I had a whisper to her I'm sure she would agree for him to sit and talk to her while Alicia and I do the shopping. Don't you think that would be extra good for him?'

'I'm in good time; I'll stop off as I pass and ask her if she'll be the one to suggest it. If she doesn't say anything, you'll know she isn't in favour.'

'Do you mind? That would be so much easier than having to engineer a chance to whisper to her. And I'm sure he's ready. It's not good for him to feel we're always watching him. Come and say goodbye before you go.'

After he'd heard her footsteps running down the stairs he sat on the edge of the unmade bed. Was it having the baby that had changed her? She had found a new confidence and surely he should be glad. Yet he felt excluded. The girl she had been a year ago had been overtaken by an adoring young mother, a kind and thoughtful daughter-in-law, the mistress of this old barn of a house – but where was the wife whose love for him had been there in her every expression, her pride in him for all the world to see? It used to irritate him; it used to put him in mind of an adolescent with a crush on a film star. One of his many pre-marriage liaisons had been with a war widow and he remembered going into her fourteen-year-old daughter's bedroom one evening to change an electric light bulb and seeing pictures attached to the wall with drawing pins: Clark Gable, Gary Cooper and Fred Astaire. The very young have but a limited image of love, an image based on glamour and happy endings. But life wasn't like that. He had told himself that he would never fail Bella, and neither would he. But with the arrival of Alicia he no longer felt he played the most vital role in her life. Surely he ought to be relieved. He had never loved her as he believed a man should love his wife, so what better than that she filled her life without being entirely dependent on him? Soon she would move back into their shared bedroom, and she would be there for him if not with any fire of passion then at least with generosity and tenderness. For God's sake, think about something else, man – you've got a meeting that David says is important in a couple of hours and a thirty-mile drive before then, so collect the drawings and get going.

First, though, he had promised to call on Louisa.

As usual he walked round to the back door and went straight into the kitchen unannounced where, to his surprise, he found her sitting at the wooden table with the coffee maker in front of her, idly watching as the dark liquid hissed down the funnel to the bowl below. The room was filled with that magic aroma: freshly percolated coffee and mentholated spirit from the lamp that heated it. But it wasn't the tempting smell that took his attention – it was the sight of Louisa. Half past nine in the morning and she was without make-up and wearing a dark green velvet housecoat – like so much else, previously belonging to Violet.

'Don't tell me you were driving by and happened to smell the coffee?' she greeted him, forcing a laugh.

'I wouldn't dream of lying to you at this hour of day. I bring a message from Bella.' And so he put forward the suggestion. 'She thought it would be a stride on Dad's journey of getting used to seeing you here – probably the first time he'd been alone with you barring the night he caused such a rumpus. I honestly think she has brought him here sufficient times since then to know you are not his Violet and that this place belongs to you. But if you feel uncomfortable about it, then when Bella says she has to go to the shops just say nothing and she will know you don't want him here on his own. It may be a useless idea anyway. His mind wanders.' She understood more than those last simple words told her and saw Leo's helplessness that he could do nothing to bring back the man he had always known. Giving help in the only way she could think of, she took another cup and saucer and poured him his favourite strong, black coffee. Immediately the mask of cheerfulness (if, indeed, it was a mask) was back in place. 'That's my girl,' he said, his eye half closing in a hint of a wink, 'I knew you wouldn't turn me out into the morning air without sharing your nectar of the gods. No one brews coffee like you do.'

'Perhaps you should widen your visiting circle, then you might find they do.' She took the cigarette he offered and waited while he lit it, only then seeing herself as he must be seeing her – sitting around in a dressing gown, smoking instead of eating breakfast. What sort of a slattern must he think her? She was conscious that under the dressing gown she was naked; she imagined he must be aware of it too. And without her daily armour of make-up she felt vulnerable. 'I don't usually breakfast before I dress,' she told him, and then wished she hadn't drawn attention to her state of undress.

'Sometimes one should break with routine or life gets tedious.'

'There's something comforting about habit,' she retorted. 'I don't like lounging.'

He smiled, his eyes shining with merriment. 'You ought to try it more often. I promise you, it grows on you.'

She opened her mouth to speak, intending to knock him off his perch, but then realized that he wasn't serious.

'From one who knows?'

'From one who believes there is a time to work and a time to play — even a time just to lounge. I'm glad Bella asked me to call in — quite apart from the coffee and ciggy. If I'd driven straight past the house I shouldn't have seen you this morning, no make-up to hide behind, just as nature made you. And you know what? Louisa Harding, you are a very lovely woman.' There was no teasing note in his voice as he made the statement. She felt horribly gauche and uncomfortable, unfamiliar with compliments as she was. She could think of no light remark that would turn the subject. Instead she took a drink of coffee in an attempt to hide her confusion. But she swallowed it the wrong way and it made her choke. Coughing, spluttering, fighting for breath, she wanted him gone so that she could be alone as she coughed from the depth of her being. Her eyes were running; her nose was running.

He fetched a glass of tap water and held it to her. 'See if this helps.'

Her hands were shaking as she took the glass so, although she gripped it herself, he still held on to it as she drank. It did help but, even though she no longer coughed uncontrollably, her quick, short breath caught in her throat and she was embarrassed as she tried to clear the air passage, at the same time digging in her pocket to find a handkerchief to mop her face.

Watching her, he was aware of a strange sensation. He couldn't put a name to it, nor yet could he recognize what prompted it. For a second his mind jumped back to the night he had first held Alicia, and yet what he felt now was very different. The similarity was in his inability to control his own emotion. And just as had happened on that night with Alicia, so now he felt the sting of tears, tears that wouldn't fall but would make this a moment to be remembered. How could she not be aware of it? But clearly she wasn't, as she blew her nose in an attempt to restore herself and draw a line under the unfortunate episode.

'Better?' he asked gently.

She nodded. 'Can't think what I did,' she gasped, still not quite in control of her voice and panting as though she had run a race. 'Sorry. What an exhibition. Thanks for the water.'

'My pleasure, m'am. And now I must prove to you that I am indeed part of the working community. I have to get to Ludlow. Nice morning for a drive. Pity you're not dressed, or you could have come too.'

'You forget, I'm expecting your family this morning.' She made sure her reply was in a tone as light as his, despite the fact that her heart was still pounding, so that he would know she hadn't taken his remark seriously.

Just for a second he hesitated, as if loath to leave, and then he said with a hint of anxiety in his voice, 'You're sure you're better?'

'Completely.' And with that one word she drew a line under the last moments, even though she knew they would haunt her in the wee small hours, bringing both comfort and shame. Bella was her friend – good, sweet Bella, who hadn't a selfish thought in her head.

As she listened to the sound of his car drawing away she stared unseeingly at where, a minute before, he had been. It was as if he had left an imprint behind. She recalled his words, the tone of his voice, the sudden merriment in his eyes, as if he were still with her. Then, realizing where she was allowing her thoughts to stray, she pulled herself together, took their cups to the sink and went upstairs to run her bath and start the morning afresh.

Tiny babies were out of Louisa's field of experience, but there was something enchanting about Alicia. But then Louisa only saw her when she had been fed and watered and was snug in her pram. In the eyes of the world the baby might have been no more advanced than her peers and, perhaps, no more beautiful; but to Bella she was the most precious thing on earth and, as for Leo, he sometimes wondered at his sanity as he

bent over her pram or cot when she'd been put down to sleep
and, alone with her, talked softly to her as he never had to
any living soul. So her parents both loved her deeply, deeply
and separately. Neither thought of her as 'our baby' – to each
she was '*my* little girl'. Of course, it wasn't just her parents
who loved her; at the farm she was never without someone
or other stopping to play with her. Harold adored her and if
there was one way of being certain where he was it was to
ask him to keep an eye on her, for him keeping an eye meant
to be within six foot of his charge. He nursed her, he sang
nursery rhymes to her and as soon as she could sit up, one of
their favourite games was for him to bounce her on his knee
singing 'Ride a Cock Horse' while she chuckled with delight.

Bella was utterly content. Alicia was the hub on which her
wheel of life turned, but there was so much more. She took
it for granted that she adored Leo – of course she did – and
really she found him much easier than she had in the first
months of their marriage. As Alicia started to sleep longer at
night there was no need to be on hand for three hourly or
even four hourly feeds. By the time the baby was almost six
months old she woke at about eleven or midnight, half-heart-
edly took her mother's breast and then slept until six in the
morning or after. With all the excitement and trepidation of
an innocent young bride, Bella told Leo she was ready to go
back to their original sleeping arrangements.

He raised his eyebrows and looked at her teasingly.

'If you want me, I mean,' she said, some of her confidence
deserting her. For over the last few months their relationship
had been so different that they might have been friendly and
caring siblings. She felt uncomfortably shy, as if she were forcing
herself on him. After all, they'd become used to the arrangement of separate rooms. It had worked very well and he hadn't
pressed her to come back to him.

'Is that all right, darling, or do you prefer having the room
to yourself?'

He sensed her embarrassment. 'Sweet Bella, I look forward
to sharing my lonely bed with you.' Reassured, she nuzzled
against his shoulder.

'It'll be lovely to cuddle up together,' she said, contentment

in every word. For through those months since their return
to the farm she had been utterly happy in her role. The old
and rambling house had to be kept clean and tidy, the meals
had to be cooked and cleared away, the baby had to be cared
for and Harold, even in his home surroundings, had to be
watched to make sure he wasn't doing anything dangerous.
Now, with her return to her wifely role, she felt her cup of
happiness was full to the brim. Secretly she hoped that darling
Leo would be content just to snuggle down to sleep most
nights, although if he moved towards her she would never
refuse him. But she had a romantic notion that lovemaking
should be reserved for moments of high emotional devotion,
with the light off and the act of union almost like a religious
benediction, taken in silence and deep peace. In any case, while
she was still nursing the baby she didn't feel it was right for
him to want to touch a part of her body that belonged just
to Alicia and herself.

He honestly tried not to overstep her limits, but he was not
a man to set one or even two nights a week aside for permitted
sex and be content to 'snuggle up' for the rest. Had she no
natural sex drive? Her dutiful availability had the effect on him
of finding her nearness less than alluring. Lying with his back
to her as if settled for the night, he had no control over his
wayward thoughts. Was this how it had been for his father?
Had he been haunted by thoughts of the woman in the house
at the end of the lane, so near and yet so impossibly distant?
But for his father the situation had been different – he had
brought Violet to The Retreat – and, for him, it had indeed
been a retreat. Leo's thoughts turned to them more and more,
remembering how as an adolescent he had loved going to the
house, sometimes when Violet was alone and sometimes when
his father was there too. He remembered the atmosphere he
always knew he would find there. Even now, after so many
years, he recalled how during school holidays he used to escape
there from the many jobs waiting in the fields or packing sheds,
and how pleased with himself he had felt when he decided to
call The Retreat a stress-free zone. But that was more than a
quarter of a century ago. What about now? It was not stress
that made him take every opportunity to go there. Sometimes

his visit would be no more than a few minutes but he found it impossible to pass the house.

Was he a fool to let Louisa have such a hold over his thoughts? She was invariably friendly, happy to sit an hour discussing topics of interest from the news . . . the latest thoughts on the suspected damage done to the ozone layer, whether it was caused by testing the atomic bomb or the increase in jet aircraft; the latest budget and the recovery of the business world – the country seemed full of hope in this new Elizabethan Age, and in his mind he saw Louisa as the epitome of all that entailed. She was intelligent, confident, independent – a self-sufficient woman. Little did he suspect there was a side to her that she kept hidden from the world.

Of the three of them, Louisa, Bella and Leo, the most contented was Bella. For the first time in her life she knew she had an essential purpose.

There were various occasions when Harold's worsening mental state became obvious, but Bella always tried to cover his failings and boost his flagging confidence. One such occasion was a cold March morning when Alicia was hardly more than six months old. Upstairs tidying the bedrooms, with one eye on Alicia, who was at the crawling stage, Bella had no idea that Harold had decided he would light the fire in the sitting room, even though it wasn't usually lit until the afternoon.

The first she knew that something was wrong was when he called out to her. 'You'd better come down, Bella, I need some help!' he shouted from the bottom of the stairs, and from his voice she knew he needed it quickly.

Carrying Alicia, she ran down the stairs to find him standing in the doorway of the sitting room, a burnt-out sheet of newspaper in the fireplace with tentative flames licking the edge of the smouldering hearthrug. Her first thought was the baby, so she dumped her on her bottom in her playpen in the kitchen where, offended, Alicia screamed angrily. But there was no time to spare.

'Move the chairs!' Bella yelled to Harold, remembering what she had read about burning upholstery being the cause of so many house fires. 'No! Not that way! Away from the fire, off the rug.' Her heart was pounding; in her imagination she could see those small half-hearted flames bursting into furious life. She stamped hard on the edge of the rug as she called her next instructions to Harold, who stood helplessly. Even in her moment of fright, pity for him made her lower her tone. 'It's all right, Dad. I want you to get me a bowl of water and a brush, any brush — even a nail brush if you can't lay your hands on anything bigger. Be as quick as you can, there's a dear.' Somehow, talking gently to him had driven away some of her own fear. Thank goodness he had shouted for her when he had. The rug was still smoking but if she scrubbed water deep into it, it should go out. Then she'd get him to help her carry it outside.

'Here's the water. Alicia wants to come in, shall I get her?'

'No, leave her in her pen. When I've scrubbed water into the pile you and I can carry the rug outside. It's a blessing you shouted when you did, Dad. I think we're going to be OK. Now then, ready? Let's lift it gently and make sure it's not still burning or the fresh air might set it off again. Then straight out of the front door.'

'You're a good girl, Bella, my dear. I don't know how I let the paper catch fire.'

'It was an accident, Dad. But it's better to use the bellows than hold a newspaper in front of the fire to make it draw properly. Promise that next time that's what you'll do.'

'Don't seem to be able to do anything properly these days. Don't know what's the matter with me.'

'You take that end and I'll take this,' she said, picking up her end of the large hearthrug as she spoke. 'The matter with you? I can't see anything the matter with you. You look in pretty good nick from where I stand.' She said it with a saucy smile but silently she thought, *Poor old darling. He must be so frightened. I've got to try and take his mind off what he did.*

His natural love of having the admiration of a pretty young girl helped to restore his self-esteem.

'Let's roll it. I can get it outside on my own if it's rolled. I'll see I take it right away from the house. You go off and sort our little girl out, eh?' His fright was fading and already he began to see himself as master of the situation.

'Thanks, Dad, you're a honey.'

So the honey, feeling completely restored and forgetting he'd been the cause of the short-lived drama, picked up the rolled rug and staggered off with it while she went to restore peace in the kitchen. That was one of the more dramatic of his muddled wrong-doings, but a day never passed without something: he would go into the hall to pick up the post and come back carrying her coat taken from the rack instead; he would go outside to the shed to fetch the vegetables needed for her to cook and then catch sight of one of the men in the field and forget his mission. When Eva Johnson came to 'give the silver a real good clean' he decided to help her; being with Eva always made him forget recent times and think himself back when they were all young, but even that was changing. For, his offer of help accepted, he disappeared to find a nice soft cloth for polishing and came back with a nightgown of Alicia's he'd taken from the top of the pile in the ironing basket. And so it went on, each day bringing something different. The men who worked the fields were very patient and encouraged him to join them, but during the cold weather there was less activity and he was often to be found indoors with Bella.

Leo had looked forward to 'working from home'. But boredom soon made him restless – which in some ways benefited the business, for he spent more time visiting dealers who were agents for their implements. And it was as he covered the miles on his own that he gave full rein to his thoughts. His heart wasn't in his work; it never had been. He envied David his wholehearted interest and yet the thought of having a life as narrow as was his elder brother's appalled him. Married to Lilian for more than fifteen years, and childless, his only break from work was his Sunday morning round of golf, after which he and Lilian would have lunch at the golf club with a couple of longstanding and similarly-minded friends before returning home to read the Sunday paper and perhaps have the same couple in for a game of bridge in the evening; only on a Sunday would David let his mind wander from the affairs of Carters' Agricultural Implements. Week after week, month after month, that was his life, and yet he seemed almost smugly satisfied with his lot. Were they childless from choice? A reserved couple, Leo felt he could never really know either of them. But who does one ever know? And here his mind would always jump in the same direction: Louisa Harding. There were moments when he felt they came closer to a true and understanding friendship than he believed possible. Or was that his imagination? What was certain was that he was never bored with her. A good-looking woman, not pretty, not beautiful in a feminine way, but striking. If she walked into any room she would be noticed. Yet there was nothing flamboyant in her style of dress. It was the way she walked, the way she held her head, her self-assurance that set her apart. She was over thirty . . . never mentioned any male friends . . . fastidious in every way . . . and yet, and yet . . . under that cool exterior he was certain there was a fire waiting to be ignited. Had she ever had a man? Perhaps during the war there had been someone, perhaps she had lost a sweetheart . . . so had she known love, physical love? Just for a moment he thought of Bella, beautiful Bella, yet where was the passion, where was the drive in her that knew only one goal? Still, what a godsend it was to know she was looking after Dad.

At the thought of his father Leo felt real sadness. Alive and healthy, and yet it was as if each day he slipped further away from them. He had been a role model as long as Leo could remember. And here his mind took a sideways jump as he thought of Violet and the *rightness* of the two of them being together. And yet what about his mother? She too had been a truly good woman and a loving wife in the only way she knew. But that could never have been enough for Dad; the most important thing in his life had been the love he shared with Violet. And was it to happen again? Was he to find the joy and true union with Louisa that his father had known with her aunt? And then there was Bella. He had promised himself that he would be a good husband to her. But couldn't he still be a good husband to her, and father to Alicia, if he found happiness elsewhere? Bella would still have everything she wanted: a family, a home, security. His being with Louisa would be completely separate from his marriage. Surely Louisa would see it that way, too?

Louisa was Bella's friend – although what they had in

common was beyond his understanding – and instinct warned him that if he tried to gain her interest in any way except platonic friendship he would lose what he had of her. Even though what he had could never be enough, he couldn't think of his life without her. But in his mind, especially at the end of the day, as he gave the impression of settling for sleep, he gazed on her imagined nakedness, he held her firm rounded breasts, he covered her mouth with his and felt her lips part as her tongue escaped like a caged animal finding freedom. She may be Bella's friend, but she was *his woman*. Most of his short-term girlfriends through the years had been easy prey; Bella had been different – easy prey indeed but with such innocent purity that she had touched finer feelings he'd not known he possessed. But Louisa was like no other; she was the best companion, she was the most desirable, the most physically aloof and, he was certain, the most sensual woman he had ever known.

His nocturnal thoughts stayed with him through the day as he drove westward to one of the firm's established agents near Taunton, and on through his discussion and lunch which was Carters' way of showing appreciation to a worthwhile customer. Charm was second nature to Leo and no one listening to him would have guessed that his mind was anywhere but on the new and improved design of the two-furrow plough for which he was hoping to be given a good order. Uppermost in his mind was how quickly he could decently get away. He could be back in Lexleigh by late afternoon. He'd never been used to being rebuffed. Surely she would give him a sign that under her façade of ice maiden she was as hungry for love as he was.

That same day had been unexpectedly exciting for Louisa. After spending an hour with a client in town she'd decided to call at the nursery and see what she could find to add colour to her still drab apology for a garden. Last year she had made a bed for annuals and been pleased with the result, but now, with summer approaching, by no stretch of the imagination could her miserable patch be called a garden, despite the hours she had spent in it. Maybe she just hadn't got green fingers. Sometimes she felt that all she saw for her efforts were broken fingernails and a stiff back. But she was determined not to be beaten. McLaren's Garden Centre was a mile or so off her road home, and she remembered how pleased she had been on the day she had first discovered it when she'd been touring the district and gathering confidence and experience at the wheel. How distant all that seemed, and her days in Reading might have been in another life altogether.

Each time she'd been to the nursery the same girl had served her; in fact, she appeared to be the only person there except for a couple of men working outside. Part of the pleasure of going there had been talking to the assistant, who appeared knowledgeable and was friendly. She was a girl with red curly hair (red bordering on auburn) and a crop of freckles over the bridge of her nose, but it was her smile that drew Louisa back. So late that morning she was disappointed to find a young man in the shed that doubled as a shop. A tall man, about her own age or perhaps even younger, his gingery brown eyes in keeping with his hair, and when he turned to greet her and introduce himself as Hamish McLaren, she saw he had the same ready smile as the girl.

'Good morning to you.' He greeted Louisa in a voice that, like the girl's, held a hint that he came from north of the border. 'Are you wanting help or do you prefer to wander around and see what there is?'

'I suppose I want both. I bought a load of annuals here last year and they almost persuaded me I was turning my wilderness into a garden. But it'll take more than that.' Then, as if she owed him an explanation, 'It's the first time I've ever had a garden – and it's the first time my patch of scrub has been expected to try to look like a garden too.'

'A new house with an uncultivated area round it? On some of the new estates where I've been called in, you wouldn't believe the state of the ground. Dig just below the surface and do you find soil? More likely builders' rubble. Some developers put a bit of turf on top; turf can cover a multitude of sins.'

'The house isn't new. But the land used to be part of a farm and they took a strip near the road and fenced it off as an independent dwelling. It's really hard work to try to turn what used to be a field into a lawn.'

'Would that be at Lexleigh?' When she nodded in surprise, he continued, 'My gran used to live the other end of the High Street and when my sister and I were bairns we liked nothing better than to go home with her for the night. So I remember her telling us how the house used to belong to the farm. Whenever I've driven that way I've always wondered why the folk who owned it didn't have the garden sorted out. Now Gran has gone, I don't go that way often, although last year I did some landscaping in the big house, Lakeside. I dare say you know it?'

'Not really. I've seen it from the road, but it's the other end of the village from The Retreat.'

'Surely. Now then, would it be the grass that's bothering you? Or are you thinking of more annuals? That's a big area, big enough for a tennis court and still room to spare.'

'In your dreams! No one could play tennis on that lumpy ground.' She had meant to knock him off his perch, but from his chuckle knew she hadn't succeeded.

'You're right there. But with the old field ploughed, the soil turned and then a harrow over it, it could be turfed and, hey presto, you have the basis of a garden. Flower beds, an ornamental tree or two and the transformation would be complete.'

'You make it sound so easy. My tools don't go beyond a spade, a hoe, a rake and a pair of blunt shears.'

Again he chuckled. 'Even with the tools it's no job for a lady. That's where I could help if you're interested. After that we could think of bedding plants or maybe a flowering tree or two.'

Louisa's imagination was working double time, but she had been an accountant long enough to know that dreams on this scale cost money.

'Can you give me some idea of the cost for having the land turfed?'

'Off the top of my head that's not easy. I've seen it sure enough, but I wouldn't like to guess the area. If you're seriously interested, how about I drive over and take a look? There's no job I'd like better than to turn that neglected patch into a garden. Will you be there this afternoon if I bring my measure and we try to envisage what can be done?' Then, his

businesslike manner giving way to an impish grin, 'No obliga-
tion, I promise.'

With his foot hard down on the accelerator, Leo headed home.
He felt almost lightheaded, but determined, driven by feelings
he couldn't control. He'd park a little further up the lane so
that he could surprise her. She was sure to be gardening, probably with the lengthening rays of the sun warm on her. He
was sure that behind the never altering manner of 'just good
friends' there must be moments when she'd read his thoughts
– read them and let hers follow where his own led. Well, today
he would tell her the truth – that he wanted her more than
he had ever wanted any woman. She would remind him that
Bella was her friend, but surely she would understand that
what he felt for Bella was something quite different. He would
always be fond of her, but there was no fire in his love for
her, and none in hers for him. Was that what marriage should
be? It couldn't be enough that she never refused him? Imagine
if it were Louisa, strong, tall, long limbed, honest, uninhibited
(how could he be so sure? And yet he had no doubt – he saw
it in her every movement). Bella doesn't come into it; I'll never
let her down. The miles slipped by. Sometimes two people are
made for each other; surely that's how it is for Louisa and me.
This must have been how Dad felt – and it worked well. Mum
had the husband she wanted, but Dad and Violet were one of
those rare couples – they belonged together. Nothing to do
with marriage; they simply existed for each other. And that's
how it could be for Louisa and me. So his thoughts went as
he came towards Lexleigh. He didn't ask himself what made
him so certain it was the same for her, for there was no logic
in his certainty.

   Instead of parking at her gate he stopped nearer the start of
the village High Street meaning to walk to the house, subcon-
sciously feeling that an occasion such as this demanded an
element of surprise. But in the event the surprise was his.
Approaching the gate he could hear voices, Louisa's and a
man's. He slowed his step, trying to recognize whose it was,
but he had no idea. Through a thin patch of the hedge he
could see the two of them leaning over the garden table where

they were reading something. He couldn't hear what was said, and to say they were laughing would be an exaggeration, but their tone told him they were enjoying themselves. The young man was writing on the paper spread out before them. Louisa said something that seemed to give them pause for thought before the conversation went on. Leo felt shut out, a sensation new to him. He told himself he ought to walk in. On any other occasion that's what he would have done but this, of all times, should have been so different. This evening was to have been like none before it.

He turned round and walked back towards High Street, where he bought cigarettes before returning to the waiting car. This time he didn't attempt to stop at The Retreat, nor even to glance as he drove past before turning into the lane leading to the farm. The timing was bad, for just at that moment the young man reversed his car out of Louisa's side entrance then, seeing Leo turning into the lane, pulled back into her garden to give room to let the car pass.

Trying to appear disinterested, Leo raised a hand in casual greeting to Louisa, who was seeing her guest off. In fact, he also had a good look at the visitor, a young man with curly red hair and a cheery voice, who in farewell to her called, 'Till tomorrow then, a bit before eleven.'

Five

Making the most of the fading light, Louisa strolled the length of the field-like strip. In her imagination she was seeing it as Hamish McLaren had drawn in his sketch, right down to the group of fruit trees he suggested planting in a mini-orchard at the far end. She had been surprised that the transformation they planned wasn't going to cost her more and she had a suspicion that he wanted to do it for his own sake as much as for hers. More than once he had referred to how he had seen the neglected plot when he'd been a child, even going to the length of peering through a thin patch in the hedge, always hoping someone would have started working on it. He was as keen as she was herself for the work to begin and had promised to bring his equipment over the following morning, which was Friday, and work the whole day on Sunday. At that stage there would be nothing she could do to help him, but she offered to prepare food. Looking back at his visit it struck her, as it hadn't at the time, how unlike a business visit it had been. Nine hours ago she hadn't even met him and yet it had been like two friends planning an adventure. But of course that was ridiculous, she told herself sensibly; she was his client so naturally he made himself as pleasant as he could. She wished Leo had gone past just a few minutes later, say as Hamish had disappeared up the road and she had been fastening the side gate. Then he would have stopped and she could have told him everything that was planned. He had never been interested in her plan to turn the wilderness into a garden, but then he had known it for so many years and always in the same miserable state (for by that time she had forgotten how pleased she had been with her meagre splash of annual colour last summer).

It would soon be dark; she had better go back indoors. Normally the house welcomed her and she was never lonely, but that evening she felt like an outcast from the human race. It must be the contrast with this afternoon, she told herself.

We didn't talk about ourselves at all, so I've no idea if he has a wife at home. And Leo, he will be sitting talking to Bella and his father, telling them about his day as they have dinner. It wasn't like Louisa to feel sorry for herself, but as she ate her solitary ham salad meal she was in the mood to look facts in the face. Thirty-one years old, and alone – alone in the way that matters. And it does matter, if I have the courage to be honest; it always did, but never as much as now, now that I know Leo. And that's dreadful. It's humiliating. Leo's a friend, and that's all he can ever be. She knew what was developing between them, but when she was with him she always pushed those thoughts aside – was determined to. Now her thoughts turned to the evening ahead. What shall I be doing? I shall be imagining the joy of lying close to someone who loves me and who shares my life. But there is no one. It's the same here as it was in Reading, except that I am older and with each month I slip further into the realization that my destiny is to be alone, finding my own way to quieten the aching longing. If it were just that, I wouldn't be haunted by shame. But I can't hold my thoughts in check. Each time I pretend it's *him*. And then it's awful, the shame, the self-disgust – not for doing what I do, but for pretending it's Bella's husband. Dear Bella. Lucky Bella, she's the mother of the child who casts a spell on him, and rightly so. Alicia is sweet – pretty, too – but with the parents she has she is bound to be. I've seen him with her; I've seen the look on his face. How proud Bella must be.

Her thoughts died even as they were born as she recognized footsteps coming towards her back door. As Leo came in she felt he must know from looking at her just where her imagination had been taking her even as he opened her front gate.

'You're a late visitor.' She made sure that her tone was casual. 'But I'm glad you've come. I have lots to tell you. It's been quite a day.'

'You're going to tell me who your friend was and satisfy my curiosity? Or tell me it's not my business, perhaps?'

She reached to pull another chair towards the kitchen table where she had been eating her salad.

'Here, look at the plan. The man you saw keeps McLaren Gardens. He's coming to work a miracle on my piece of scrubland. Nothing less than a miracle will make a garden of it. What do you think?'

He pushed the plan to one side and, taking her by surprise, grasped her hand. 'I think I can't go any longer without saying – oh, God, I'm no good at this sort of thing. Don't you know why I come here every minute, every second that I can? It's because I can't keep away. Sometimes I think what's happened to me has happened to you too.' Then, his unusually serious expression changing as the more familiar impish smile tugged the corner of his mouth. 'Don't sit with your mouth open – you look like a guppy fish.'

She laughed. She wanted to shout for joy. Then, just as suddenly, the wonder of what he was saying was lost. 'We mustn't, Leo. We can't. Yes, it's happened to me. I think of you every waking hour, I can't sleep for – for—'

'For wanting me, like I want you.'

'Leo, I've never felt like this in my life. There has never been anyone for me until I met you.' She was talking softly, each syllable clear as if to stress the importance of what she said. 'But you are Bella's husband; Bella is faithful and adores you. We can't take what we want without hurting her. Bella is my friend, and your wife. We can't do it.' For a second or two neither spoke, then she said in a voice that refused to stay as calm and clear, 'But with all my heart – with all that I am – I wish it were different.'

'I hear what you say,' he said softly, still holding both her hands, 'and if you thought differently you wouldn't be the woman I love. But Bella doesn't come into this – she won't get hurt. She is my wife and that's how she will remain. If she were different I would want us to give her grounds to divorce me, but Bella is a hundred per cent good and we can neither of us do that to her. Perhaps it's this house that casts a spell. Didn't we say that ages ago, the first time we met? Remember? My father and your aunt were meant for each other, just as we are. Yet my parents lived a normal home life. Mum must have realized, but the home was a happy one. I never heard them quarrel. I think perhaps she was relieved to think he looked elsewhere for something he couldn't find in her. Except for the fact that Bella is extraordinarily lovely to look at, she and Mum are very similar. They are born to create comfort in the home and security for the family; it's what makes their lives satisfying. I'm at fault just as my father was, but love overrides everything.'

The first wild joy had faded when faced with the reality of the situation. They sat in silence at the kitchen table, the grip of his hands not loosening, neither of them speaking and the only sound the ticking of the old-fashioned school clock on the wall.

At last it was Louisa who broke the silence, her voice warning him that tears were fighting to gain the upper hand.

'It was such an exciting day. I wanted to share it with you.' It was a childish thing to say and she felt ashamed, yet she grasped at any excuse for tears rather than face the truth. But it was no use. 'I haven't cried for years. Why now, when I ought to be happy?' She wiped the palms of her hands across her face, smearing her mascara and not caring. 'You've just told me the thing I wanted to hear more than anything in the world, and I sit here behaving like a five-year-old.'

Leo got up from his chair and, pulling her to her feet, forced her to meet his gaze as he drew her into his arms.

'Darling, darling Louisa,' he whispered, moving his chin on her head. 'We could both cry for the moon but it would still be out of our reach. We have to take what life offers. Forget tomorrow – forget everything except that now at last we are honest with each other. I swear I have never felt for a living soul as I do for you. We can never be together as we want, but what we have this evening is more than we've ever had before. Friendship, yes, and that is still as precious; but now we have no secrets, we know that it can't be enough.' Again there was silence as the clock ticked on. She raised her face to his; her lips parted. And then it happened. His mouth covered hers and all her restraint was gone. Clinging to him and following instinct she moved her mouth on his; he felt her tongue on his lips just as he had imagined as he drove home with only one thing on his mind. There was no question now of what was right or what was fair, no thought of Bella or of anything except where love and passion was driving them.

If they'd put it into words, to walk together up the narrow stairs side by side and still clinging to each other knowing where they were heading might have sounded sordid. But there was nothing sordid in their emotions, nor did Louisa feel any coyness as together they took off their clothes and stood before each other. Except for poorly endowed statues or oil paintings she had never before seen a naked man. She was living a dream and longed for the next moments. She wished she were experienced and could give him everything he wanted, but this wasn't a moment for wishing; this was what she'd dreamed of. Following instinct, she held nothing back.

If she was lacking in experience, Leo wasn't. At his touch her passion mounted. In her lonely bed as she'd followed her instinct, always thinking of him, it had never been like this. She cried out in pure ecstasy when the final moment came and then, panting but exultant, they lay close in each other's arms.

'I see the man has brought his machines and tools,' Bella said as she found Louisa tidying the shed late the next morning. 'Leo told me all about it at breakfast. I was surprised. You'd never said anything to me about having it landscaped. How grand that makes it sound,' she added with a chuckle.

'I'd never considered it. It all cropped up so suddenly. But Hamish McLaren, the man who owns the garden place, is going to do it himself and it's not nearly as expensive as I would have imagined. The fruit trees will be quite dear if I get enough to make a little orchard. But come and look at the plan.'

Unlike Leo, Bella gave it her full attention and, watching her as she knelt on the kitchen chair with her elbows on the table as she concentrated on the sketch, Louisa was touched with a feeling of real affection for her. And yet she had no guilt about what had happened the previous evening. It was as if Bella was removed from what existed between herself and Leo. She told herself she *ought* to feel guilty; she *ought* to feel shame that she could deceive someone so innocently trusting; someone who was her friend. But Leo was right when he said that Bella didn't come into it; she wouldn't get hurt. For her,

nothing would change. Louisa's friendship with Bella and relationship with him were two entirely separate things.

'He's home today – Leo, I mean. He's working on some
drawing or other. So I left Dad with him and Ali and I came
by ourselves.' From her expression it was clear her thoughts
had suddenly jumped in another direction. 'Alicia is such a
mouthful for a tiny tot like she is, don't you agree? Ali sounds
so much more *friendly*. Oh, good, I think she's waking up. Can
I get her out of the pram in a minute? I want you to see how
she pulls herself right up on to her feet if she has something
to hang on to. I hope she'll do it for you. She's getting so
clever.' Yes, Bella was untouched by what had happened between
Leo and her, not just yesterday evening but over the months
when he had spent so much time at The Retreat. 'Aren't men
funny – Leo has never been interested in gardening. But he
seemed quite excited – no, perhaps that's silly, not exactly
excited, but really keen about what you intend to have done
here. I expect it's from a design angle, don't you? He'll like to
see the implements Mr McLaren uses, even though gardening
isn't the same as farming. He said to tell you he'd probably
look in later. When he works at home he likes to go walking.
I expect it helps him to work out in his mind what he is
designing, don't you? You know what I think, Louisa? I think
he is much more wrapped up in Carters' than he even realizes.
It's probably all to do with being the younger brother; David
– oh, I'm not criticizing, honestly, but he is so terribly *serious*
so everyone thinks he's the important one. And tomorrow
morning he is fetching Dad and they are going into Gloucester
to see the solicitor about arranging Power of Attorney. It's not
for both of them – David and Leo too – but just for David.
Leo says he isn't upset about it, but surely he must be hurt.
It's not fair.'

'It seems a bit hard, but don't get upset about it, Bella. Mr
Carter may be getting forgetful, but he's far from needing
anyone to have Power of Attorney. Come on, let's get Alicia;
I want her to show me how well she can stand.'

Bella's morning visits were never long and the remainder of
that one was spent admiring Alicia's latest achievement. While
Louisa encouraged and praised, her thoughts were already on

the afternoon, when she knew Leo would be with her. And so, with the exception of the strand that was Hamish McLaren, the pattern that was to shape their lives over the months to come was formed.

From eight o'clock in the morning of that first Sunday until daylight faded, Hamish worked on the area that was to be transformed from weedy coarse grass to lawn. First, he guided a motor driven single furrow plough, leaving the ground in straight lines of mounds and trenches.

'No turning back now,' he told Louisa, who had been watching from the sidelines where she had erected the garden table and brought out a tray of sandwiches, a jug of coffee and a bottle of beer.

'I certainly don't want to turn back. I can picture what it's going to be like even better than from your drawing. It all looks so much bigger now the earth has been turned. If you want to scrub your hands before you eat, you'll find a downstairs cloakroom to the left of the back porch. Don't be long or the coffee will get cold.'

'Food? Och! But that's mighty civil of you. I intended to work straight through the day, but since you press me . . .' They both laughed, not so much because he had said something funny as because the sun was shining and this a very fine way to spend a Sunday. By the end of the day the erstwhile, unkempt plot was transformed into raked soil, ready for the next stage.

'Have you given any thought to the suggestion of a small orchard at the far end?' he asked as he loaded his implements on to his pick-up truck. 'If you don't want it then I'll get down to laying turf next time. But if you do, the trees would be better to be in first and I can turf round them.'

'I've thought about it and I know it will cost a lot but, yes, I think the idea of an orchard, even a small one, is . . .' She hesitated, aware of how stupid it would sound put into words to someone who was almost a stranger, '. . . is lovely,' she concluded lamely, aware that he was watching her closely, as if he knew she was holding something back.

'To my mind it's what this garden needs – something to

raise your vision at the end of the long strip of grass. It's an
odd shape for a garden, as if someone decided to chop off the
end of the meadow and build a house.'

She nodded. 'I believe that is exactly what they did, years
ago, of course. Perhaps the owner was getting beyond looking
after the place and decided to take on a manager.' She
was aware that she had come very close to telling her new
acquaintance what had made her decide to spend as much as
she had on the garden. But temptation had been overcome
and she was glad; such inner feelings weren't to be shared
simply by way of conversation. 'Do you have trees in stock?'
Her momentary weakness overcome, she was once again the
business woman.

'Indeed I do. When would you find it convenient to come
and make a selection?'

'Tomorrow. I'll come tomorrow morning. Will you be there
or will your sister be able to give me some advice?'

He had sensed her sudden businesslike aloofness and was at
a loss to understand the reason. Funny creatures, women.

'I can't be sure without looking at my diary. But if I'm out
Margaret can answer any questions. I'll tell her you're coming.
But I may be around the place.' Then, satisfied that he had
been sufficiently cool to hide from her that she had been in
his thoughts ever since his chance meeting with her at the
centre on Friday, he gave her the boyish smile that was part
of his nature and bid her goodbye.

She had enjoyed her day but by that time she just wanted
to get ready for the evening. Although he never arranged his
visits in advance, she was sure Leo would come and she meant
to spend the next half hour indulging in a deep, scented bath
before dressing in her most alluring underwear.

The bathroom was steamy so that as she stood up ready to
step out of the water she couldn't even see her reflection, but
she didn't have to look at it to know that she was a different
person from the frustrated woman she had been before Leo
had brought reality to her dreams and imaginings. It was like
looking back at another life to think of how miserably scared
she had been that the future would hold nothing more for her
than fantasy. In her lonely desperation as she had pretended,

imagined, strived towards attaining what she yearned, she hadn't
known how far from the truth was what she had experienced.
Now she knew the truth, now she was a new woman; Leo
had set her free and made her whole.

She towelled herself dry and leant over the bath to pull out
the plug so that the scented water gurgled its way down the
pipe while, in her habitually methodical way, she rinsed away
the remaining bubbles. She seemed hypnotized by the water
as it rushed away, but in truth she hardly saw it; her thoughts
had carried her back forty-eight hours. She didn't hear a voice
call from downstairs, or footsteps or the opening of the bathroom door. The first she knew that Leo was there was his
warm hands taking the weight of her breasts as she bent over
the bath.

Instinctively she gasped before she realized who it was then,
just as instinctively, she made a soft sound in her throat that
told him more than any words could.

'I would have come sooner had I known where you were,'
he whispered. 'I wanted to be sure your young friend had
gone.'

'I hoped you'd come,' she whispered. 'I wanted to be ready
– scented bath oil – the lot.'

'You don't need any of that, my beautiful Louisa.' He turned
her round and moved his hands down her body before dropping to his knees. She pressed his head close against her, even
though this had never been part of her dreams, never something
she had even imagined as part of lovemaking. But as his tongue
moved and caressed her it awakened sensuality such as she
hadn't known possible. With her eyes closed she moved her
body against him as she drew him close. She had neither the
will nor the power to stop herself. There was no past and no
future – only this. She heard Leo breathing fast, she felt his
hands holding her to him just as hers pressed his head close
as she moved against him, yet she seemed removed from everything except what drove her. Closer and closer she came to
what she knew would happen . . . yes . . . yes . . . she wanted
it to last forever and yet she wanted the moment to come. It
must . . . yes . . . yes. She heard her voice as she cried out,
then, so soon, the moment was gone. Had they been lying

close, then the wonder would have stayed with her. But here in the bathroom, the moment reason returned so too did . . . was it embarrassment or shame? She slumped forward and fell to her knees, wanting him to hold her. Instead, breathless, he sat back on his heels, laughing.

'Wow!' he chuckled, but there was admiration in his mirth. 'I didn't expect *that*. I thought we were just warming up. You recovered?'

She felt hurt, ashamed of what she had allowed to happen. More than that she was embarrassed by her nakedness, feeling it was nakedness of her soul as well as her body. As she had been consumed by something she'd had no power to stop, where had *his* thoughts been? Had he watched her and been pleased with himself that he had such power? Had he been laughing even then?

Reaching for the bath towel she stood up, wrapping it around her.

'Go down and put the coffee on,' she said, her casually friendly tone making it clear that she was moving on, the brief interlude over. 'I won't be two minutes throwing some clothes on.'

He looked at her quizzically, his eyes shining with merriment. 'I can think of much better ways of thanking me than giving me coffee,' he teased.

But she wasn't to be drawn. Later, she would think about it, but in truth she felt confused by what had happened. To be dressed and sitting together discussing something from the news, something too far removed from their personal lives to stir their emotions, was what she wanted. And that's exactly what they did, neither of them expecting to find the ease in each other's company that they had known until so recently. But surprisingly they both enjoyed airing their views on France's recent turmoil arising from the revolt in Algeria, and their own impression of newly elected President de Gaulle. If they expected the incident upstairs would have made their usual almost platonic friendship impossible, they were proved wrong.

For more than an hour they sat smoking and talking, the conversation moving easily from current affairs to the progress in the garden. When finally she walked with him to the front door he cradled her face in his hands and tenderly kissed her mouth.

'May I come tomorrow?' he asked softly, confident of her reply.

'You know you may.'

Walking back along the lane to the farmhouse, he looked back at the evening and frowned. What was the matter with him that he could have been content to spend an evening with her just as he used to before their relationship altered? The truth was that he had never known a woman like Louisa. He had confidently believed that behind the calm exterior she presented to the world there was passion she held in check, and he had proved that to be true. But even after that he hadn't expected her to respond as she had this evening. God, but what a woman!

Next morning she drove to the nursery, telling herself that Hamish would have gone off to keep an appointment and her choice of trees would be guided by his sister Margaret. She also told herself that her only reason for preparing herself for his absence was that, despite his assurance of Margaret's knowledge – and despite reminding herself of her strong opinion that a woman was every bit as capable as a man – she wanted Hamish to advise her. He was doing the work, so his should be the choice. As she drove on to the gravel patch that served as a car park she had an upturn of spirit as he came towards the car.

'I've been making my personal selection,' he greeted her as he held open the door. 'I remembered what you told me you were prepared to lay out on trees, and I've spent the lot.' There was a laugh lurking just beneath his words and immediately her mood rose to match his. 'But I want you to make your own choice without being told mine first and then we'll compare. We go this way, down to the end of the field.'

It was a morning such as she'd never spent before. The sky was a summertime pale blue even though it was only spring, and the sun shining down on them was pleasantly warm. A nursery at that season of the year was filled with promise. If in the days when Louisa had worked in that dingy office in

Reading she had been told she would find excitement, yes, real excitement in walking among rows of potted flowering shrubs and plants waiting to be taken to adorn gardens as spring gave way to summer, she would have brushed the idea aside without a second thought. Yet on that morning the atmosphere seemed to cast a spell on her. She found herself chattering to Hamish as if they had known each other all their lives and when Margaret left the 'shop', as they rather grandly called the large wooden shed where she manned the till and served small utensils such as hoes, rakes, pails, garden twine, packets of seeds etc., she felt that in both brother and sister she had friends.

'You wouldn't believe this, Mags,' Hamish greeted her. 'You saw the trees I thought would suit this lady. Well, I didn't say a word, I just left her to look for herself and, you know what?'

'From the cocky look on your ugly mug, my guess would be that she chose the same ones you had.'

Louisa looked from one to the other, both of them enjoying the moment. Her initial resentment that he must have been discussing his work on her garden with Margaret, or Mags as he called her, was so short-lived that she was barely aware of it. With these two it would be difficult for ill humour to get a foothold.

'I hadn't realized you two were so alike,' she said, speaking her thoughts aloud as they came into her head.

'Och!' Hamish answered with a grin. 'But isn't that the way with twins?'

'Well, I didn't know you were twins. I might have guessed.'

'We look alike, and mostly we think alike,' Margaret told her. 'What I lack in brawn I have to make up for with my ability to put the heels back in his socks. Isn't that so, Hamish?'

'That's about it. But your brawn is pretty good, and how would it be if you put it to use on the garden at The Retreat in Lexleigh this evening? Two spades would work quicker than one, and the sooner we can get the trees out of their pots and into good earth the better. We could get the digging done this evening while the weather holds.'

'Great,' Margaret said, real pleasure in her voice at the thought of digging the newly turned ground. Then to Louisa: 'We could never make that garden out, just a long strip of nothing. But wait till Hamish has knocked it into shape, and with the trees at the far end to take off the narrow look, it'll be great. He came home yesterday full of enthusiasm for the job.'

Louisa thought what a lovely couple they were. They seemed to her to exude contentment and happiness for where life had brought them.

'Do you both live at the house here?' she found herself asking, speaking before she stopped to consider that she hardly knew them.

'Yes,' Margaret was first to answer, 'no travelling to work for us. Aunt Hilda keeps house and looks after things, bless her. We'll tell her that we shall be coming to you straight from closing up here at six o'clock.'

Louisa's mind took a leap; she was with Leo. The atmosphere in the garden lost its appeal and she knew that this evening should belong to Leo and her. The last thing they'd want would be a pair of strangers working in the garden. He hadn't said he'd be there this evening but he always arrived unexpectedly and she had no doubt at all that he would come.

'Not this evening. I've already arranged to be out.' Her answer was spontaneous, spoken without thought.

'We can manage without coming to the house,' Hamish assured her, and this time she didn't argue for fear it sounded as though she felt she should be there to watch them. The idea that she and Leo might enjoy the evening knowing that these two were working outside was impossible. Her mind started making plans.

So it was that after another quarter of an hour or so of amiable chatter she set off back to Lexleigh not knowing exactly what her next move would be. But as she stepped in through the front door she found a note on the floor and saw a pointer towards her next move.

'Sorry I missed you. I called to say hello but couldn't hang around as Dad wasn't up to coming with Ali and me this morning. Leo is keeping an eye on him.'

That was reason enough for Louisa to visit the farm, but not before she had touched up her make-up and re-combed her hair. Partly, it was second nature for her to check her appearance, but she knew on this occasion she was doing it for the impression she would make on Leo.

When she arrived she found him with Harold and Ted Johnson. This was a side of Leo's character she hadn't seen before, for while Harold stood close to them nodding his head and with a smile of encouragement on his face, the other two were deep in conversation as they did she knew not what to a piece of equipment she later learnt was a potato riddle. Whether they were carrying out a repair or an adjustment and what it was for she had no idea. If she expected Leo to leave what he was doing and come to meet her she was disappointed, for it was Harold who left the little group and came over.

'This is nice,' he greeted her. They were words that might have been spoken by anyone and yet she knew what Bella had meant when she had written that he wasn't up to coming out with her. His smile was bright even though his eyes made her believe he was frightened. But why should he be? Here in his own home, in the surroundings he had known nearly all his adult life, what could give him that haunted look?

'I was out when Bella called. I wanted to tell her about the work I'm having done in the garden. I've just ordered fruit trees for it. Is she home yet?'

'Ah . . . yes . . . home . . . is she home . . . we'd better ask Leo. I saw her earlier, but don't know what she was up to . . . best we ask Leo . . . I don't seem to . . . don't seem to . . . muddled . . .' He looked at her directly, holding her gaze and letting his unfinished sentences hang between them.

'I expect she would have come out if she were home, don't you?' Louisa answered, careful not to let him suspect she had understood just what Bella had meant when she'd written that he hadn't been up to walking with her to the village. 'But we'll go and ask Leo. I've had such an exciting morning at the garden centre I simply had to tell her – well, all of you – about it.'

Linking her arm through his, she steered him back to the two with the potato riddle.

'Your father wasn't sure whether Bella was back, Leo. Do you know?'

'Not to my knowledge, she isn't. Is there any message for

her?' They might have been mere acquaintances. He didn't quite meet her eyes when he answered her, just as when she spoke it was as if her words were for all three of them.

'It's about the garden. You remember when you looked in yesterday you saw it had been ploughed up ready. Well, this morning I went to the nursery and this evening – the same day as I told them the trees I want – as soon as they close the place to customers Hamish McLaren and his sister are coming to dig the holes. They say if they work hard they can get the digging done in the one evening. I don't want to hang around watching them working. I'll probably go to town and see if there's anything worth seeing at the pictures.'

Leo looked up from what he was doing and their glances met, so briefly she almost thought she had imagined it.

'At this rate, in another week you'll have the place transformed,' he said, just as he might to any casual acquaintance.

'I hope so,' she replied, in the same vein.

'Pictures? Pictures on your own and not even knowing what rubbish you are going to see. Better than that, my dear, come over to us and share some supper. How's that, Leo? Like things used to be. Your aunt used to come here. Times change, nothing lasts . . .' His voice grew softer as he spoke, almost as though he were talking to himself.

Again, Louisa glanced at Leo, as if his consent were needed.

'A good idea, Dad. Bella will be delighted, that I can promise you.'

Surely it was a charade as much to Leo as it was to her, and yet he spoke with the sort of natural friendliness he would have used to any of Bella's friends – except that in Lexleigh Bella had none except for Louisa.

So it was that just as the McLaren twins arrived, Louisa was leaving the house to walk up the track to the farm. Despite her lack of guilt, she had a sneaking feeling of shame that she had taken extra care over her always immaculate appearance. She would be careful that no glance or comment between herself and Leo aroused Bella's suspicions. This would be her first time in the same room as them both since her affair with Leo had started and she felt dreadful, her confidence in her ability to separate her feelings for Leo from her friendship with

Bella waning. The situation went round and round in her mind
as she walked to the farm. How could Bella not know that
her husband had fallen in love with someone else? How much
did Harold understand? For she had been sure that morning
he was aware of something between Leo and her, been aware
of it and encouraged it as if in them he was carried back down
the years. And where had those years got Violet? Had she been
content with what she had had of Harold, or had she felt she
could never be nearer than on the periphery of his life? Of
one thing there was no doubt: both Leo and Bella adored little
Alicia, or Ali as they called her. If the rest of their world fell
apart Ali would hold them together. And there Louisa came
back to the beginning of the conundrum, knowing that she,
like Violet, must always be on the outside of the family circle
– the spinster lady who lived at the end of the lane, the object
of the village gossip once word got around from the prying
neighbours who were probably already suspicious and taking
note of how often Leo visited.

By the time she came to the farmhouse her mood was such
that she wished she had stayed at home and watched Margaret
and Hamish McLaren preparing the ground for the trees. The
sight of Bella did nothing to restore her spirit. It was one thing
to mull the situation over in her mind, but seeing Bella so
happy and content at the farm, she knew she couldn't honestly
believe that what she was doing wouldn't hurt Leo's wife and,
ultimately, Alicia too. What if Bella sensed something between
them? Louisa thought, miserably, that even if she did, her
loyalty to both her husband and her friend would be such that
she would probably dismiss it straight away. Aware of her own
selfishness, an inner resolve started to take hold of Louisa: she
would tell him that she wanted it to stop. But that was a lie;
she wanted it never to stop.

'You'd never believe it, Lou. Leo has had a call from some
farmer who took a place not long ago and wants to buy lots.
Leo met him recently and they got along like a house on fire.
He said the phone rang just as you drove away this morning.
They've asked him to dinner and then to stay the night so that
he and the farmer can discuss things in the morning. He's a
long way away, in Surrey, I think Leo said. So he was going

by train and then in the morning the farmer will drive him to the factory and decide on his order, then Leo will get the train home. Isn't it a shame he's not here? It would have felt like a real party with all of us together.' Then, her thoughts jumping towards her life's greatest interest: 'Before we eat I'm going up to make sure that Ali is asleep and covered properly. I expect you'd like to creep in with me for a peep. There is something so . . . so . . . is it silly to say heart-wrenching? – but honestly that about describes it, doesn't it, Dad? – about seeing such innocence.' All the time she talked she busied herself laying the table, lifting saucepan lids, stabbing boiling potatoes with a fork to see if they were ready to mash, filling a large glass jug with water and managing to do it all while her mind was on what she was saying. 'Heart-wrenching, it sounds like something out of a "penny dreadful" but it's the honest truth. Leo would understand; I know he would because I've seen the say he looks at her. It's funny though, Lou. I can say these things to you but I would feel embarrassed saying them to him even though I *know* he feels the same. But he'd never tell me. Now, everything is ready to take up, so shall we creep up and see our little princess? Better take those high heels off or she'll hear you. My sandals are quiet.'

With Leo not there, although the evening had lost the magic Louisa had anticipated, it was much easier and the three of them ate their meal, washed up together with Harold doing the washing, Louisa the drying and Bella putting things away. Then they played Monopoly. The clock was striking eleven as Bella put the game away and Louisa put on her jacket to go.

'I'm not letting you walk down that dark lane alone,' Harold told her. And when she laughed at the thought of being unable to take care of herself or, indeed, of minding the dark, moonless night, he became more insistent. If Leo had been there he would have seen her home so, in his absence, Harold wouldn't let his offer be refused. She would have been much happier on her own for, even though it was some time since she had consciously thought of that night when he had believed Violet had come back to him, it took no more than the thought of being alone with him in the dark and empty lane to bring back the memory she had tried to put out of her mind.

However, his behaviour was perfectly normal and as soon as she had the front door open and the hall light on he bid her goodnight. With relief she closed the door, only then allowing herself to acknowledge how nervous she had been.

That's when she heard a gentle but persistent tapping on the front door.

Six

The caller wasn't using the knocker, but simply tapping softly on the wood of the door itself, about half-a-dozen taps, a pause, then another half dozen or so. Standing alone in the hallway, Louisa felt helpless. If she left him out there long enough surely he would go home or, if he remembered Violet had kept her extending steps in the shed, was he sufficiently unbalanced that he would climb to the bedroom? The Johnsons had no telephone and if she rang the farm there was no one there except Bella and the baby.

'Turn out the lights and open the door.' Relief flooded over her as she recognized the voice whispering the words.

'But you went away,' she answered stupidly.

'Put out the lights, then let me in.'

'Wait.' She found herself speaking quietly too as she switched off the hall light, then in the dark ran up to the bedroom. There, first she flooded the room with light before opening the window and closing the curtains. Instinct made her aware that nothing was missed by the neighbours across the lane, and surely that would satisfy them that she had come home and gone straight to bed. Then, closing the bedroom door and running back down the stairs in darkness, she reached the front door and quietly opened it.

He'd gone away for the night; they had hours, with no one to disturb them. She had longed for love for so long, hiding her lonely longing behind a façade of ice-cold grooming and a businesslike manner that gave no hint of the yearning she only half understood. No man had attracted her nor yet been attracted by her despite her faultless appearance, or perhaps because of it. And then she had met Leo and her defences had tumbled.

None of these things were in her mind as she quietly closed the front door and felt herself taken into his arms.

'Yes,' he whispered, 'I'm away for the night, away from

everything that keeps me from you. We have hours; no one to disturb us, nothing to come between us. I've been waiting for you, thinking of you. I want to know every inch of your beautiful body.'

'I want it too. Everything. It's so right, so perfect.' For surely when they had made love it had been the most wonderful thing she had ever experienced. And tonight it would be like that again. Her evening at the farm with Bella was forgotten; there was nothing except these hours.

In the darkness they went up the narrow stairs and then into the bedroom where in the soft light they looked at each other as if for the first time. This was no furtive half hour; this was the luxury of endless night. '. . . to know every inch of your beautiful body', his words echoed.

Whatever her half-understood fantasies had been, she found they were nothing compared to the reality. History was repeating itself. Alice Carter had objected to what she thought of as Harold's bestial urges; Bella would never refuse Leo, but she felt uncomfortable with anything more than 'lights off gentle lovemaking', Leo called it. Louisa resembled her aunt Violet in more than appearance. Her appetite seemed insatiable. She wanted nothing but their two bodies as nature intended; for her the night was filled with wonder. She tried not to look when Leo adeptly introduced a sheath, for she wanted nothing to come between them as they followed where nature beckoned. But it was only a momentary thought and nothing could hamper the excitement and exhilaration that drove her. She knew nothing of the art of sex; her only guide was uninhibited nature.

Hours later, while he slept, she got out of bed and drew back the curtains, letting in the first light of dawn. She had never been more aware of her good health, of her strength. This was the first day of her true understanding of being a woman, being needed by a man she loved. Then, for the first time in so many hours, she remembered Bella and what he had said about nothing changing between Bella and him; his love for her, Louisa, was something apart. After last night surely he wouldn't still feel like that? Yet how could they take away Bella's happiness? Louisa imagined her at the farm, so content with running the home and looking after Ali, and knew that, while she was unable to put an end to her affair with Leo, she would not allow her friend to suffer. And Leo? Ali's father, Ali's adoring father? Hadn't Harold Carter told her how, so many years ago, he had begged Violet to come away with him so that Alice would divorce him, and Violet had refused because she wouldn't let him lose his sons, and she had been right. If Violet could be strong, then so must she.

'What are you thinking?' Leo's voice surprised her.

'In words it sounds silly. But I was thinking that I am *alive*, *really alive*. Last night has made me *whole*. Does that make any sense to you?'

'Come back to bed and I'll show you what sense it makes. Louisa Harding, you are whole, perfect and complete.'

She felt the sting of tears. Surely this was the culmination of everything she had lived for. Willingly, she went back to bed.

It was a strange morning. Deceit didn't come easily to her, but wisdom told her that Leo should keep out of sight.

'They don't miss a trick from across the lane,' she said when she at last got out of bed, 'so we have to be sure they don't know you're here or it'll be common knowledge by elevenses time. I bet by now everyone has heard that your car was left overnight outside the railway station.'

'Tell me about it,' he laughed. 'This house has always been their main source of scandal. Do I don some of your aunt's clothes and drive off in your car? Or – and this sounds a tempting proposition – do I lie in bed and restore my poor worn-out body, then creep out just as I crept in under cover of darkness? I could do with some rest after the energy I expended last night.' His expression teased, but his words momentarily took away some of Louisa's joy as he added: 'Perhaps you're akin to nature's female creatures who gain strength from mating with the male and then killing the poor chap. God, I'm shattered. What time do you reckon we finally accepted defeat and went to sleep?'

'I've really no idea. I'm going to run a bath so I'll leave you to sleep.' More hurt by his remarks than angry, she locked the bathroom door. If he attempted to follow her he would be disappointed.

When, just after half past nine, Bella and Ali called on the way to the butcher's, Louisa was surprised to find that, as before, she had no feelings of guilt. As the baby was dumped on the sitting-room carpet where she crawled, cooed and managed to pull herself to her feet holding the arm of an easy chair, she was admired just the same as any other morning.

'You're not driving into Gloucester by any chance today, are you?' Bella wanted to know. 'I want to get Ali her first pair of shoes – just soft ones, but they will protect her feet now she is trying to stand. I thought it would be a good opportunity with Leo away.'

'Wouldn't he wonder where you all were if he got home and found all of you away? But in any case,' she added, making a sudden decision, 'I have a new client I have an appointment with later today in Swindon—'

'Gosh, Lou, how did that come about?' Bella's lovely face beamed her pleasure. 'Your fame is spreading.'

Louisa's laugh was perfectly natural. She was acting out a charade, but even though she was lying to innocent and trusting Bella, she could think of nothing but her time with Leo.

'He is the brother of someone who deals with me already, so what could be more natural? But it would be stupid for me to drive back from Swindon tonight as tomorrow I want to be in Reading. Want to be, did I say? When I left there I never wanted to go back, but I had always done the annual accounts for Hill and Perkins, a bakery, so Mr Hill asked me to continue. I shall be back late in the day tomorrow.'

'We shall miss you, won't we, Ali?' to which the baby answered with a loud shout and a big grin. 'Perhaps it's better for me to wait until Leo is home before I gad off to Gloucester. If it had been today it would have meant taking Dad and I don't expect he would have thought much of shopping for tiny shoes. Next time you have to go there, when Leo is there to keep Dad company, we'd love to come. And when you've taken your work to your client we could have a lovely time, three girls together.'

Louisa smiled and nodded in agreement, but her thoughts

were on something very different. As soon as Bella had left she ran upstairs to tell her plan to Leo.

She backed the car out of the garage then, like a thief in the night, got out, closed the driver's door almost silently and just as quietly opened the passenger one behind it before going back into the house.

'OK,' she told Leo, 'the coast is clear. There's a coffee morning in the village hall and I saw all three of them from opposite go off in that direction.'

'The Lexleigh Ladies,' he chuckled. 'It would take an earthquake or worse to keep any of them away from their get-together. Once a month they meet; you must have seen the notices on the door of the hall. I bet you none of them has ever suggested you might join them?'

She wished she could have told him that she had been invited but had declined.

'You bet right. But why haven't they invited Bella? And I'm sure they haven't or she would have said.'

'Mum used to go when she wasn't too busy. She used to say they only minded other people's business because they had nothing interesting in their own lives; she was a wise woman, my mother.'

'And Bella?'

'A wise woman? Give her another ten years and I might know.'

Louisa tried to ignore the implication of his remark. 'I didn't mean that,' she told him, irritated by any slight of Bella. 'I meant why haven't they suggested she join them, especially if your mother used to go?'

'Obvious, don't you think? She comes in and out of here nearly every day and often with Dad, so they link Bella with you and therefore with Violet. But forget all of them; today belongs just to us. Are you sure you have to waste time calling on this chap in Swindon? We could go down to the coast, find a seafront hotel for the night.'

Louisa had believed herself to be a new woman, but his suggestion proved her wrong.

'Perhaps another time we'll do that. But I made a definite

appointment and even for you I won't break my word. I'll not
be long and you can take the car and search out somewhere
nice for lunch.'

'You could phone him and tell him you're not well.' Then,
with that mischievous twinkle in his eyes, 'Tell him you were
awake nearly all night.'

Louisa said nothing; he read his answer in her expression.
Last night Miss Louisa Harding, business woman of Reading,
had no chance. Clearly by morning light, wearing her tailored
suit and ready with her briefcase, she wasn't prepared to be
trifled with. Leo said no more.

They knew the car would be recognized in the village, but
there was no other way. The coffee drinkers were already
coming out of the village hall and, making sure she was seen,
she waved a friendly 'good morning' to her neighbours while
Leo kept down low on the back seat, out of sight. It was only
as they turned on to the empty open road with Lexleigh well
behind them that she drew up so he could come and sit by
her side.

'That was fun,' he chuckled, taking two cigarettes and holding
them between his lips. Both of them lit, he passed one to her.
Such a small act, and yet it relaxed her and put paid to any
flicker of conscience that had threatened. She knew that her
situation would be akin to that of Violet. Did it matter so much?
Harold had loved Violet above all else and so it would be with
Leo and her. But for the present she would take a day at a time,
a day and each precious night they could manage to steal.

The further they drove from Lexleigh, the better their day
become. Everything went according to the plan they had made
and, her introductory visit to her new client over, they drove to
Marlborough. Cars were parked in the middle of the wide
High Street, so they added theirs to the line and went in search
of food. Too late for lunch, but a traditional lunch could never
have been as exciting as the tea that was served to them at
half past three in the afternoon. They ate toasted teacakes with
jam full of strawberries, then delicious creamy pastries. Louisa
poured the tea into delicate china cups. There was something
highly indulgent about such a meal at mid-afternoon, and it
was just one more thing that set the day apart.

When Leo phoned the farm Harold answered his call.

'I'll tell Bella you've decided to stay another night. She's upstairs with Alicia. She's a dear child – Bella, I mean. We knew you hadn't been to the factory; David was on the phone. Leo, don't mess around, son. I had no regrets, couldn't have done things any other way. But hearts get broken. I'm fond of Bella, you know.'

Standing outside the telephone kiosk, Louisa could tell from Leo's expression that he was worried about the conversation. Had Bella guessed why he was staying away a second night? No, of course she hadn't – how could she? Walking away from the kiosk, Louisa gazed at the darkening sky, desperately hoping nothing was going to spoil their stolen time. When Leo caught up with her he still looked worried.

'You made a plausible excuse why you hadn't taken your client to the factory? But what about tomorrow?'

'It's all taken care of. I can be quite efficient when necessary. While you were with your chap in Swindon I telephoned my laddo to tell him I'd had an emergency dental appointment so everything would be running a day late. He was quite agreeable. You can lob me off at the railway station where he's meeting me as you go on to Reading.'

'I wish it didn't sound so sordid,' she said, speaking her thoughts aloud. 'The only one who comes out of it squeaky clean is Bella. And so she should. Bella is pure gold – she never has a mean thought in her head.' She paused, knowing that while she would do whatever she could to make sure Bella didn't get hurt, she deserved much more from both of them. 'Perhaps we owe it to her to be honest, Leo. Surely it's better to know than to be deceived.'

'I've told you, my feelings for Bella haven't changed and she is all the things you say. I may be a heel, but I will never let her down. And as for telling her about us, what is the point? Isn't the fact that she doesn't know without being told enough to prove that the vital chemistry is missing in our marriage?' He stopped walking and turned her to face him, holding up her chin so that they held each other's gaze in the fast-fading light. 'My mother held our home together; even as a child I knew there was something special between your aunt and Dad.

But David and I were brought up by two parents in what we saw as a happy home. I understand now just how much of that was thanks to Mum. Perhaps she was blind to what was between Violet and Dad. It would never have been in her nature to be unfaithful and she probably never suspected they were anything but companionable friends, which is exactly how Bella sees us. Is that so bad? Surely it gives us freedom and no one gets hurt. Most of all, it gives little Alicia the security she deserves.' He was silent and Louisa thought he was waiting for her to say something in agreement, so she was surprised when he spoke again; she was even more surprised by something in his voice she had never heard before. 'I know I'm deceiving Bella, but I couldn't bear for Alicia not to have a perfect home, a home warm with love. Does that sound silly?'

Louisa shrugged her shoulders. 'I don't know much about that sort of thinking. Emotion had no place in our family. My parents never made rules for me that they were unprepared to stick to themselves: work hard, speak the truth, Sundays were for chapel and weekdays were for duty. Fun and laughter were not welcome in our house.'

Privately Leo wasn't surprised by her angry tone, and neither was he surprised by what she had said.

'So, my darling Louisa,' he said, that teasing note in his voice, 'it's time we made up for your wasted youth. Let's go back to the car and get on our way to that pub where we booked in for the night. Mr and Mrs Harding, that's what I told them.'

'More than a pub,' she corrected him, 'it's an old coaching inn. And the dining room looked promising. I don't know about you but I'm starved. Nothing much for breakfast, no lunch, a delicate and expensive tea; my energy is flagging.'

''We can't allow that.' Back in step again, as they'd talked they had walked briskly back down the hill to the High Street and the car. She got into the driver's seat and before he closed the door he bent and kissed her forehead. 'We're at the beginning of a long road. It won't always be easy, but one thing I know for certain and that's that in or out of wedlock, even with no more than stolen days and nights, a life can be truly fulfilled. I saw it with Dad and Violet.' His sudden smile was full of confidence. 'And anything they can do, we can do better. Now, let's get on the road.'

The meal at the old coaching inn was as good as the appearance of the dining room had promised; the bedroom even sported a four-poster bed, and the furniture was antique and in keeping. But there all comfort came to a halt. The wardrobe door squeaked, the bulb in the bedside light didn't work, and when Leo went to turn off the switch on the wall by the door each step he took on the creaking floorboards must have been audible in the room below. The springs in the mattress were evidence of its age and twanged with the slightest movement. Even if they kept still there were unrelenting lumps.

In such a situation the previous night together, laughter would have been impossible. But on their first stolen night far from the prying eyes of Lexleigh, they lay side by side, holding hands and relieving their frustrated disappointment with laughter.

'We'll be all right, you and me, won't we?' she said, surprisingly contented despite everything.

'I'm sure of it. Dad knows, you know. Forgets the day of the week and yet he sensed what had happened between you and me.'

She thought about it, remembering Harold on the first night she had come to the house, how he had talked to her about Violet and his fear of a future without her. She was quiet for so long that Leo began to think she must have gone to sleep, but then she said, 'I'm glad he knows. I wonder if Aunt Violet knows too.' But for Leo, the thought was a step too far.

Next morning, half an hour before the time for the train he had told Carters' perspective client he would be arriving on, Louisa dropped him off before turning on to the road to Reading. It was as if the ghost of the woman she used to be travelled with her, perhaps exaggerating how changed she had become since moving away. Glancing in the driving mirror she reassured herself that her appearance hadn't altered, but what about her outlook on life? Reared in a home of strict morality, how could she be the same as she had been before

the advent of Leo? Just Leo? Surely Bella had made some sort
of impression too – one that probed her conscience. Suppose
Leo had been married to someone else, someone she had never
met – would she have the same feeling of shame casting a
shadow on the joy it struggled to suppress? She thought of
how Bella's constant reference to Leo, her seeming inability to
see anything but the best in everyone and everything and her
constant chatter about her wonderful marriage had irritated
her in the early days. Now she felt real affection for the girl,
and respect, too. And how could she not feel shame? Watching
the tactful way Bella handled Harold, never robbing him of
his self-respect as his behaviour become ever more erratic,
made Louisa aware of how far short her own behaviour would
fall if their positions were reversed. Imagine if their positions
were reversed . . . it would be *she* who was married to Leo,
she who was the mother of the little girl he idolized, and she
who would have to spend her days caring for an ageing man
whose mind was forever on the love he had shared with Violet.
It must have been his understanding of that relationship that
had opened his eyes to what had happened to Leo and her
– or was it obvious to anyone who knew them, even to trusting
and innocent Bella? She quickly pushed the thought from her
mind.

By the time Louisa parked the car in Reading's Market Place
and walked the short distance to where she had her appointment, it took all her concentration and willpower to muster
up the expected image of Miss Louisa Harding, precise in
thought, deed and personal appearance. At the back of her
mind, ready for the first opportunity to push to the fore, were
images of Leo and of the journey of discovery they had travelled together. All of it new to her, but how familiar was it
to him, and who had he travelled it with? There was no doubt
there had been many women in his life before Bella. Perhaps
with the same instinct that had told Harold what was between
Leo and her, Louisa knew without a doubt that Bella wouldn't
have understood the wild joy she had felt in giving all that she
was, holding nothing back and begging for more. She forced
her mind back into line and glanced at her wristwatch, satisfied that she was exactly on time for her appointment. Her

working life took over; only later would she allow memories of the past two days to intrude.

The rough area around The Retreat soon began to resemble a garden. The turf was well laid, the fruit trees giving shape to the ribbon of land to one side of the house. Right from first moving into the house Louisa had surprised herself with how enthusiastic she had felt about bringing life and colour to it, but with the lawn as a backdrop there was no stopping her.

'Here's our best customer,' Margaret called to Hamish. 'I wonder she has a patch of earth with nothing growing in it, the boxes of plants she collects.'

'Och, but there's space and to spare there. It's taking shape though, Mags, and she works like a Trojan.'

'Well, she's just parking. Best you come and serve her.' Then, with a saucy wink, 'Reckon it's you she's after more than the plants. Come on, she'll be in in a minute.'

'Chump! Tell her I'm out in the potting shed. If she needs a bit of advice with her choice she'll know where to find me.'

Margaret was disappointed. She and her twin could almost read each other's thoughts and she was sure he was sweet on Louisa Harding. And what could be better? It was time he was thinking of something outside the nursery. By this time next year she and Dennis would have enough saved to put down a deposit on their first home, and once they were married she wouldn't find it so easy to spend all her days working. But, of course, Louisa was a professional woman – she might not want to be tied to serving in a shop or helping outside.

'The sunshine's brought you out early, Louisa. I've only just got the place set up. Did you want plants or have you come to see Hamish?'

'Both. Or maybe hanging baskets are more in your line than his?'

'Sometimes I make them up for folk, but it's best if you have a word with Hamish if you're choosing what to put in them. You don't want to mix things that like a lot of water with others that are averse to it.'

'I don't know about that sort of thing. I just go for colour,'

Louisa answered. 'Petunias are always a bright splash, don't you think?'

'They last well, too, as long as you dead head them every day. But they do tend to get a bit leggy and can make the basket look untidy as the season goes on. Have a word with Hamish – he's out in the potting shed.'

As Louisa made her way between the tables of plants, Margaret stood back from the open doorway but made sure she still had a view of the potting shed. Come on now, brother Hamish, she's a strong-minded woman if ever I saw one, and if you want to make an impression don't pussyfoot about.

Maybe he pussyfooted and maybe he didn't, she had no way of knowing, but they were a long time in the shed and then both came out to make the choice. By the time they came back into the shop, each pushing a barrow filled with colourful plants, nearly half an hour had gone by.

'How soon can you get them ready, Mags? By this evening?'

'If I don't get too many interruptions, but on a day like this we may be busy.'

'Don't rush for this evening. Suppose I come and get them tomorrow afternoon? I have to go to the ironmonger in town to buy brackets to put on the walls. I may not have them up as soon as this evening.' Louisa meant to keep the evening free. Sometimes she was disappointed but often Leo came out on the pretext of having a drink at the Pig and Whistle. Occasionally that's what he did too, taking Louisa with him and enjoying the passing glances and raised eyebrows. Those were the times when, back at the farm, he would casually say he had 'dug Louisa out' to come with him to the pub. Her favourite evenings were those when he made no mention of her at home, and neither did he go to the Pig and Whistle.

On that particular evening Louisa had given up hope of his coming and was in her workroom when he arrived.

'I'd just decided you'd stood me up this evening.'

'Um? Stood you up? No, nothing of the sort.' Clearly his mind was somewhere else.

'What's the matter? Trouble?' In her mind trouble meant had Bella realized how they spent their time.

'It's Dad. Something is different about him. I know his

memory lets him down, but it's more than that. It sounds uncaring to say he looks cunning – anyway, of course he isn't cunning. He's lost and frightened, poor old boy.' For a moment he seemed deep in his worried thoughts before he visibly brightened. Even his voice sounded normal again. 'One thing is certain: he absolutely dotes on Ali. Well, of course he does; as soon as he comes near her she beams at him and holds up her arms.'

'I know. Bella told me.' She hoped he wasn't going to spend the evening with his mind on what was going on at the farm. 'Shall I get you a drink?'

'No, thanks. I'm not staying this evening. Bella was putting Ali to bed and Dad was gazing at a very flickering picture on the television. I must get the chap from Sewards to come and look at it. That set has been nothing but trouble. Is yours all right? Can it be the weather? I know nothing at all about the wretched things and neither do I want to.'

'I watched the news and that was OK. Anyway, I mustn't keep you; I can see you're anxious to get home.'

He looked surprised by her tone, and then his expression changed as he held his hand out to her. 'Anxious, yes; but wanting to get home, no. I want to stay with you, that's all I want. But the old man worries me. Lou, I wish I could help him. I can feel his sadness, his fear at what's happening to him.'

'Sorry, I sounded snappy. I hate the way we have to live – the pretence, the *cheating.*'

'And you think I don't? Listen, I came so that I could tell you this – just between ourselves, mind. Not a word to the others. An old friend – we go back to school and then college together – lives in London and writes for an engineering monthly magazine, but he has a cottage near Leominster where he often spends his weekends. He says we can use it any time we like except weekends. See, I have the key here,' he added with the smile of a triumphant schoolboy.

She knew she should resist him but was powerless, and found herself moving to perch on the arm of his chair, bending to kiss his brow.

'A very useful friend to have.' She said it to please him, as what he said had only added to her sense of shame. Shame that she wanted to be at the cottage, somewhere cut off from everyone who knew them, shame that she was stealing temporary happiness to which she had no right, and shame that of the two sentiments it was the first, the eagerness to cut themselves off from everything but each other that was predominant.

'I told them at home that I'd had a long talk on the phone to Gerald Sinclair – that's his name – and he'd invited me over to see the place. I said I'm going tomorrow and shall stay the night. They accepted it without question. It'll mean driving separately, of course, but we can meet up for lunch. There's a really good café I know called The Copper Kettle – their steak and kidney pie is out of this world and always on the menu. I'll draw you a map of how to get to an arranged spot and from there you can follow me in.'

'Not tomorrow, Leo. I've arranged with Hamish McLaren that he's going to town to get the brackets on his way here and then he's hanging three baskets of flowers his sister has promised to get done. I thought one near the front door and one either side of the front window. What do you think?'

'I think you'll just have to phone this gardener chap and tell him something has cropped up. Tell him where you want him to hang them and when you get home you'll find them waiting. Agree?'

'Most certainly not. They are putting a lot of work into these hanging baskets and I'm not clearing off without even seeing them put in place. You can use the cottage any weekday, so let's go the next one.'

'If that's your answer I shall have to go without you. I've already told Gerald we shall be there tomorrow. I'm sorry you think it more important not to hurt this gardener fellow's feelings than mine.' With that he stood up, ready to leave. Her immediate reaction was panic but it didn't last. One look at the sulky expression on his face and she started to laugh.

'Oh, Leo, darling Leo, you're being a prima donna. Hamish won't be here above an hour, I shouldn't think. Have your steak and kidney pie and I'll meet you later.'

Just for a couple of seconds the expression hung on, then it was gone and she found herself pulled into his arms. Shame had no place in her mind, nor did hanging baskets; she wanted just to be with him, whether it was right or wrong mattered not at all.

Five minutes later she was alone, a piece of paper in her hand telling her where to find The Copper Kettle, which was the rendezvous where he would wait for her.

A few days later it was Bella who told her that Leo had given up the flat where they'd lived before Ali was born.

'I persuaded him it was greedy to keep it. I heard the other day that the council has a list a mile long of people waiting to be housed, so to hang on to a place he only used if he didn't want to drive home seemed immoral. That's what I told him, expecting him to argue that the flat we'd rented wouldn't help anyone on the council list. But he took it like a lamb and even agreed.'

'Perhaps if he doesn't want to drive home he could stay with David occasionally,' Louisa suggested, her mind journeying in an entirely different direction. Sometimes, through the months she had suggested they should find a way to spend the night in his flat when they had found a plausible excuse to both be away at the same time, but he had always preferred to find somewhere new to both of them. Booking in as Mr and Mrs Harding they had managed a few escapes, always setting off at different times and in different directions, and returning an hour or two apart. The cottage near Leominster put a new complexion on their situation. It may not alter the lies they had to tell, or the care they had to take to set off in different directions, but it was a little home waiting for them, somewhere they could return to knowing they could shut the door on the outside world and have nothing but each other for a whole night. Compared with couples who lived together permanently, that was so little to ask. It would be no more than an hour's drive to the cottage, and there would be occasions when they could meet there even for a couple of daytime hours. No more booking in as Mr and Mrs Harding and having to familiarize themselves with unknown surroundings.

So a new era began. More often than not they were only in the cottage together for two or three hours, but for Louisa those brief periods were like a drug she couldn't live without.

Their relationship was changing; the hours of intellectual discussion grew less frequent. Their time together was driven by physical need. It wasn't a case of one leading and the other following. Louisa knew nothing of his past, and neither did she want to know. For her, until he came into her life she had been aware of the biological facts but for all her half-understood yearning and lonely self-indulgence, she had found nothing compared with the wonder Leo brought to her. It was as if she had been but half alive until he made her a whole person. Now that part of her life belonged to him and only to him but, even so, it wasn't in her nature to wait idly for the hours they could be together.

It sometimes seemed to her that her life was divided into sections, each of them separate. By far the most important was Leo but the others all played their part. By word of mouth and recommendation her business was growing so that she had sufficient work to fill as much of her time as she needed; then there was Bella who came to see her most days, sometimes just with Alicia but occasionally, if there was no one around who could 'keep an eye' on Harold, bringing him with her; and then, increasingly as that year of 1958 drew to a close, there was Hamish.

Sitting up in bed, Louisa wrote something on those lines to her friend Jess. Some people keep diaries, some drift through life never putting their true feelings on paper. Louisa supposed she fell somewhere between the two for, ever since Jess had set sail for Australia, letters to her had been a safety valve. Had they met face-to-face after so long would she have opened her heart in the same way? She suspected she wouldn't, for Jess's years in another country, first single and then married, would have held them apart. But, on paper, life changes didn't come between them; they'd been kindred spirits for too long for altered circumstances to put up a barrier.

If Louisa could have read her earlier letters it would have brought alive the memory of how she had contrived to make her life sound more exciting than it was. What was there to tell of a weekly routine that never changed? That was before Violet had lifted her out of the tedium set to continue in the same colourless way. If only she'd had more self-confidence she would have forced herself to join some society, any society; but to do that would have meant trying to find a way into a closed circle of friends, or so she had imagined. So she had hidden behind a façade of austere efficiency. And then she had fallen under the spell of Lexleigh where, on her first afternoon, she had met Bella. No longer had she struggled to fill the pages of her letters to Australia. Indeed, to her they were like a confessional, a place to put into words that she had fallen desperately in love with her friend's husband, that her life revolved around the hours she spent with him hidden from the prying eyes of a world which would condemn what they did. Then into her letters there crept another character, one about whom she had no guilt: Hamish. As the months went by his name appeared more often as she described a day fossil hunting on the Dorset cliffs, a visit to the glorious gardens of an ancestral home in Cornwall, a Sunday spent helping in the potting shed at the garden centre, all written as the happy memories tumbled back into her mind.

Jess's reaction to her friendship with Hamish was to suggest that he was in love with her, something Louisa immediately rejected. From his enthusiasm for the transformation of her garden there had developed a friendship that became increasingly important to her. He was such an easy companion and informative, too. Often at weekends when the garden centre was closed they would drive on some outing or other, her interest developing as she learnt from his greater knowledge. Then with the coming of spring they would walk in the countryside. She was grateful to have her Sundays filled, for it was the one day of the week when work stopped at the farm and in the factory too, a day when Leo had no excuse to have to keep appointments. So his freedom was curtailed. He kept an eye on Harold – and Harold kept an eye on him – while Louisa became ever more involved with the McLarens. Occasionally Margaret and her fiancé Dennis would make a foursome with Louisa and Hamish. Even after what Jess wrote, it didn't occur to Louisa that Margaret had hopes – even expectations – that they were forming a quartet that would be permanent. Their outings were always happy times and from the McLaren twins she was absorbing a lot of knowledge about plants and gardening technique. Had she read Margaret's mind and realized the hope that one day she would be included in the McLaren family and even be part of the garden centre, she would have felt less at ease with them.

It was a Friday in April, the morning of a day that seemed to have forgotten the season and taken them straight into summer. Leo had gone to keep an appointment with one of Carters' important agents in Shropshire, saying he anticipated being away all day.

'He likes days like that,' Bella told Louisa when she called on her way to the butcher. 'I expect they could get through their business in half the time if they wanted, but he's been asked to stay to lunch and then there will be more chat. He's so much happier now he has an office at home and doesn't have to spend his working hours in that dingy office at the factory. I know he always had days out like today, but even they must have been spoilt by the thought that tomorrow he'd be back in the factory. He gets a lot of work done at home too.'

Louisa nodded. 'Much better. People must always work better when they are happy in their surroundings, I expect. I know I do as much here, mornings, evenings, any time I want, and yet I always feel a free agent.'

Bella smiled and nodded. 'It's Lexleigh's magic. I love it here, don't you?' It didn't need an answer. 'I dragged you out of your workroom and I expect you want to get on. Can I pick up anything for your lunch?'

'No, I'm OK. I'm warming up a casserole from yesterday. But I must get on. This afternoon I want to take back the papers I've been working on.'

'We won't hinder you. I just wanted you to see Ali in her new jacket. Remember, it's the one we bought in Gloucester back in the winter and it was much too big for her then.'

'She looks gorgeous. She really is the prettiest baby. Couldn't fail, I suppose, with you and Leo for parents.'

Bella chuckled appreciatively, told twenty-one-month-old Alicia to wave goodbye to Auntie Lou, and then they were off. Watching her carefully close the gate after them, Louisa was flooded with shame once more. Sometimes it happened to her; it was a physical feeling of emptiness, hopelessness. Going back into the workroom she put away the papers she had been working on. To lie to Bella was to betray a friend who had never shown anything but kindness to her, and that she could do it filled her with self-disgust. Her mouth felt dry; her hands were shaking. She lit a cigarette and drew on it deeply. *Forget Bella, forget the lies, none of it matters. Put it all out of your mind and think of the afternoon that's ahead.* What if Leo had lied about having lunch with Carters' agent – no one was hurt by it. No wife could be happier or blinder to the truth than Bella and, as for an order, he would use all his charm and knowledge and come back with that safely in his pocket.

Those were the thoughts in her head as she got ready for her trip. Yesterday's casserole would stay just where it was until it was heated this evening, for all she would have time for would be a sandwich and a cup of coffee. The last thing she needed was to waste time eating; she meant to make herself as attractive as possible (which in fact was very attractive indeed, but she was far too used to her appearance to appreciate it). Her make-up must be applied with extra care, her hair perfect, her oatmeal-coloured dress and jacket set off by her red neckerchief, shoes and handbag. All this was done to her satisfaction, all thoughts of Bella and deceit pushed to the back of her mind as, just when the clock on the tower of St John's Church at the far end of the High Street struck midday, she came out of the front door, remembering to carry her briefcase lest the neighbours were on watching duty. Another minute and she was in the car, reversing into the lane when she heard the front gate slam shut and Hamish was waving to attract her attention.

'This is unexpected. What a shame, Hamish. I'm just off to keep an appointment.'

'Look, Louisa. I mean, well, I mustn't keep you if you're in a rush. Um . . .' Clearly, something was wrong. She switched off the engine and wound the window right down.

'Is something wrong? You look bothered. What's up, Hamish?'

'Now I've got here it's hard to find the right words. And

you're off working somewhere. Perhaps I should wait for a better time.'

'A better time for what? I can wait five minutes. Tell me what's troubling you.' She had grown so fond of him and hated to see him upset about something. He was usually sure of himself. Whatever could have thrown him like this?

'It's not trouble, Lou. It's finding the right words.'

'Right or wrong, just tell me what it is. Is it something to do with Margaret? Or are things bad at the nursery? You always seem busy.'

'No Mags is fine and trade's pretty good too. What sort of a man must you think me, stammering and stuttering like some kid. Lou, you're not blind, you must have seen how I feel about you. You and me, we get along so well. What I'm trying to say is that I love you and I reckon we'd make a good couple. Say you'll agree for us to get married. We're fine together; all the times we've been together we've always got on. We could build happy lives.' He hadn't been able to form the first words, but once he'd started he sounded set to talk uninterrupted. 'Think of all the good times we've had; it'd work. If you wanted to set aside a bit of time each day to the work you do, then I wouldn't stop you. But I'm old fashioned and I'd expect to pay the bills. If you earned anything then that would be extra pocket money for you. I've been wanting to say this for so long . . .'

'I had no idea,' she interrupted. 'Hamish, I'm truly so fond of you, but I had no idea. I've never thought of us in that way.'

'I've made a mess of it. I did it badly.'

'I can't say yes, Hamish. I've never thought of you as anything but a friend, a very, very special friend.'

'That'll do to be going on with. But think now, Lou, darling Lou.' There! He'd said it; he'd called her his darling.

'Friendship isn't enough to marry on. You are very dear to me, honestly you are. Marriage needs friendship, but it's so much more.'

'I know and so it could be. I'd always be good to you; I hold you on such a high pedestal I promise I'd always cherish you.' Then, with a grin that was so much part of his character, his and Margaret's too, 'Imagine what perfect children we could have – pure pedigree.'

Despite herself she laughed, but all she said was, 'Hamish, I'm dreadfully late. I must go.'

'Think about it, Louisa. Promise me you'll think about it.'

'I promise. But Hamish, you promise me something too. Don't let any of this spoil what we have.'

'I promise *that* easily enough. Better half a slice of bread than none at all. May I call round this evening and give you a hand weeding the bed?'

'Thanks, friend.' And she let out the clutch and reversed out on to the lane.

Seven

The afternoon at the cottage cleared Louisa's mind of any thought of Hamish, any thought at all except the need to fill the time she and Leo had with the joy of living and loving. From the first moments they both knew what the culmination of their brief hours together would be, yet something held them back from rushing. It was as if into one afternoon they had to cram every aspect of how their shared lives could be. She made coffee, he twiddled with the knobs of the radio until he found music, they talked, yet all the while their imagination was drawing them forward. Perhaps something in Louisa's nature still clung to her hidebound past and prevented her letting him know where her imagination had been as she had driven from Lexleigh; in truth where it still was as she sipped her coffee and tried to give the appearance of relaxing while they smoked and talked. But he understood her better than she realized and, stubbing out his cigarette, he looked at her with that teasing light in his eyes.

'I think we've paid our dues to convention.' Holding out his hand as she came towards him, he pulled her to lie across his lap where he sat on the settee. She felt the warmth of his hand through the silk of her blouse.

'To hell with convention,' she muttered. 'Some people have all their lives, we have just these hours.'

'Methinks the lady is tempting me,' he said softly and she heard his voice as a caress.

'Your lady is wanting you,' she answered, scarcely moving her lips as she lay across him with her eyes closed and felt his hands move on her, 'every day and every night.' Her eyes suddenly opened and she looked very directly at him. 'What's the matter with me that I can say these things to you?'

'The same as is the matter with me, Lou, my beautiful Lou, every day and every night.'

By now her blouse was unfastened, then her bra; his tie was

off and she unbuttoned his shirt; his shirt was off and easing her on to the settee he unfastened his trousers and wriggled out of them just as she did with her skirt. That was just the beginning: in seconds they were stripped, their excitement mounting by the second for never before had they faced each other unclothed anywhere except the bedroom.

The cottage was far off the road down a narrow lane, but even so they pulled down the blinds and shut themselves off from the world. They wanted the afternoon never to end – this was what they had imagined each day and each night since they'd last been to the cottage nearly a fortnight before. Of course, Leo had a dutiful wife who had no idea where his imagination was carrying him as she held him tenderly and sent up a prayer of thanks that he seemed to have forgotten 'all that nasty nonsense' and hoped he wouldn't need to take too long. How different were Louisa's thoughts as she gloried in every act, every caress, wanting these moments never to end, even though at the same time she strained towards the climax she knew she would attain. And when that moment came she was driven by ecstasy, triumph and relief, hardly aware of her cry which expressed all three.

They dressed without speaking then, in her methodical way, she cleared away the coffee cups, plumped up the cushions and restored order to the room as if no one had been there while Leo lay back in an armchair with his eyes closed. It was Friday afternoon – the weekend lay ahead when they seldom saw each other. Why it was that the weekend should make any difference to their days made no sense – except that from Friday teatime until Monday morning the cottage was out of bounds – but because the routine at the farm was different and the village shops closed it affected all their lives. That was how it had come about that Louisa often saw Hamish and Margaret on Sunday, for on that day the nursery gate stayed shut to the public.

'I'd better start first.' Her voice brought Leo out of his exhausted half-sleep. 'Everything is cleared up; all you have to do is lock up when you leave. And don't forget that you haven't put your tie back on.'

'Where do you get your energy from? You seem to have

more get-up-and-go than you arrived with. As for me, I'm shattered beyond belief.'

Gazing in the mirror above the mantelpiece, she touched up her make-up. 'When shall we see each other?'

'I'll call and suggest you come to the pub this evening. Probably I'll bring Dad with me – he'd like that.'

'I'll be appropriately surprised when I open the door.' She bent over him and kissed his forehead. 'It was wonderful,' she said softly, the matter-of-fact Louisa overtaken by the woman who would live on memories of these hours until the next time. 'Each time is better than the last.'

His Adam's apple seemed too large for his throat as he recovered from his exhaustion.

'No use looking at me like that,' she told him, her voice light but with an underlying note of seriousness. 'I'm off. You know your friend Gerald often comes early on Fridays and I'd feel at a disadvantage to meet him for the first time after rollicking on his rug.'

'Tut tut, woman, where's your decorum?' he teased, wide awake by this time.

'I'll make sure I find it ready for when you and your father call for me.' And with one more fleetingly light kiss that missed his forehead and landed above his hairline, she was gone.

All the way back to Lexleigh she sang, something for which she had no talent. But alone in the car there was no one to hear when she slipped out of tune. It was simply an expression of her inner contentment. Life was good. She and Leo may never live together as any ordinary couple but, with days like today, as if that mattered! Wasn't what they had more exciting than love that might become part of habit and routine? Like Violet and Harold they would be lovers as long as they lived – lovers who found supreme joy in what surely in the average marriage became comfortable routine. No wonder she sang.

She took a detour a mile or two from Lexleigh, bringing her in beyond the village so that she had to drive down the High Street. It was unlikely that anyone was out shopping by that hour, for it was almost time to close, but the fact that she hadn't come via the direct route added to her feeling of mystery and excitement. And, when one of her opposite neighbours looked round from clipping the front hedge, she made a point of waving as she turned first into the lane and then her garage. Ten minutes later and approaching from the opposite direction, she heard Leo's car drive up the lane on his way to the farm. Harold and Bella would listen with pride as he regaled them with a description of his day and what a successful order he had been given.

Half an hour later she was lying in the bath, freshening up after that 'rollick on the rug'. After a warm day the evening was turning chilly as the sun sank and she dressed in slacks and a jumper. Where so many women would have looked as though they hadn't bothered, this could never be said of Louisa. Her lilac-coloured slacks and jumper were an exact match, and with them she wore a neckerchief of lilac, fawn and deep violet. Her only ornamentation was a pair of small pearl earrings. With her face freshly made up she was satisfied with her appearance when there was a knock at her front door. That's when she remembered Hamish for the first time since she had set out for Leominster and, as so often, she was ashamed. Dear Hamish. She was truly fond of him and yet, even after his visit that morning she hadn't cared enough, even at the back of her mind, to hang on to the memory of his visit. When Leo had said he would pick her up on the way to the Pig and Whistle nothing had triggered the memory that she had agreed to spend the evening in the garden with Hamish.

When she opened the front door there was nothing in her expression to hint that his arrival hadn't been expected.

'You'll think me a rotten friend. If you want to let the weeds have their own way until another day, of course I shall understand. But something has cropped up and it would have been unkind to refuse.'

'Och, but I can see from your get-up that gardening won't be for you this evening.'

'You know my friend Bella, of course, but I'm not sure whether you've met her husband, Leo Carter? You may have. He often pops in.'

'Not to my knowledge,' Hamish answered, his tone giving nothing away. 'Is he the lucky man who has merited this casual elegance?'

'Yes and no. He popped round to say that he was walking to the Pig and Whistle for a drink this evening and taking his father. Poor Mr Carter, his memory is failing and he's losing his grip, but Leo thinks it's good for him to get amongst people sometimes. Bella couldn't go, of course, because of the baby, so Mr Carter suggested they call here on the way and take me with them.'

'The old lad has a shine for you?'

She laughed at the unexpectedness of the question. 'Most unlikely, I should think. But Bella often brings him here, so he is used to me. Going into a crowded pub might be a strain on him. Leo is very social, he'll chat to all the locals, but I can see that Mr Carter is OK.'

'That's kind of you, Louisa. Rumour has it that he used to be a pretty frequent visitor here.'

'Yes, my aunt was very fond of him. It would sadden her to see him now.'

Hamish nodded. 'Shall we make it another evening or shall I spend an hour or so scratching around out here?'

'That seems an awful cheek. When they arrive, why don't you come with us to the pub? We can garden together another evening.'

It was said on the spur of the moment and with no thought as to what Leo might make of the idea. But as it worked out, it was at just that moment that Carter father and son arrived. If she'd expected Leo to resent her having invited Hamish to join them she had misjudged him.

'I saw the van outside,' he said as they came up the path. 'Are you the miracle man who transformed this wilderness into a garden?'

'Och, but I am no more than the in-between man.'

'You aren't McLaren?'

'Indeed I am.' Louisa noticed that his sometimes hardly noticeable Scottish dialect was more pronounced than usual. 'I put in the plants but the miracle comes after that; it is the rain and the light, the sunshine too, that gives us what we see. Mr Carter, sir,' addressing Harold, 'you have been a grower for many years; you know how dependent anyone working the land is upon the weather.'

Harold seemed to grow an inch or two. It was a long time since anyone had referred to him in that way; indeed, as regards his experience on the land it was more than a long time – more likely it was the first time.

'You're right, my boy,' his answered in a strong voice, smiling at the three of them as if he were the founder of all knowledge. 'We're off to the Pig and Whistle for a wee dram of something. How about you coming with us, eh?'

'Thank you, sir. Some other time I should enjoy it, but this evening I have my work lined up. The hedge is to be trimmed. You agree that is no job for a lady.'

Harold looked at the long hedge, memories alive in his mind.

'Like painting the Forth Bridge, by the time you reach the end the beginning is waiting for you to start again. Many an hour – and day – I've spent with the shears on that hedge. We never did much to make it a garden, but Violet loved a neat hedge.' As he spoke his voice changed – he seemed to be speaking just to himself as he recalled how his life used to be. Pulling himself out of his reverie, he looked at the three of them and said, 'It all goes too quickly. Where does time go? Before you know it you'll all be looking back . . . too late by then . . . now, *now* has to be what matters.'

'Come on, Dad, we'd better get to that pub or Bella will think we're lost. Are you in the mood for a drink, Louisa, or do you want to watch the hedge cutting?'

'Of course she's coming,' Hamish answered for her, 'she'd already told me you were picking her up. I must get my trimmer out of the van. Can you leave the door unlocked so that I can plug it in? Or the garage, that will do.'

Louisa noticed Leo's quick frown and had a feeling of satisfaction. At least he must have had a twinge of resentment that another man had access to her house.

'You can plug it in in the kitchen if you're sure you don't want to come.'

'Indeed, I am sure. I'll start on the hedge; the weeds can live another day.'

They left him to his labours and set off towards the Pig and Whistle, but they'd not gone many steps before Leo told her,

'You ought to be careful who you let have the run of the house like that.'

'Hamish is a friend, a very dear friend.'

Harold was walking between the two of them and Louisa was aware that he smiled to himself as he looked from one to the other.

'A very nice young man,' was his opinion, 'as trustworthy as they come. And if you want my opinion, I'd say his pleasure in doing that garden comes from seeing the delight Louisa gets from it. Different with Violet. No, gardens didn't appeal to her. She liked the size of it, though, and the hedge. A good hedge keeps you private. I planted it, you know. Then I used to keep it trimmed – not cut right back, but clipping it helps to thicken it up. Long time ago.' Once again, and only momentarily, he was back in all his yesterdays. But they'd reached the Pig and Whistle, so the past gave way to the present.

On that evening, Harold was good company. He might have been a different man from the one who had invaded Louisa's (previously Violet's) bedroom all those months ago. She wondered if they were mistaken in watching over him so carefully, for perhaps it was that which took away his confidence. If he were treated as he was this evening where it was clear most of the drinkers had known him for years and were glad to see him, then she believed he would respond. She would talk to Bella about him after the weekend and suggest that none of them would be normal if they were watched continually and looked on as being incapable. But as they were walking home along the ill-lit village street she realized it was she who had misjudged the situation.

'What is it, Dad? Are we walking too fast?' Leo's question alerted her to the fact that something was different about Harold. Instead of walking in step he was shuffling and his breathing was different, each breath like a suppressed moan. 'You take one arm, Lou, and I'll take the other.'

'No, no, don't hold me.' By then all three had stopped, Louisa and Leo peering at Harold in the gloom.

'Did those friends he met give him too much to drink?' she whispered to Leo, believing Harold was unlikely to follow the question.

'Didn't you see her? Must be blind, the pair of you.' He peered at them, first one and then the other, at the same time pulling his arms free of their hold. But it was fear, not anger she heard in his voice.

'I didn't see anyone, Mr Carter. Who did you think you saw?'

'Think? *Think?* You believe I'm off my bloody head, don't you? Just because you're too wrapped up in your own tiny world to see. I tell you, I saw her.'

'Who did you see?' What was she asking it for? She knew who it was he believed he saw. But she had to ask it anyhow.

'You wouldn't know. You and your lot were no family to her. You spoilt her life, made her feel like she was a sinner. My precious Vi, my preci—' His words were swallowed in a near silent sob.

What a moment for Louisa's thoughts to turn away from Harold and Violet and on to Leo and herself. Surely it was the same story repeating itself. If one day she were to be lost to him Leo would feel there was nothing left in his own life, just as Harold did. Was she being fanciful? She had such a strange feeling. It was as if for the first time she was conscious of overwhelming love between Leo and herself. Lovemaking was the way it manifested itself, lovemaking was wonderful and beautiful but it was only part of what held them together. She wished they were on their own instead of poor, broken Harold standing in between them, shaken and frightened. Was Leo thinking the same as she was? To what extent did he see their story as a repetition of his father's with her aunt?

'Leo?' It was no more than a whisper but she felt he must hear her and understand all that one word conveyed.

'Come on, Dad, we'll soon be home. Or it might be a good idea if we stopped off at your place for a few minutes, Lou. Don't take to heart what he said about your family – I guess he was bitter on her account. He's been so good all evening.'

Louisa shook her head, as if to warn him not to talk as though his father couldn't hear.

'Don't worry,' Leo whispered, 'he won't be hearing a thing. When he gets like this you can't get through to him. If he can come in to your place, see *you* there where she used to

be and perhaps have a good strong coffee or something, that
should help. He'd been so good all evening too,' he said, just
as he had a moment earlier. She felt he spoke out of love for
his father, making sure that she didn't condemn him for the
change in his behaviour.

For months Harold had been coming in and out of The
Retreat with Bella and seemed to be quite used to it no longer
being Violet's home, but Louisa was less certain of him this
evening, and couldn't put that other evening out of her mind
when he had looked at her and seen her aunt. Not that anything
like that could happen tonight, and Leo could be right in
thinking that it might lay the ghost to bring him in to the
home that was no longer Violet's.

'Let's all get in step and on we march,' she said cheerfully,
linking her arm through Harold's. This time he didn't pull
away, but neither did he seem aware of his surroundings.
With one each side of him he walked at their pace, a pace
slowed down from the strides they would normally take. He
didn't speak and now all they could hear as they progressed
along the quiet street was the effort he made at each intake
of breath.

Once in the sitting room, which had been such a familiar
part of his life in happier days, he went straight to his usual
chair, where he sat with his eyes closed. The other two looked
at him, saying nothing but following their own thoughts.

Louisa felt sorry for him, but reason got the upper hand. It
wasn't fair on Bella to expect her to look after him day after
day. Either he ought to be sent to a nursing home – one which
catered for people with dementia – or, failing that, they ought
to engage a man to look after him, a strong man, for Harold
still had plenty of fight in him.

Leo's thoughts weren't so simple. As a child he had looked
on his father as some sort of godlike creature, and had tried
to emulate him in every way. Whereas David, two years his
senior, had ignored Violet Harding's presence, it had been very
different for Leo. He had always been welcomed at The Retreat,
sometimes with Harold and sometimes on his own. Remembering
those days, even after so many years, he could recall the atmosphere in the house, the feeling of love, both the love of life

and of each other. Remembering, he was ashamed, for to think as he did must suggest there was less love in their own home. His mother had never been a woman to show affection, yet there had been no doubt in their minds that they had been loved. Time had been her enemy; there had never been enough hours in the day for all she had to cram into them. Now, Dad – Dad had been different. Seeing the slight smile tug at the corners of Leo's mouth, Louisa tried to guess where his thoughts had taken him. But guess all night and she could never have been right. Yes, Dad had been different. Leo let his mind slip back a quarter of a century: Dad had been full of fun, full of the joy of living, such good company. If there was an outing to be had, then sure enough Dad would be there. Poor old Mum – no chance of any outings for her. But then, she wouldn't have enjoyed them; her interests were with the work in the fields or with the village. Not Dad, though, the old rascal. And now look at the poor old lad – never has anyone gone downhill so quickly. A good job Bella is there to look after him. She's a good girl. Thank God for Louisa, though. There must be something about this house. Fate was kind in making Violet leave it to her. If she hadn't come here and if we hadn't met, what would our future have been?

He realized she was watching him and half closed his eyes as their glances met, his expression telling her everything she wanted to know. She nodded her head slightly in answer to his silent message, as if to confirm that her thoughts had moved with his.

'All right to walk home now, Dad?' Leo said, realizing that Harold had opened his eyes and was watching them, his expression alert.

'I'm all right on my own if you want to stay a bit longer.' Harold's thinking had cleared. Looking at the pair of them put him so much in mind of himself and Violet. By God, he would have stayed a bit longer, and if Leo was the man he thought he was, then that's what he'd want to do too.

'No,' Leo told him. 'We'll walk together. Louisa has had a busy day and I expect she's ready for bed.'

'The young these days – they've got no stamina,' Harold chuckled.

Their goodnights said, the men started towards the garage and the double gates opening on to the track to the farm.

'Just a second, Dad,' Leo said, 'I want a quick word with Louisa before she bolts the door.' He hurried back just as Louisa started to close the door, so he didn't see his father's satisfied smile or guess the thoughts that filled his mind. The boy must think I was born yesterday. But it's good to see history repeating itself; brings it all back. I don't want to forget, but I'm getting so silly, can't hang on to things for two minutes. Can you see it too, Violet, my lovely? If only it were us, you and me, young, dear God, but we had some good times. Youth, where does it go? What's happening to me? I feel as strong as an ox one minute and the next . . . so frightened, don't understand where I am, don't know what to do . . . I'll just hang on to thinking about young Leo and Louisa . . . your Louisa, my Leo . . . she and my boy . . . just like us again, eh?

In the doorway, Leo was whispering urgently to Louisa. 'I'll see him safely indoors and then come back. You go on to bed. Just for an hour, Lou. Think of how it was for us this afternoon.'

'No. You must go home. Bella's waiting for you.'

'It's *you* I want. Please. I'll tell her I've dropped my wallet, and that I think it must have fallen out because I took my jacket off here. She'll not doubt it's the truth.'

Probably it was that last sentence that clinched Louisa's reply. 'She'll not doubt it's the truth.' How true that was. Bella would believe him no matter what lie he invented. That one sentence had even wiped away some of the wonder of the afternoon. Louisa felt cheap, deceitful and unworthy of Bella's trusting friendship.

'Then let's stick to the truth. Go home, Leo. Take care of your father – and tell Bella that I went with you to the Pig and Whistle. Be sure she'll hear anyway and she'd be hurt and think we have something to hide.'

After he'd gone she thought of her words and felt even worse than she had at Leo's suggestion.

Harold appeared to have recovered from his earlier confusion and was in what appeared to be good spirits when they got back to the house and found David's car parked there.

'We would have come earlier if we'd known you were coming,' he told his elder son, accompanying his words with a welcoming smile and a kiss for Lily, David's wife with whom he never felt entirely at ease, although he had never been heard to admit it. She was a thin woman, bony and angular. He could never understand how David had got any pleasure from bedding her, be damned if he could. Bony she may be, but strong. No, not for him, Harold thought as he planted a paternal kiss on her cheek; it would take a braver man than him to tumble her in bed. He wondered what Bella made of her, such a sweet child. So his rambling thoughts went as the others made conversation that went over his head.

'Bella told us where you'd gone,' Lily was saying, 'so we drove down to look for you. When she said you'd walked, we thought we'd give you a lift home. In the bar they said you'd been gone half an hour or so.'

'Ah,' Harold brought his mind back from where it had slipped and sensed trouble, 'my fault you missed us. I wanted us to collect Louisa. Living alone I doubt if she goes out much in the evening. After we'd had a drink we dropped her back home and stayed talking a while.' He caught Bella's eye and his smile dropped. He suddenly looked crushed. 'We drop in there a lot, don't we?'

'That's right, Dad. Mostly we call when we go into the village. Louisa is a very good friend.' There was a defiant note in Bella's voice.

'I was telling Bella,' David said to Leo, 'that I saw your car today outside a cottage, yours and another one. I'd driven to collect Lily from staying with a friend.'

'I'd been in the ATS with her,' Lily interrupted. 'All through the war we were together and then lost touch. Quite by chance from an acquaintance I heard where she was and got in touch with her again. I had two days there, two days to catch up on about thirteen years. It was so nice. But, sorry David, I cut in on what you were saying.'

'That's all right. I was simply saying I was surprised when I saw your car, Leo. I understood you were going to meet with George Middleton. And Bella was telling us you got a big order. Is that where he lives? That's a long way from the firm in Shropshire.'

'The firm is in Shropshire,' Leo answered coolly, 'and I've no idea where he lives. You must have seen me parked outside Gerald Sinclair's weekend cottage. You must remember him.'

'You mean that was *his* car parked by yours? If I'd known that I would have banged on the door. Lily's friend is walking distance from there; in fact, we were walking when we passed the cottage. I couldn't make it out. The blinds were drawn and yet both cars were there.'

'You missed your vocation,' Leo laughed, 'you ought to have been a detective. I expect he leaves the blinds drawn while he's away during the week. He's in London all the week but gets home Friday afternoon. I caught sight of him shopping in town and had a word, then followed him home. I can't say I went inside – we walked straight round to the back garden and sat and nattered for a while. It's very isolated there. You say your friend lives nearby, Lily? Surprising. It's a real hideaway, just what he likes after a week in London.'

'I must ask her if she knows him. I expect she must do in an isolated place like that. What a small world it is.'

Leo and Louisa's glory days at the cottage had been spoilt after David reported seeing his car parked there next to another. They had gone a few more times, both leaving their cars in a public car park about a mile's walk away, but nothing had been the same. Most of their time spent together was at The Retreat, usually when he knew Bella was busy at home, for with a large house, a young child and a father-in-law who needed constant watching, she had very little spare time and mostly only called to see Louisa when she was shopping in the village.

But on the morning following David's unexpected visit to Ridgeway, Louisa knew nothing about his having recognized Leo's car at the cottage, and the previous afternoon was clear and bright in her mind.

She saw that almost half of the hedge had been trimmed before the fading light had cut short the work. It was a comforting thought that Hamish would come back and finish the job as soon as the nursery closed. He must have known it was more than one evening's work even with the electric cutters, but no arrangements had yet been made. She was certain he would come and found herself looking forward to it. At the weekend she never saw Leo or Bella either. At the farm Sundays had always been set apart from the rest of the week, not for religious reasons, but because Sunday was family time; and especially for Bella, for whom being part of a family was something she'd always dreamt of, so it was a rule she approved of wholeheartedly. If Louisa were honest with herself, she would have admitted that was the reason it had become natural over the months to spend her weekend time with Hamish and Margaret.

Looking back at her years in Reading after Jess had gone to Australia, she never let her mind dwell on the weekends. Living alone through a busy week she liked the orderliness of her flat, but at the weekend her footsteps had seemed to echo – every sound of passers-by emphasized her solitude as the years ahead mocked her. A successful professional woman? Or a lonely spinster?

But it was all very different at Lexlcigh. Even before she had become acquainted with the couple from the garden centre she had never been lonely at the weekends. So what was the difference? Perhaps it had to do with having a front door that led to the big outside, a place where (even before the advent of Hamish) plants and weeds could grow. It was a living place. She would sit on her garden bench, in those days freshly painted by Ted Johnson, and know herself to be part of the living world. Then change had come in the form of the McLaren twins and friendship had developed so naturally she accepted it without conscious thought. Sometimes she would spend Saturday at the nursery, helping to prick out seedlings, even serving in the shop, sharing the makeshift snack which replaced lunch on what was the busiest day of the week. An easy friendship had developed and she was frightened that Hamish's proposal and her refusal might have changed their relationship. But it mustn't. She wouldn't even let herself imagine the gap there would be in her life without the McLarens.

So on that Saturday morning she dressed in a well cut but simple skirt and tailored blouse – the best she could muster for casual wear – made up her face and did her hair with the usual precision, then slipped her stockinged feet into a pair of her habitual high-heeled court shoes. She would go over and offer her services. If Margaret was too busy to leave the shop she would offer to sort something out for a snack lunch. She felt entirely content with her lot. She let her mind slip back to the previous afternoon, half smiling at the memory. Last night she had fallen asleep almost as her head had touched the pillow. How different it had been from the nights that had gone before. Yesterday with Leo she had been like a starving man at a banquet, greedy for every morsel. And afterwards, her hunger sated, she was content, a sentiment still with her as she drove towards the nursery.

That summer set the pattern for the months ahead. Of all of them the biggest changes were in Alicia: from taking her first tentative step and then landing back on her bottom to becoming a toddler firm on her feet was a steady progress, as steady as the changes in the seasons – autumn, winter, spring and then into the beginning of another summer.

Lexleigh was a village set in its ways and happy with itself. It wouldn't be true to say there were no teenagers there but their numbers were few, and if they wanted to kick their heels up they had little opportunity for it in the village. They tried to emulate their contemporaries in town, but the nearest they managed to get to being part of the new teenage world was a monthly dance in the village hall with no licence for alcohol. Soon they would be old enough to spread their wings and so they dreamed as they danced to music on a record player, the traditional quickstep giving way to the twist as they imagined themselves to be part of the modern age.

At the farm, Harold lived in his own private world. Physically he appeared less frustrated by his lapses than in the early days, for the further he withdrew into a world of his own the less he experienced the misery and humiliation of realizing what was happening to him. Bella looked after him almost as if he were a dependent child, always seeing he was as careful about how he was turned out as he had been all his life. She shaved him each morning, knotted his tie for him, tied his shoelaces, all the time talking to him as she would have in the days he had been capable of holding a conversation. She was quite touched to see a side of Leo's nature she hadn't known, for it was he who helped his father in and out of the bath and into his pyjamas each night. But there were nights when Leo wasn't there, and on those he had to skip a bath and Bella made sure he was snug in bed. He felt loved and protected. While they took care of him he slipped into a kind of contented stupor, forgetting his inner misery or, if not forgetting it, letting it lie dormant at the back of his mind. There was just one person who gave him real pleasure, which had nothing to do with his own personal comfort, and that person was Alicia. At two years old she was enchantingly pretty, something that appealed to Harold whatever the age, but more than her physical appearance what held him spellbound was the way she followed him like a shadow. Sometimes they would play with a ball together on the small grassy patch they called the garden; at other times he would carry her on his shoulders to find the men working in the fields for, despite his mental deterioration, physically he was still strong. Everyone loved Ali and she responded by being her most delightful. At two years old she knew without being taught how to use her eyes to advantage, whether her expression was one of shyness and she lowered her gaze in a demure way, or whether she opened her mouth, showing two rows of pearly white perfect teeth, threw back her head and laughed. To make her laugh the men would stop working amongst the rows of produce and come to speak to her as she sat high on either her father's shoulders or her grandfather's. She would enter into the spirit and laugh uproariously as they performed any antic, be it hopping, singing a snatch of a song accompanied by pulling a funny face – anything that would bring peals of mirth. Jo Marsh, a seasonal worker who spent his days gathering fruit or vegetables according to where he was needed, considered himself something of a comedian. He was Alicia's star turn and she would chuckle with anticipation and delight when he approached.

It was early in September, soon after Ali's second birthday when Leo called 'casually' while Bella and Ali were in the garden at The Retreat and Harold half dozing on the bench.

Nothing in either Leo's manner or Louisa's hinted that the scene had been pre-arranged so that he would be there when she told them about her forthcoming visit to her parents.

'One night would be long enough, but it's a long way to go for such a short time, so I shall stay for a second,' she said, not looking at Leo and pleased with herself and with him too for playing their parts so well.

'On Tuesday, you say?' Leo commented with no real interest in his voice. 'That means there will be nowhere for you to retreat to on the Wednesday, Bella. That's the day I have arranged to go to Reading to chat up our main agents there. Then I thought I'd look in at the Cattle Market, remember? You and Dad will be on your own.'

'I'm quite capable of looking after Dad,' Bella answered, her tone telling them that in her opinion it was usually *she* who looked after him.

So, following their plans, on the Tuesday afternoon Louisa headed towards Newquay where she would spend the night with her parents, and on the following morning Leo set off as if for Reading. Once he had travelled far enough to be free of being recognized he changed course as planned and they met on the seafront in Weymouth. It was a town neither of them knew, so it gave them a feeling of being cut off from everyday life and people. The place was quietening down for autumn now that the school term had started and they had no trouble in booking a room for the night for Mr and Mrs Harding.

There was no better way of putting distance between herself and the duty visit to Cornwall, and Louisa meant to enjoy every minute. Walking along the promenade with Leo, the thumb of her left hand almost caressed the cheap gold band she wore on her third finger. It was as make-believe as everything else in their relationship but into the few brief times they had together they had to cram enough to give them memories to keep forever. Like addicts puffing greedily on their drugged cigarettes, so they filled every moment day and night. The sun shone on them and they lay on the golden sand as though they hadn't a care in the world – she wearing the bathing costume she had remembered to pack, he in trunks he had had to buy. They swam in the sea. Their day was magic; there was a quality of unreality about it, for never had they spent what might be seen as typical seaside holiday time together. But if the day was magic, by night they were firmly on earth, two human beings hungry for every bodily pleasure, whether driven by love or lust.

At about the time Leo and Louisa were meeting in Weymouth, little Ali tugged hopefully on Harold's trouser leg, looking up at him appealingly. It was a morning of brilliant sunshine, very different from the storms of the previous two days.

'Ball? We take the ball, Grandpa?'

'The grass will still be wet – don't let her sit on it, Dad,' Bella called as she saw them making towards the grassy patch.

'Right you are, my dear; I'll take care of her. We're going to have a game of football, eh, Ali?'

Drawn to the window, Bella watched them, a smile playing at the corners of her mouth. In a minute she'd go up and tidy the bedrooms, but there was no hurry – Leo had set off early for his drive to Berkshire, where he'd told them he had an appointment to see a supplier. After that, as it was sale day in Reading Cattle Market, he was looking forward to going on there, sure to meet farmers of his acquaintance. Harold and Bella knew this was a part of his job he liked best. Mixing with the farmers was always good for business. He had said he would be home by tea time. With Louisa visiting her parents, Bella had nothing to hurry for. Without realizing it, the smile spread across her face as she watched the two playing on the postage stamp lawn, hearing the whoops of excitement from both of them as they kicked the ball. She took up her cleaning tools and went upstairs. Dad was a darling, she thought, and had a momentary feeling of shame at how often she was irritated when he seemed not to know what he was doing. She honestly tried her hardest not to let it show when she felt angry and frustrated; he couldn't help being the way he was, and she thought of how much he loved Ali. Really Ali was his salvation – when he was with her he forgot to be frightened that he couldn't remember things. Hearing them playing together, Bella smiled again as she started her daily bedroom tidying.

About an hour later she came back down, beds made and
bedrooms tidied. She went to the pantry to start to assemble
what she needed to cook for lunch. It was then that the silence
was broken by the telephone bell.

'Bella, it's me,' came Leo's voice. 'This must be a quick call
– I'm in a kiosk and haven't much change. I've just arrived at
the Cattle Market and who should I bump into but Eric and
Jane Gibbons—'

'Who?' He spoke so enthusiastically about these friends,
people she had never heard of. She felt shut out.

'Gibbons, Eric and Jane Gibbons – you remember. I must
have told you I was best man at their wedding. Haven't seen
them for ages. Dreadful how we get swamped with daily living
and forget to keep up with old friends. Anyway, we're going
to make the most of it. They want to see how much they get
for their cattle and then they're taking me home for the night.
A thick head night unless I'm mistaken,' he added, laughing.
'Is everything all right at home? Tell Dad who I'm with,
although he probably won't remember.'

'Of course I'll tell him. Have a good—' but before she could
finish her sentence she heard the pips and they were cut off.

She went back to cutting what looked like being the last of
the runner beans. After a few minutes it struck her that Harold
and Ali were very quiet outside and curiosity took her to the
window that had been her vantage point earlier, expecting to
see that they had finished with the ball and found another,
quieter game. There was no sign of them. He must have carried
her to the fields. She smiled to herself as she dug in the sack
of home-grown potatoes to count out enough to make a
topping for the cottage pie. Ali loved cottage pie and she was
such a neat little person, sitting in her highchair she could feed
herself beautifully and seldom tipped her spoon upside down
when she put it in her mouth.

With Leo out all day there were only the three of them for
lunch and so, with everything ready to be put on the table,
she started out to the field to fetch them back. The only person
in the first field was Ted Johnson, busy collecting bean poles
to be cleaned and stored for the following year.

'I thought I'd find Dad and Ali here, Ted. Did they go on

to the next field? That's a long way for him to carry her on his shoulders and she couldn't walk it on this uneven ground.' She started down the edge of that field towards the gate into the next.

'You won't find them there. I'd know right enough if they'd crossed my patch. Perhaps he's taken her to see Miss Harding – more likely there than walked off down the lane by the wood.'

'She's away. She went yesterday to stay with her parents. But still, Dad wouldn't think of that. I expect that's where they are. I'll go and fetch them back. Thanks, Ted.'

But she soon found there was no trace of them in the direction of The Retreat. If it had been just Harold she might have been vaguely concerned but not really worried; he had lived here for the best part of his life, and couldn't get lost even if he tried. But what was he doing with Ali? She wasn't a girl given to hysterical panic, but in that moment Bella's mind was filled with ghastly images: he wasn't normal, half the time he seemed not to know what he was doing. And he had Ali . . . he'd taken Ali . . . but where? Perhaps they were in the wood on the far side of the farm. She would be frightened – she'd never been there before. It wasn't a nice wood with space between the trees, it was dark and there were no tracks made by use. 'Ali!' she shouted, not once but over and over again.

'No sign?' she heard Ted calling after her. 'We'll give you a hand looking.'

Seeing the three of them, Ted, Geoff and Jo Marsh, the only remaining seasonal worker who would be with them for another month or so, Bella's spirit lifted. With all four looking, in no time they would find where Harold had taken her. And in that same second, as her confidence took a boost from the sight of them, Jo shouted, 'Look, there he is. He's seen us, he's waving.'

Eight

'Good. You can help us. We've lost the ball, you see.' Harold's voice held a note of excitement, as if they had come to join in the game and now the fun would be in looking for the ball.

'Where's Ali? What have you done with Ali?' Never in her life had Bella known such a sick feeling of fear, but Harold didn't recognize it.

'Looking for the ball. Now you've all come we'll soon find—'

Terror destroyed all Bella's previous efforts to be gentle with him, to remember what he was like when first she met him.

'Damn the ball! *Where have you left Ali?*'

Her shrill voice was so unlike anything he was used to that it at least turned his mind away from looking for the lost ball. Instead he looked first to the right and then the left, as if he would trigger a memory of where he had been.

Ted Johnson took command. 'You three spread out and look. He may have taken her into the wood. I'll take the guv'nor home and leave him with Eva. She'll give him a bite to eat. Don't you worry, Bella, we'll find her. Soon as I've handed him over I'll come straight back.'

'Dad, try and think. Try and remember, please.' Bella voice was no more than a croak, evidence of her battle to hold back her tears.

'Did you go in the wood?' This from Jo Marsh. 'You can get in just down further, there are planks cross the ditch. Did you do that? If she's in the wood we shall hear her screaming, she'll be getting scratched to bits. It's a right jungle in there and she's just a wee mite.'

'Come on, Guv,' Ted took Harold's arm, 'you and me'll get back home where Eva's waiting to give you a bit of lunch.' Then, to the others: 'If you've found her before I get back, just make for home the way we came and I'll meet you.'

'She can't be lost, Ted, not really *lost* – you know what I mean?' For recently they had all read a lot in the paper about a child who had gone missing, disappeared without trace while playing in her own back garden which backed on to common land, and the police could find no clues. The word 'kidnapped' sent a chill of dread through Bella.

Yes, Ted knew what she meant right enough. 'What? Here? This land all belongs to the farm. He'd have registered if he'd seen any stranger about. Don't let yourself get ideas like that. We shall bring her home, never you fear. Come on now, Guv, or your dinner'll be getting chilled.'

Like an obedient child, Harold let himself be 'quick marched' back to a surprised Eva waiting for Ted with dinner ready in her cottage while the other three split up. But there was nowhere to search except the wood and, as Jo had said, if that's where she was she would surely be screaming.

When Ted Johnson returned from delivering Harold to Eva he could hear voices from various parts of the wood as they called Ali's name. So they hadn't found her. They must have crossed the ditch on that narrow bridge consisting of two planks, so he decided not to cross it but to follow the grassy, uncultivated edge to the field and continue on the same side. Surely if Harold had dumped her on the ground she would have been more likely to have stayed in the open than go into a dark and overgrown wood. Ted imagined the scene: the ball thrown and lost and the little girl being put on her own feet so that they could both look for it. Poor old Harold, Ted thought, despite the trouble his forgetfulness was causing. His heart may never have been in working the land, but young or old you couldn't help liking him. Leo was a chip off the old block, too. Wonder if there's any truth in the word that's going around about him and Louisa Harding. Most men would give anything for a wife like Bella – and to be fair to Leo, he always seems nice enough to the girl. But from the gossip Eva had heard in the village store he was always stuck round at that Retreat place, just like his old man before him.

For all Ted let his thoughts wander, he looked around him as he walked. Perhaps the little lass had wriggled through a gap in the hedge and was wandering in the field of sweetcorn.

But it was while that thought was forming that he noticed something colourful in the ditch. This was the first good day for a while and the constant rain had filled it. But there was something . . . something pink . . . Oh, God, no, don't let it be too late. Oh, God, please, God, help me . . . He slid down into the ditch, which held about eighteen inches of water, and paddled towards the little body lying where it had fallen.

'Bella!' he yelled at the top of his powerful voice. 'Bella, back here.'

In what seemed like no more than seconds Bella had fought her way through the dark and neglected wood and appeared on that side of the ditch near the plank bridge.

'You've found her. Thank God—' She stood stock still, breaking off mid-sentence as she saw the two of them, the tiny figure lying on the ground with Ted kneeling over her, trying everything he knew to try and empty her lungs of water from the ditch and start her breathing. Seeing Bella, he shook his head helplessly. She must have run towards him but she wasn't aware of what she did as she fell to her knees and lifted Ali, cradling her in her arms.

'No, no, please God, no.' Sobbing, she crushed the inert little body against her, knowing that all her cries for help couldn't bring life back. 'It's my fault. Oh, Ali, I let you go with him. Please, God, don't take her, anything else but not Ali. She's just little – she's not even had a life yet.'

The other two had heard Ted's shout too and were standing helplessly by. If Ted were honest he felt useless too, but he knew it had to be up to him to help Bella, so standing up he bent over her as he said, 'Stand up, Bella, my dear, I'll help you. Give her to me to carry.'

'No! I want her.' She stood up with Ted's help but her grip on Ali didn't loosen; in life Ali would have fought against being crushed like it. And so the procession back to the house started.

The next few hours passed like a dream, or more truthfully, like a nightmare. Eva Johnson kept Harold out of the way. With the exception of Ted, the men returned to the fields. They had orders to fill, vegetables to be prepared and boxed and taken to the station. Usually it was Ted who wrote the labels and checked the packing before the crates were loaded into the lorry, but on that Wednesday the two men worked without supervision. Neither put it into words; in fact, they went about their work in silence, but they felt this was the only way they could show their sympathy for the tragedy that had befallen Ridgeway.

Where do tears come from? Even in her misery Bella wondered whether she would ever find she had used them all, for although her crying had grown quieter it certainly hadn't stopped. She took off all of Ali's sodden clothes and washed her, even her hair, in the bath. Then, lifting her out, alone with her in the bathroom, she moved her face over the wet little body, smothering it with kisses. And all the while she cried, making her face red and blotchy, her eyes almost closed by their swollen and reddened lids. She neither knew nor cared what she looked like – she had only one objective and that was to make sure Ali had every trace of the ditch washed away. Then she re-dressed the little girl, putting on her best sunshine-yellow dress, little yellow socks and patent leather shoes, which brought a further torrent of tears as she remembered the excitement there had been when they had bought them only the previous week. For the last time she brushed Ali's hair and then lowered her to lay her down in her cot.

Hearing a step by the door, for a moment she thought Leo must be home. In her present state it didn't even occur to her that until that moment she hadn't thought about him and now it had gone from her mind completely that he wouldn't be home until the next day. But of course, it wasn't Leo. Ted had telephoned the surgery and been told Dr Saunders was on his round of house visits, but Mrs Saunders suggested she could make an appointment for his evening surgery.

'No, Mrs Saunders m'am, it's not an illness.' And then he'd told her. She'd remembered the baby and her gentle and sweet mother; she had seen them on one or two occasions when the young baby had had her first vaccinations and more recently another against polio.

'Oh, my dear,' she had said, her hushed tone telling him her genuine shock at the news he had had to tell her. 'I know where he's visiting, I'll telephone immediately.'

And so when Bella looked up from where she was bending over the cot, it was the doctor she saw. She shook her head, her face contorting as she tried to speak.

'No good.' Somehow she managed to get the words out. 'Gone. Ali's gone.'

The doctor was no stranger to death and his manner was always kindly, but on that occasion he found himself taking Bella in his arms as though she were his own daughter. He felt helpless. Indeed, anyone, even Leo, would have been helpless against heartbreak such as this. Bella just wanted to die with her.

'She's all alone . . . doesn't know about dying . . . be frightened . . . want me . . .' It was beyond her to make a proper sentence. What words she could manage came out in bursts as she sobbed from the depths of her being.

'She'll never be alone, my dear. You may not see her but you will never lose her. As long as you love her – and you will love her as long as you live – she will know.'

'How can she?' It wasn't like gentle Bella to sound so aggressive. 'She can't know anything if she isn't alive.'

'Listen to me, child.' Dr Saunders' tone was a complete contradiction to hers. A man nearing retirement, he had dealt with life at its most joyful and its most despairing. 'Think of her lying each night in that cot, asleep. Are you saying that while she slept she didn't know she was loved? When she woke and cried out for you, that was because something had disturbed her contented sleep. Sleeping she felt loved; waking she was temporarily alone and needed reassurance. Look at her, my dear,' he turned her towards the cot, 'does she look frightened? No, she is content and peaceful, wrapped in the love that will never fail her.'

'And what about *me*?' After so much crying, Bella's face felt stiff and she could barely form the words.

'I have no such comforting words for you, child. I wish I had. You will feel lost, empty, the purpose gone from your days. I know because I have travelled that road myself when my wife and I lost our son. He was eight. By now he would have been thirty-six. Like you, I didn't know how to face the rest of my life. But from somewhere there comes an inner strength. You never forget. That's how I know it's true when I tell you that your Alicia—'

'Ali,' Bella interrupted, the single word coming out with unexpected force.

'. . . your Ali will never be alone. She will be loved as long as you draw breath.'

Bella looked at the kindly man, seeming to see him afresh. 'You lost your little boy?' she said. 'How did you bear it?'

The doctor held her gaze steadily. He knew truth was the only way.

'There is no easy way. Each day was a battle and so it will be for you and your husband. There is no magic cure. Just go on loving little Ali, don't try and escape the pain by not thinking of her. Remember her laugh, remember every blessed day you've had her. And wrap her in love. What happened today will leave a scar on you for as long as you live, but one day you will find you are able to find comfort in memory. But before you reach that stage, you have a difficult road to tread.'

'Every day she was happy. No more days.' Her voice was flat. Dr Saunders couldn't tell whether he had been able to help her.

'I'm afraid I have to examine her before I can confirm the cause of death.' This was one of the moments when he would rather be doing any work than his own.

Bella's misery had been overtaken by numbness. Standing by, she appeared to be watching as the kindly doctor handled her little girl. Indeed, she saw his every movement and yet she couldn't take in the truth of what was happening. With the certificate written he turned his attention back to her.

'Your husband has been contacted, no doubt.' It was a statement, not a question.

'He went to Reading – working, you see. He telephoned to say he wouldn't be back until tomorrow.'

'But, my dear, can't you contact him? It's not fair to you and not to him either. He should be here.'

'He's staying the night with friends. That's why he phoned. I don't know where they live or what their phone number is.'

He was puzzled. In the circumstances she described he would

have expected her to be distraught that he wasn't with her, but she replied like a child saying what she had been taught was the polite thing.

'Try and think of a way of finding him. Do you know these friends' name?'

She nodded. 'But I don't know where they live. He didn't tell me.'

For one brief moment the doctor imagined the patients waiting for him, but he thrust the thought from his mind. This girl's needs were greater than theirs.

'Would Mr Carter Senior be able to throw any light on it? I know his mind isn't what it was, but sometimes people remember unexpected things from the past even when they can't—'

'No!' Her voice was shrill, and he saw the terror in her eyes. 'No! I can't see him! Don't let him come in here!' She was shaken with hard, dry sobs. 'I should have watched him. They were in the garden. "Shall we play ball, Grandpa?" That's what she said. Then they were gone. I didn't know where he'd taken her. Hate him! He didn't even care. He was just looking for a ball.'

There could be no words of comfort.

'Shall we go downstairs and see if you can lay your hands on an address book? Or perhaps there is the telephone number of these friends listed. Come, my dear, let's try to find your husband.'

As suddenly as her outburst had started, so it quietened, leaving only the occasional hiccough as she took a gasping breath. Without protest she let the doctor guide her out of Ali's room. As they made for the stairs he was relieved to see through the landing window that Ted Johnson was hovering outside the house. A thoroughly good man and one young Mrs Carter would be comfortable with. On the way out he would stop and have a word with him. But first he would help the poor girl find her husband.

The up-to-date house telephone book listed no one called Gibbins, but when Bella went to replace it she saw that there was an older version still kept. And there she found the number.

'I'll leave you to talk with him, my dear. If there is anything,

anything at all you want me for, you have my number. I made sure it was in your book,' he added with a smile.

Perhaps it was the smile that helped her remember how indebted she was to him for the way he had talked to her. Whatever the reason, she managed to force her face into a grimace, which she intended to show her gratitude.

'You have been so kind – the things you told me. I'll try – I won't fail her, my poor ba—' But she couldn't say it. With the corners of her mouth clenched tightly between her teeth she made herself ask, 'How much would she have known? She must have called for me.' Her words were hardly audible; it took every bit of her willpower to ask the question.

'In my opinion she would have known nothing, and certainly she wouldn't have been conscious to call. The bump on her temple tells me that she was unconscious before she fell right into the water. A happy little girl on an adventure.'

'Why couldn't he have watched her? Damned old fool. He promised.'

'He loved her dearly. Each time he comes to me he talks about her with great love and pride. My dear, make your phone call. Share your grief with Leo. Alicia – Ali – was the most precious thing in his life, as she was in yours.' After he'd said it he wondered at his choice of words, but she seemed not to have noticed. So he let himself out and, while she was asking to be put through to the Gibbins' number, he stopped for a word with Ted.

'Hello. This is Jane Gibbins.'

'Mrs Gibbins, may I speak to Leo? It's urgent, terribly urgent.'

'Leo? Leo who?'

'Leo Carter, from Lexleigh. He's staying with you for the night.'

'Is that his mother? I didn't recognize your voice, Mrs Carter. But I expect we all sound different after all these years. How are you?'

'She's been dead for ages. I'm his wife. I thought it was you he said he was with in Reading this morning and you were taking him home for the night. It must have been another name.'

'Fancy Leo married. We haven't heard anything from him

for quite fifteen years. And neither have we been to Reading market except to buy bits for the machines. We gave up livestock years ago.'

But Bella wasn't listening. Gently, she replaced the receiver. Leo wasn't there . . . he'd lied to her . . . he probably hadn't even been to Reading. She stepped back from where the telephone was attached to the hall wall and sat on the bottom stairs. She knew he spent many hours with Louisa, and she had never felt a bit jealous. She knew they were both far cleverer than she was – both of them interested in things that went on in the world. She couldn't compete with all that; she didn't even want to. She'd found all she wanted in Ali . . . and warm tears escaped to roll down her cheeks. Then she pulled her mind back to Leo. Louisa was with her parents – wasn't she? – but if she knew about Ali she would come straight home. Bella was ashamed that she could be so weak, but she couldn't face the night alone here. If Louisa didn't say she would come back this evening, then Bella would lock herself in Ali's room. Dad would be home. She didn't want to see him.

Hardly conscious of what she was doing, she got up from her seat on the stairs and went again to the telephone. Directory Enquiries would tell her the Hardings' number if she gave them the name of the town and the road where they lived.

And so a few minutes later she was answered by a none-too-friendly male voice. When he heard that it was Louisa she wanted, he told her, 'She was on the road by just after nine this morning. She must have reached home by lunchtime. Try her there. Now, if you'll excuse me, I had just turned on the wireless for the early evening news.'

She found herself again sitting on the stairs with no recollection of how she got there. Louisa must have known she was only staying in Newquay for one night . . . Leo had lied about the Gibbins . . . Louisa and Leo . . .

Yet she felt they were removed from her, just two people she had been fond of – *was still fond of* – but were removed from the thing that had taken the foundations away from her world.

'Bella, is it all right if I come in? Did you get Leo on the buzzer?'

She shook her head. 'No. I can't contact him.'

'Look m'dear, there are things that have to be done. Not things for you to see to. If you give me the certificate the doctor has left with you, once the Registry Office opens in the morning I can get things sorted for you. If Leo is away all night we shan't see him before midday tomorrow and there are arrangements to be made. Let me be the one to do all that for you, won't you?'

'Doesn't seem real, Ted. Does it to you?'

'I'd give my right arm for it not to be true, and that's the honest truth. But it's no good our wishing and pretending. The little lassie needs us to look after things. We'll do her proud, just see if we don't. If she could see the pair of us — and I tell you, I've had a few tears too — but if she could see us, I reckon she would be a bit scared. This isn't the mum she calls when she wants something, no, and no more is it the old Ted she always had a smile for. We've got to keep going, child, make her proud of us, eh?'

So how was it that when, at his words, her body was shaken with sobs and he sat by her side and held her in his arms, his cheeks were also wet? She believed her tears were all for Ali, for the loss of all the years of childhood, of adolescence, of growing into a woman, for the unfairness that it should have been snatched from a little person who had brought nothing but joy to the world. But they were for more than that, because in the moments after she spoke to Louisa's father she had faced what in her heart she had been aware of for a long time. Leo had never really loved her; he had married her because of the baby. Those visits to The Retreat were what gave his life purpose.

Limp and weak from her bout of crying, Bella forced herself to face what had to be done. She was thankful for Ted's offer to register the death in the morning and call at the undertaker's on his way out of town.

'Then there's the guv'nor,' he said, conscious that she seemed to draw back at his words. 'Me and Eva had a word with him. Told him you weren't feeling too good and with Leo away it would be best he kipped at our place.'

'He killed Ali.' The words came out hardly more than a

whisper; certainly she didn't speak them as if to someone other than herself.

'He's not himself, Bella. His body may be strong, but he doesn't know what he's up to. You know that better than anyone, the hours you watch over him. He loved Ali. He wouldn't have hurt a hair on her head. But you can't be expected to have to take care of him here until after Leo gets back from these friends of his. Are you going to ring the number again later on? They may have been out looking round the farm. Even later still – say they go out to dinner and you don't get hold of him till they get home – he'll get straight in the car, you can be sure. I wouldn't want his drive after what you'll have told him. Poor lad.' Nearly forty years old but still a lad as far as Ted was concerned.

'Ted, I got through to the Gibbins. They haven't seen him for years.' She made herself look directly at him, willing him to meet her gaze. 'So I phoned Louisa's parents so that I could talk to her. She only went for one night.'

There was no escaping what they were both thinking. His only comment was a grunt, while he thought that the local gossip Eva had picked up seemed to have been nearer the truth than they'd wanted to believe. And what about this poor girl? Pure gold she was and let down not just by her husband but by her friend too. It wasn't right.

'I can look after the guv'nor if you'd like Eva to come over for the night. She could bring a sleeping bag and put it on top of a spare, no need to make a bed up. She'd come like a shot, you know she would.'

'I know, Ted. And I'm grateful for the offer. But, no, I've got to face it by myself. You know what you said about us having to do Ali proud. So for *her*, I'm going to show that her mum isn't a wimp.'

Later, when she could see from the window that the lights in the workers' cottages had been put out for the night, she got ready for bed. But the thought of climbing into her side of the double bed and sleeping was impossible. She pulled on her thick dressing gown and crept back into Ali's room, half expecting to see the little girl had moved, changed the way she was lying, even though reason told her that could never happen. And so started the longest night of Bella's life. She lowered the side of the cot, letting her hand take Ali's in its grasp. How cold she was to touch. Of course she was cold, all she was wearing was her best sunshine dress and socks . . . and her new shoes . . . not the first time they'd been in the cot with her, for the first night she'd had them she'd been so proud of them that she had kept them on her pillow.

Reaching to lift her from her cot, Bella was shocked at the change in the feeling of the little body. Whenever she'd picked her up Ali would wrap her arms and legs around her, would nuzzle against her neck; but now the inert body lay stiffly in her arms. It was Bella who nuzzled, hardly aware that she was crying, her wet face against Ali's. She had never felt more at one with her, shut off from everyone, her tears damp on the baby-soft face. This was grief that belonged just to the two of them, something that would stay with Bella as long as she lived.

The put-u-up where she had slept for the first months of Ali's life was barely used through that long night.

So much happened the next morning. True to his word, Ted registered the death and then called at the premises of the undertaker, glad that he remembered the firm Harold had used for Alice. So by the time Leo's car parked at the front of the house, Ali's little body had already been taken away.

Bella was upstairs in the nursery bedroom when she heard him come, but she made no effort to go down. Sitting in the low nursing chair near the empty cot she was removed from anything that went on, held apart from it by a wall of misery. She knew he was searching, arriving home ready to play his role and tell his endless lies. Although the image seemed distant, as far away as though it were a dream, she pictured his disappointment that no one was there to greet him. There was nothing attractive in her smile.

'Hello? Where are you all? I'm home,' he shouted from the hall.

She was glad to think of his disappointment, or as glad as it was possible for her to be when she was numb with misery. Then his footsteps on the stairs. Her mouth felt dry. In seconds she would have to tell him; she would have to form the words that her heart refused to accept.

'Didn't you hear me call? Whatever's the matter, you look awful. Are you ill?'

Bella shook her head.

'Where's Dad? And Ali? I didn't see them when I parked. Bella, for Christ's sake, what's the matter with you?'

'Ali,' she managed to get the word out even though her tongue was almost too dry to form the right sound, 'dead.'

'What are you saying?' He must have misheard her. 'It sounded like—'

'Dead!' This time she shouted. She needed to yell, to hit out as if by hurting someone else she would ease her own pain. 'He killed her, Dad killed her.' Her voice rose hysterically as loud sobs shook her body.

'What are you saying? Where is Dad? For Christ's sake, tell me what's happened.'

Bella tried to find the words, but when she spoke it came out a jumbled mess. 'Ask *him*. Promised to look after her, just playing ball . . . then they were gone . . . he took her . . . I want to die . . . please, God, let me die . . .' Bella, gentle, kind, pure gold, but in those moments she was screaming, bellowing as she cried. When he shook her it made no difference. His hand hit her sharply, leaving finger marks on her cheek. It made her gasp and that gasp broke her hysteria, leaving her trembling and weak, her strength gone as she flopped back into the nursing chair.

'Now, quietly tell me exactly what happened. And where is she? Was she taken to hospital?'

Sitting hunched with her knees apart and her arms hanging limply between them, Bella told him what had happened the previous day, ending with the visit from the undertaker this morning when Ali was taken away. Leo listened in silence. If she'd glanced up at him the sight of his face might have cut across her own isolation and she might have remembered that it wasn't for her alone that Ali had been precious beyond words. But she didn't look at him.

'How long have you been up here? Where's Dad? He's not downstairs.'

'He's staying with the Johnsons.'

'But why? This is his home. He must be devastated.'

She shrugged her shoulders.

'This happened yesterday,' he muttered. To her? To himself? She neither knew nor cared about him or anyone else. She wanted him to go away and leave her sitting silently on her own. When she'd listened very hard she'd thought she had heard Ali's laugh. Laughing, not crying. Please, God, make her happy, don't let her feel lost and frightened. Or is there nothing? If you die, is there nothing? There must be something. People you've loved must be there for you. But she was just a baby, she only knew *us*, she'd hardly started life. Why couldn't Leo stop talking? Something about his father . . . going to get him back from Eva. I can't take care of him. I won't!

'Yesterday . . . all those hours and I didn't know.'

'You would have known,' she replied, surprising herself that she could answer in a voice of such cool clarity, 'if you'd gone to the Gibbins people. I telephoned them.'

Did she imagine it or was there a brief pause before he told her, 'I imagine they hadn't got home. My visit fell through. Someone backed into their car. I left them at a repair garage. Then, having said I wasn't going to be here last night, I thought I'd take the opportunity of looking up a fellow I was in the army with. He's a lecturer at Reading University.'

'Don't bother lying,' she said, her voice expressionless. 'I really don't care where you were – or where Louisa was either.' And she meant it.

'You know very well where Louisa was.'

'Not precisely, but I know she wasn't with her parents. Can't you understand? I don't care. I'm only here because of Ali. You had to make the best of marrying me because of Ali.'

He suspected hysteria was still very near the surface. Damn her, why did she have to make a scene now of all times – now, when all he could think about was Alicia, Ali, the most precious thing ever to have come into his life, and not Bella's own distress. Damn her, taking over Ali's room, filled with the toys she'd played with, the books he had often read to her, just as if he hadn't lost the dearest, most perfect thing in his world. Grown men don't cry, he told himself, as misery seemed to flood over him. He turned away and left the room. She heard him going across the corridor and into the bedroom they shared; she heard the firm click of the latch as he closed the door behind him and then the key turning in the lock.

It was about a quarter of an hour later when she heard him go down the stairs and out of the front door, supposing he was on his way to bring his father home. But she soon realized she was wrong. He was walking down the track. Let him go to Louisa, she thought, shocked with herself that she could be so uninterested. They would soon have been married for three years – three years in which they had never quarrelled until that day. Was she in love with him? She loved him – he was the father of her child – but she wasn't *in* love with him, she knew that now. It had all seemed so perfect, more than she could have hoped for – a husband, a child – but while her love for Ali had been real and overwhelming, had she ever been more than infatuated with Leo? She didn't understand how his mind worked, but perhaps that was the same with most marriages. The way he wanted to make love – not the way she liked it, but doing things she didn't think had anything to do with loving someone . . . was his way really the way it should be? Should she want those things too? Was the fact she didn't a sign that she didn't feel for him the way she should? She knew what he was suffering. She knew he had really loved Ali and always would. He hadn't tried any of those things for ages; perhaps it had been just a phase he'd been going through? Or perhaps Lou liked what he did. It's all wrong, she told herself, I can't be normal that I can think things like that and honestly, *honestly*, not care that he has a lover, or that his lover is my friend. If anything it's a relief, really, that he has one, because even when I've thought how special and cosy it has been when he has made love to me in our nice warm bed when we're ready to snuggle up for sleep, I have always been worried that he will be leading towards something I think in his heart he would really like to do. Real love should be gentle and tender – well, that's what I think anyway. None of it matters now. Ali was the most important thing in our marriage. Ali, poor darling little Ali, she'll never have a chance to know about living. Just a baby still. And Leo was forgotten as Bella moved to the small chest of drawers and took out a pile of neatly folded clothes. Burying her face against them, she seemed to smell the sweet baby smell. Wherever she is, please, please, don't let her be lost and sad. If only I could hear her voice, or her laugh, just once.

That night, the second since she had lost Ali, she slept – or more accurately for most of the time she lay awake – on the put-u-up. Leo didn't come to say goodnight to her, but she heard him come up the stairs and go to their room, closing the door firmly behind him.

When morning came, Bella woke from a fitful sleep and thought with foreboding about the day ahead. The first day of the rest of her life, she told herself, and she had no choice but to face it. She got up and tidied her makeshift bed, bathed, dressed and met herself face-to-face in the mirror for the first time in forty-eight hours. The sight shocked her, but it restored some of her mettle. Breakfast could wait; it was more important to disguise the effect her misery had had on her face. We have to do Ali proud, she seemed to hear Ted telling her, and she certainly wasn't going to be the one to let her down.

As she went downstairs she could smell coffee. Leo was never the first down in the morning, but perhaps he, too, was doing it for Ali.

'The coffee smells good,' she greeted him by way of a 'good morning'.

'It's just ready. Black or white?'

'Milk, please. Leo,' and then she didn't know what it was she wanted to say to him. 'We have to talk, about everything. Ali, Dad, me and what we're going to do.'

'Of course we have to talk. I've been left out of everything. She's *my* daughter too; you seem to forget. How could you have neglected to watch what he was up to? You know how it is with him. He can't help it. How could you have left him long enough for him to get right to the edge of the wood?'

She clenched her fists and held her chin rigid; anything to keep back the tears that seemed permanently ready.

'I supposed he'd taken her to the fields. He did that most days. When their food was ready that's where I went to find them.'

They looked directly at each other, and in that moment they were close, drawn together by the pain of loss.

He reached out and took her hand. 'Let's not quarrel,' he said. 'Life is hell enough without our adding to it.'

She nodded. 'Did you tell Lou?'

'Of course. She has a right to know. She's Ali's godmother and almost family.'

It was those last words that brought the situation home to Bella. Did 'almost family' mean that he wanted his freedom to marry her? Well, of course, he must do. Apart from being in love with Louisa, he must want to be free of a marriage that had only happened because of the baby coming.

'Are you going to give me grounds to divorce you then?'

'What the hell are you talking about? For Christ's sake, Bella, haven't we got misery enough without you wanting to upset everything?'

'That's not fair. You can't be happy with our marriage – not without Ali—' How hard it was to say that, but she made herself go on, 'Or you wouldn't spend half your life at The Retreat.'

He weighed up her words and before he answered he poured a second cup of coffee and lit a cigarette, pushing the packet and his lighter across the table to her.

'There must be something about these Harding women that touches a chord with us Carters.' And then he told her about Violet and his father, even about the night Harold had let himself into the house with the key he still kept.

'How horrible for her. Poor Lou. How did she get rid of him? She didn't tell me.'

'We were living in the flat. David brought him back here, you remember. The next day I came meaning to fetch him back, but instead I saw the light and realized the solution was for us to come and look after him here. Poor Dad. His whole world fell to pieces.'

She nodded. 'And now, so has ours. He's old – well, by our standards – but we have so many years to live. I can't even imagine them. Everything was so perfect.'

'Was it?' And surprisingly she found there was tenderness in his tone.

'Yes. You know me – I've never been ambitious for a career or anything. But I loved every day. I thought you were happy. Well, I'm sure you were; how could you not have been when Ali used to watch for you to come into the room, or run to you outside.'

'Don't.' It was her turn to reach to take *his* hand, knowing that just as she had had to fight to hold back her tears, so he had his own battle. 'Bella, we were talking about Louisa. At first, when she and I were drawn to each other – physically, not just as friends – she refused to sleep with me. "Bella is my friend", she said. But I knew, positively *knew* that what was between Louisa and me would have no bearing on our marriage. You wouldn't be touched by it; it couldn't hurt you. I knew you didn't want the things I'd have with Louisa. At last, I persuaded her and, yes, we are lovers just as her aunt and Dad were. What was between *them* never touched the home here, but that didn't belittle what they felt for each other. And you say yourself, you have been completely happy and content. So, dear Bella, don't talk of divorce. This is your home. Dad and I are your family.'

'I can't spend my days looking after him, watching his every movement. He's *your* father, not mine.' She was shocked by her own words, and yet she had no power to hold them back.

'I'll talk to David and Lily. I'll ask them if, after Ali's service' – he couldn't bring himself to say the word 'funeral' – 'they could take him back with them for a few days. I don't think he ought to be here until he gets used to what has happened. The service will drive it home to him. He loved her; she was a huge part of his life now that he is losing his grasp. A week or so with them will put other things into his mind. I don't want him ever to realize that she was with him when it happened. Poor old Dad – I never knew anyone could be so changed in such a short time.'

While he'd been speaking Bella had opened her mouth to interrupt but couldn't find the words. In the silence that followed what Leo had been saying she physically felt the anger and misery rising up in her. Poor old Dad, he had said. Bring him here, let the waters close over what has happened and go on jollying him along to make his life as free of care as they could.

'No!' Her voice was harsh and unnatural. 'If you bring him here – and I can't stop you – but I tell you I cannot and will not spend my time taking care of him. Don't you understand? It's *his* fault we lost Ali, his, *his*, **his**.'

'Bella, oh, Bella, this isn't like you. We both know Ali adored him. Grandpa can we this, Grandpa shall we that. If she were here and able to tell us, do you honestly think she would want him banished from everything that's familiar to him? She didn't see him as losing his memory, unable to think straight. Look at me, Bella, and tell me: isn't what I say the truth?'

He willed her to hold his gaze and after a second or two she nodded, frightened to trust her voice to speak. Only as her tears overspilled and rolled down her cheeks did she manage to say, 'I shouldn't have let them out of my sight.'

He didn't contradict her. As the silence grew between them she found herself looking back into the past and forward into the future he was proposing, living here where she had been happier than ever in her life. But nothing could be like that any more. There would be no Ali, and Leo was in love with Louisa. It didn't even surprise her that Fate had played her hand that way. Her first clear memories were of when she was an evacuee in a house where, although she was given her fair share of rations, kept clean, sent to Sunday school come rain or shine, she had never known any affection. With her parents killed during the war, when other evacuees had returned home she had been sent to the orphanage until she had been old enough to be found a junior job in an office and a place to live in a youth hostel. Trapped by low wages and no training, she had been unable to move anywhere else, but rather than kick against her lot she had accepted it as the way life was. And then she had met Leo and naively fallen in love as only an innocent teenager could.

She wiped away her stray tears with the back of her hand, glad that Leo gave no sign of having noticed. Part of her wanted to shout, to scream at Leo that surely she deserved better than him? Why should she be denied finding the love he had with Louisa? Sitting smoking her cigarette and letting her thoughts carry her where they would, even now, after almost three years of marriage, she still saw herself as someone who had to be grateful for any kindness shown, and she hated herself for it.

'I'll talk to David,' he repeated. 'As far as he is concerned, you and I have a perfectly full and happy marriage.'

'That was when we had Ali. It can never be like that again. We don't share anything.'

He looked genuinely surprised. 'That's not true. You are interested in the farm here – you get on well with the men and with Eva Johnson. This house is your home,' and he gave her the smile that never failed to turn things the way he wanted, 'and very well you look after it, too.'

'So would Louisa. She's much more efficient than I am.'

'I am truly sorry, Bella, but I am as I am. I wonder if my parents ever had a conversation like this. This was a happy home; I never heard them quarrel. Yet I know – and I understand completely – that what was between Dad and Violet Harding wasn't negotiable.'

Bella didn't answer. Feeling wretched, and drawing hard on her cigarette, she fought to keep her control. Her help came when there was an unexpected knock on the back door and she automatically got up from the table to answer it.

'Bella, oh Bella, Leo told me.' And Louisa's strong arms were holding her tight. At the sound of her voice Leo had come to the door too.

'Lou . . .' he began.

'Go away. I've come to see Bella.'

'She knows, she phoned your parents—'

'Go away,' Louisa repeated, not even looking at him. 'Come home with me, Bella, let's have the morning together. Leo can take his father out somewhere for lunch.'

Bella surprised herself by nodding in agreement. She felt crushed and utterly despairing, but to her the suggestion spelt escape.

'Get your coat, it's a miserable morning,' Louisa told her. And like an obedient child, she fetched her coat from the row of pegs in the lobby. Then, as if Leo didn't exist, Louisa helped her into it and they walked away. Watching from the window, he was at a loss to understand. Knowing that Louisa was his mistress, how could Bella go with her so trustingly, holding her hand as if it were a lifeline?

They walked in silence, for what was there to say? Bella didn't need to be told of Louisa's sadness about Ali; it was there in the grip of her hand. But Louisa's emotion was more complicated. It was as if Ali's death had exposed what had lain hidden in her subconscious. More than half the night she had been awake, making herself recognize what she had done to Bella's marriage. The day of their first meeting had haunted her, when all the girl could talk about was the wonders of her so-perfect husband. Then – for in the silence of night there had been no hiding place – she had recalled her own unfulfilled hunger for sexual satisfaction, not just as she had known it in the isolation of her lonely bed, but something greater, something complete that she had been sure was always just beyond her reach. She had recalled the first time Leo had made love to her – the first time and every time, it had been an out-of-this-world experience, more perfect, more wonderful, more complete than she had ever imagined possible. 'It won't hurt Bella . . . it will make no difference to my marriage . . .' and she believed that would have been the truth, if only Ali hadn't been taken. Now that Bella had found out, she knew she had been wicked in stealing from her friend – her dear friend – the happiness that had never existed for her. She had come to know and understand Bella so well and she had no doubt that living at Ridgeway, looking after the house, adoring Alicia and having such joy in watching her progress, loving Leo in the loyal, gentle way that was part of her nature – all those things added up to complete happiness for her.

Those had been her thoughts last night. Leo had said that Bella knew about them. What she didn't know and probably didn't even consider was the shame and self-loathing Louisa felt that she could have found her own happiness and gratification with no thought for anyone else.

Reaching The Retreat, as they closed the front door behind them, Bella looked around, almost as if she were seeing the familiar hallway for the first time.

'I'm glad I'm here. He wants to bring Dad home. A few days with David and then back to the farm, that's what he wants.'

Louisa studied her friend. 'Take one thing at a time, Bella. Why? Why? Why? Nothing will be the same without her. She was born in this house. Remember?'

'If he had to have a lover, I suppose it's silly of me, but I'm glad it's you.'

'Bella, oh Bella, I feel so ashamed. You are my friend, such a dear friend. What have I done?'

'I offered to give him his freedom, but he says that you and him being together doesn't make any difference to our marriage. I don't know. I don't really care. Just care about Ali.' And dropping to sit on the bottom stair, again the tears came.

As Louisa sat at her side and held her close, it struck her what an odd situation it was. And then, forcing itself into her mind and taking her by surprise, she knew something else, knew it clearly and positively.

Nine

Alicia's death was the talk of the village. In a small community where very little happens and most deaths, although reported with regret, occur when the deceased has reached years of maturity, there wasn't a person hearing the news who wasn't saddened. On the day of her funeral the church was packed; the more sensitive even shed a few tears as the tiny white coffin was carried out to the churchyard at the end of the service. Side by side Bella and Leo followed it, looking neither to the right nor the left. They must have been aware of the number of people there, but only later, perhaps much later, would they consciously think of it and be glad. Ali had had a smile for everyone right from when the local shoppers had leant over her pram and 'coo-cooed' before she'd been old enough to sit up, and by the time she had reached her second birthday she would hold court from her push chair while her admiring 'friends' gathered round. That the affection they showed her was partly aimed at her sweet, pretty mother was lost on Bella. One day in the future, when the pain of memory wasn't too raw, Bella would remember the sea of familiar faces and be glad that so many people had come because they had loved Ali.

Behind Bella and Leo walked David and Lily with Harold between them. Apparently he remembered nothing of how she had come to lose her life, and certainly had no idea that he had played any part in it, but it appeared to have registered on him – at any rate, for the time being – that they had lost her. As they walked down the aisle towards the open door and autumn sunshine he looked utterly miserable. He shed no tears, but there was about him an air of dejection; his shoulders sagged, he shuffled his feet. He had become a really old man ahead of his years.

'Are you going with the family?' Hamish McLaren had asked Louisa when he had called the previous day on the pretext of checking the hanging baskets.

'No. They suggested I should. I was her godmother, you see. No, I shall go on my own.' For herself she wasn't a bit interested in what the locals chose to gossip about, but on this occasion she had no wish to give grist to their mill of scandal.

'Then, how would it be if I came with you? I don't want to push in, but I'd seen her so often at your place that she and I had struck up quite a friendship. It is so . . . so *wrong* that a child so young and with not a stain on her character should lose her life. Och, I said this to Mags. She is a wise soul. Sometimes she surprises me with her wisdom.'

'She must have agreed with you?'

'She agreed about being sad, but she said didn't it say somewhere "Suffer little children to come unto me"?' Then, looking uncomfortable and unsure of Louisa's reaction, 'Och, something like that, anyway.'

'Certainly she was unstained with living, which is more than can be said of most of us. But life is a gift, Hamish, and it seems so unfair that hers was snatched away when she was not much more than a baby.'

He nodded. 'It must be a hell of a pill for Bella and her husband to swallow. Many a marriage would go under.' Louisa sensed that he said it purposely and was waiting for her reaction.

'And surely many a marriage is strengthened by tragedy – shared tragedy. I hope theirs comes under that category.'

Clearly the hanging baskets were no more than an excuse to lead the conversation to what had been on his mind.

'You really mean that?' he asked, looking at her so directly that she knew without having it spelt out to her that he had heard the whispers – whispers and more – that she was sure had been circulating through the last months. He was the first to lower his gaze as he added hurriedly, 'I have no business to ask you any such thing.'

She reached and took his hand in hers as she replied. 'Most sincerely, I mean it, Hamish. And you have every right to ask, and to get a truthful reply.'

'You mean you're thinking about what I asked you? I think about it; I think about it every day. But above all things what

I want for you is your happiness. And you know what folk are saying about you and the younger Mr Carter.'

'I can imagine. Not that they would have the guts to say it in my hearing. I remember the first day I met Leo. We got on; it was as if we'd known each other for ages. Our view on life is pretty much the same, and on lots of other things too, but not everything. We would sit and discuss things, politics, morals, religion, you name it – and we've had deep and lengthy conversations about it. But it's Bella who is my dear friend.'

'I would never have thought you had much in common with her. She seems so young and kind of unworldly.'

'When I first met her that was my opinion too, but I soon found I was wrong. Oh, you're right, ask her the name of the prime minister and I wouldn't put money on her knowing. But come nearer home and see her love for Leo and Ali – even for me, I truly believe – and she would defend them with her life. And now Ali has gone. Why? *Why?* If there is a god in charge of life and death, why did he let it happen, why did he take away the most precious gift in Bella's life when she is pure gold through and through? Can you tell me that?'

'No. It seems all wrong. But Mags always says not to look at things when they are too close. Let a bit of time go by and the pattern evolve, then you can see the reason.' Then, with a grin: 'I can't say I've ever tried it. My life is pretty cushy. The only big thing I've ever done is borrow money from the bank to start the business, and thankfully that's turning out OK. There's just one thing more I want, and I hope one of these days when you stand back far enough to be able to see the pattern, I may get it. Louisa, give me an honest answer: is there someone else? I supposed it must be Leo Carter, but you tell me that you and he are friends and on the same wavelength and that Bella is your dear friend. So I cross him off the list. Is there someone else or if I'm patient do I stand a chance?'

Louisa looked at his eager eyes and knew she couldn't tell him all he ought to hear. 'There was someone, but that's over now. As for being patient, the truth is I can't think straight about the future. I should tell you that somewhere out there is a young woman just right for you. You are very dear to me and I can't imagine you not being part of my life. But marriage is a life-changing commitment. Coming here to Lexleigh, for the first time in my life I felt free, independent.' Was she being completely honest? She would dearly love to know that her life was permanently knitted closely with another and she was truly fond of Hamish; but marriage? Was it wicked of her to think of the glory of the hours she had spent with Leo, how they had been the focal points of her days? Imagine being Mrs McLaren, gentle, kindly Hamish making love to her. Could any man but Leo ever release the wild passion in her that grasped greedily at every sensuous touch whether tender or crazed with lust? Yet now, a day before little Ali would be lowered into the ground while Bella and Leo saw the end of the miracle that had come into their lives, Louisa wasn't ready to think of what was in the future for Leo and her. Nothing could ever be as it had before, for Bella knew about them, Bella whose life could never again be happy and content. Suppose she had another baby – would that give her back the same joy? No. How could it? The memory was still vivid in Louisa's mind of that young bride who had been so sure she had the best husband in the world. Louisa had no illusions; she was certain that if Leo hadn't found her when he had, there would have been someone else. But he had found her, a thirty-year-old hungry for sex, probably something a man with his experience was able to recognize before he decided to give her experiences beyond her dreams. Ali's death had altered all their lives, and Louisa knew nothing could be as it had been before.

So was she making a mistake in refusing Hamish? She was thirty-three, about two years older than he. Plenty of women don't start a family until they were her age. And wouldn't moving to the house at the garden centre, starting a completely new way of life, getting involved in the business, knowing she was loved by dear, loyal Hamish – wouldn't all those things lay the ghost of the exciting and joyous love she had shared with Leo?

'Tomorrow,' Hamish went back to his original suggestion, 'may I come with you? We could leave the car here out of the way and walk to the church. There's not much parking there.'

'Yes, I'd like that. I'm not going back to Ridgeway afterwards, so you could have lunch here if you like.'

Nothing could have pleased him more. He felt he was being
wise not to press her for a reply; he would play the waiting
game, be there for her when she needed support, have fun
with her in the weekend hours they spent together and always
hope that his patience would give him what he wanted. He
was sure they could be happy together, and in his mind he
imagined her content to look after the 'shop' if, after next
year's wedding, Mags stopped work to have a family. He imagined, too, the family he and Louisa would have. But then
common sense came to the fore, that and fear of being hurt
if all he planned never came to fruition.

At Ridgeway, emotion had been high throughout the week of
Ali's death and her funeral. Leo brought Harold back to the
house from the Johnsons' cottage, but he was uncomfortable in
an atmosphere he couldn't understand. He had been told that
Ali had died but he had no idea of his part in it, and Leo insisted
that was how it must remain. A day didn't pass when he didn't
suggest he should 'take my little friend outside for a game' or
ask 'where's Ali? It's a nice morning; I thought she and I would
go and watch the men at work', things that had been part of
his life all through the summer months. There were times when
Bella remembered Ali's delight at his suggestion and made herself
answer patiently, reminding him that Ali had gone.

It was an afternoon towards the end of the month. She felt
she had to escape, and went up to Leo's workroom to tell him
that he would have to keep an eye on his father as she was
going out. She opened the door, taking him by surprise, and
found that he was standing at the window, staring unseeingly
across the field.

'Leo, I'm going out.'

'Dad too?'

'No. Three times in the last hour he has asked about Ali,
wanting to take her for a walk. Where is she? Is she having a
nap? He said he had a bowl ready and he would take her to
pick loganberries. I told him, each time I told him, and he
was upset, quite tearful because he hadn't remembered. Then

back he'd come, honestly in only a few minutes, and we'd go through the same rigmarole. Leo, it's not fair having him here. He ought to be where he is looked after properly. People are trained for it. I can't do it anymore.' He heard an ominous break in her voice and knew her appearance of anger was simply to hide her misery.

'He'd be lost if I sent him to where you say "he would be looked after". A home, you mean – somewhere for people who are mentally deranged. I can't do it, Bella. He's my father. All my life he has been a hero to me.'

'Then you'd better go down and look after him. I'm going out. He's downstairs somewhere.'

He was watching her closely. He'd taken her so much for granted over the years they'd been together that only now was he seeing her afresh. In appearance she was as lovely, but there was something harder in her manner.

'You've changed, Bella.' Gone was the way she used to look at him with love and pride in her eyes for the world to see. It used to irritate him that she could still behave like a love-struck schoolgirl. Now he would have given a good deal to see that expression again, even though he knew he didn't deserve it.

'We've all changed – Dad, me, and I expect even you. Don't forget, you're in charge.' And she was gone.

Habit dies hard, and instead of going through the front door and more quickly to the track she went through the kitchen to the back, intending to have a quick look for Harold as she went. What surprised her was that she found him in the kitchen, rummaging in the knife drawer.

'What are you looking for, Dad?' For no matter how much she complained to Leo that she wasn't prepared to spend her days taking care of his father, there was something in her nature that, even after all that had happened, wouldn't let her be anything but gentle with him.

'Just a knife. My pencil could do with a sharpen.'

'Look in the drawer of the bureau in the other room and you'll find a pencil sharpener; that'll make a much better job than a knife. I shan't be long, I'm just going out.' Then she made her escape before he could suggest coming with her.

Afterwards she felt guilty that she hadn't waited with him until Leo came downstairs with a suggestion that they should walk over to the fields together and watch the man at work. But the need to escape outweighed any guilt and she hurried down the track to the lane, keen to put space between herself and Ridgeway. Her instinct was to go to Louisa just as she had ever since she had come to live at the farm. Yet she told herself that now that she knew about the affair between Louisa and Leo she ought to shun her friend. Vividly she remembered their words the week before they had both 'happened' to be away, and now she could see clearly that the whole conversation had been simply to disguise what they were planning. She tried to whip up dislike for Louisa, but she couldn't. She thought of how she had helped her on the day Ali had been born, the easy, casual ten-minute chats they had shared when she'd gone to the village, the safe, secure feeling she had had in their friendship. Surely it had been the same for both of them? Louisa had given her confidence, made her believe she was capable of running her home efficiently and caring for Dad, Harold and Ali. But now there was no Ali, no darling Ali whose face always used to light up in a smile at the sight of her; Dad meant no harm but, whereas before her world fell to pieces she had willingly cared for him, now his presence was no more than a reminder of how things used to be. And what about Leo? Was he hankering after whatever it was that he and Louisa found in each other? She didn't know if he was still making his visits to her house, and didn't want to.

She thought of the previous night when they had both retired at the same time. When that happened she was always sure he wouldn't settle for sleep. Thinking back to the time when first she had been thankful that he seemed satisfied to make love without leading up to it by doing things that she had found so unsettling, she supposed that Louisa welcomed what she, personally, considered unnatural. Surely that ought to make her hate the girl she had looked on as her friend. But it didn't. She felt untouched by it, as if the Louisa who was such an important part of her life was a different person from the one Leo was interested in.

Reaching the double gate on to the track from Louisa's

garage, she saw the car was out and the door left open so that she could drive straight in on her return. That made the decision for her: there would be no visit to The Retreat. So, reaching the lane, she turned to the right, taking her away from the village and its few shops. She didn't care where she walked; all she needed was to get away from Leo and Harold and a house so full of memories. She wanted to stride out alone and let her thoughts go where they would. Although she was laden with grief, there was no self-pity in Bella, yet neither was there a conscious effort to fight the grief off. Her life, up until the time Leo married her, had prepared her for the hard knocks she would find through the years. When she'd been little more than a toddler she had been evacuated with a carrier bag, carrying her possessions with a label around her neck. Through the years of the war she had lived with the Skidows, two brothers and three sisters, none of them married and from her viewpoint all very elderly. In fact, they had been in their fifties when she'd been delivered into their care, but from her viewpoint that had been ancient. None of them had ever been unkind to her; she'd been given the spare bedroom, her rations had been used fairly and the few shillings they had been paid each week for her board had been saved in a post office account in her name. But they had had very little contact with her, expecting her to eat her food in the kitchen with Madge, the middle-aged maid of all works. It had been no home for a child of any age, but for one as young as Bella it had left her believing herself to be of less worth than the other children in her class when she started school. When a bomb had hit the flats that had been home to her, her father had been on leave and she had lost both parents. Miss Blanche, as she was taught to address the eldest of the Skidow sisters, had called her to the drawing room and told her that her parents had been killed, but had assured her that she had nothing to worry about as she would stay where she was until the end of the war and only then go on to an orphanage. And that was exactly what had happened. After nearly six years in the Skidows' house, when armistice came she had moved to an orphanage and her post office savings book had been given to the secretary for safe keeping until the time came for Bella to leave. Had she been older when the war began, older and living in a comfortable and loving home, she might well have been bitter and felt unjustly treated; but there were no bright memories for Bella and she had always accepted, with neither jealousy nor bitterness, that that was the way her life was destined to be. And then Leo had seen her and thought her the loveliest creature he'd ever encountered.

She had been gloriously happy as she found herself part of a family and the mother of Ali, yet when all that changed it was as if she had always known that one day her old way of life would be back. And had that day come?

Walking the country lanes, she had no conception of time. Her only hold on reality was her right heel, which was rubbing. She had been aware of it before she turned off the track but wouldn't risk going back to change her shoes. After an hour or so she could see blood where the blistered skin on her heel had broken. But she couldn't go home, she had to think, she had to try and find a way into the future. Leaning to rest against a five-barred gate, she looked across the wide field, empty except for the herd of cows grouped together in the far corner. Just like people, she thought. All this beautiful countryside and people crowd into towns, queue up to go to the pictures and then sit in great smoke-filled cinemas. Her mind was leaping ahead, anything rather than let it go back such a short time ago to when her world had been everything she had wanted, but it hadn't been real, just a dream of happiness. What can I do? Where can I go? Who would employ me? In that beastly office all I did was run errands, make the tea, take the post or, if I was really lucky, get given a pile of post to be filed away. I could always try to get a domestic job; I've had lots of practise looking after a house. But that was dangerous ground and, knowing she was being cowardly, she shied away from it.

She had almost come to a crossroads, or more accurately across-lanes, and was brought out of her reverie by the sound of a car slowing down so that the driver could check there was nothing approaching. She didn't look up, but heard it cross the junction before it stopped, reversed and turned towards where she was.

'Do you want a lift or are you walking for the good of your health?'

Without turning she recognized Louisa's voice and her troubles fell away.

'My health would do much better in a car,' she answered, determined to make her forced laugh sound natural as she crossed the grassy verge to where Louisa had pulled up. 'You know the worst thing about walking is that it's so good it makes you forget you have to walk all the way home again. See my heel. I've rubbed a blister.'

Louisa knew her too well to be fooled by the bright voice.

'Next time you'll have to come prepared with a packet of plasters,' she replied in the same vein as she reached to open the car door. 'In you hop.'

They set off in silence, both conscious of so much that was under the surface, so much that neither of them was ready to face. It was Bella who spoke first, her voice harsh with pent-up emotion.

'I can't do it, Lou. I can't look after him. Every few minutes he's asking the same thing, "Where's Ali? I'll take her for a game." Then, when I tell him – and I've said it over and over, I can't keep on. I have to pussyfoot around him and all I can think about is *her*. It's *my* fault, I should never have let him get used to playing with her and we would never have lost her. Leo thinks it's my fault.' By this time her self-control was lost and she spoke through her tears. 'I was upstairs doing the bedrooms and I left them playing in the garden.' She'd said it before so many times. The horror of it haunted her, and with each telling her guilt became more certain in her mind. 'I should have watched; I knew Dad did silly things. I should have checked they were still out there. It was my fault. When I said that to Leo he just looked at me, didn't argue or even say anything, just looked. My Ali, I would rather . . .' The rest of her words were swallowed, drowned in her tears.

Louisa drew to the side of the road and stopped the car, then drew Bella to her.

'It was *not* your fault nor Mr Carter's either. You could say it was Leo's for swanning off with me, or mine for encouraging him. You know what I believe?'

'I don't know anything,' Bella sniffed, her spate of crying giving way to utter dejection. 'I don't even care about anything anymore. Don't even want to live.'

'Ali was only a baby still, but if she were old enough to understand surely it would make her miserable to hear you talk like that. She loved you more than all the rest put together; you were her whole life. Remember the day she was born. Such a tiny scrap of humanity, and every week she grew, she did something new.'

'Shut up. Don't talk about it.' Bella sounded like a cornered animal, her reddened eyes wide with fear.

'Yes, we will talk about her. She was the most precious gift—'

'She wasn't a gift; she was on loan. She was never really mine. If there's a God, why did he take her away? Why did he make me think she was mine and then take her back?'

Louisa dug deep to try to think of something that might help, but it wasn't easy.

'I can't tell you. I don't know any more than you do. But I like to think that what you said is the truth. He sent her to you so that you learnt what it must be like to be the most important person in someone's life. I envy you that. Surely there can't be any love as pure and innocent as a baby's.'

'So what did this wonderful god let it happen for? She was always happy. She made everyone happy. She didn't deserve to die. I could stand the hurt, the wretchedness of losing her if she had wanted to be somewhere else and I knew she was happy. It's not just for me that I'm miserable, it's for *her*.'

'I know. But I can't believe that she is snuffed out like a candle. Bodies die. Yours will, Leo's will, mine will. But our souls? While we are remembered – and if we are lucky enough during our lifetime to be truly loved as she was – then surely her soul will still be close to you. Remember every little thing, Bella. I know you do, and you will continue to. You won't lose her.'

'Are you just being kind? Or is that what you truly believe, God's honour believe?'

'I truly believe that if you always think of her, don't let

yourself be frightened to remember, then she will never be far away from you.'

'Just be imagination – must be.' And yet there was a hint of pleading in her words.

'You can think that if you like, but I truly believe I must be on the right track.' Somehow Louisa had to find the right words. 'If she fell and grazed her knee, then even though she would cry it wouldn't alter the person she was. That's just a hurt on her body. Now imagine yourself walking into the room and finding her playing on the floor with that toy dog she so loved. She would look up and see you, her eyes would shine with happiness and she would give you a smile that came from her very soul. Now tell me the body is all there is.'

'I want to believe. I'd give anything, *anything*, if I could be sure she wasn't lost and lonely. So I suppose I must believe something even if I don't know what.'

'When you get to bed tonight, lying there in the dark, try to remember what I said. Picture her face when she sees you, remember her with your heart and Bella I do honestly, God's honour, believe she will be with you.' She switched on the engine and they started forward. After a minute or two she said, 'Leo has lost her too. You say he blames you, but don't you think that's the hurt in him, and the guilt, speaking? About him and me . . .' But what was she trying to say?

'He was never in love with me, but we have got along well. I didn't expect him to change his ways just because we were married. I was sure he'd had lots of lady friends and I would rather it was you than anyone else. I'd heard whispers in the village about how often he was at your place.' She shrugged her shoulders. 'On the evenings he came home late and I was in bed, I was thankful that he wouldn't wake me up when I pretended to be asleep.'

'If you were a stranger I would feel no guilt. But you are my friend. And for months the most important thing in my life has been making love with your husband. I feel ashamed and wretched.'

'It's funny, isn't it?' Despite her words there was an unfamiliar hardness in her tone. 'Here we are, his wife and his mistress, and it all seems trivial and unimportant.'

'To me it's neither of those things. It's as if your Leo and the man I know are two different people. But I've told you before – he said that anything between him and me would never make any difference to *you*. His marriage wasn't touched by it. If I'd had any pride I ought to have refused to be just his plaything, but I had no pride.'

'Home already.' Bella seemed eager to change the subject. 'Put me down at the end of the track. I'll walk the last bit.'

'What about your blister? You can get out at the end of the track when I turn the car.'

When they reached Ridgeway there was no sign of either Leo or Harold.

'Dad kept saying he wanted to take Ali to see the men in the fields. It looks as if that's what Leo has done with him. Thanks for the lift.'

Her voice sounded dull, and even her smile didn't come spontaneously.

'I have some work to clear up when I get home, but it won't take much above an hour. Why not come over this evening?' Louisa suggested, ashamed of how often she had been irritated by the girl's constant bright good humour. Now she seemed to be lost in a fog of despondency and Louisa was touched to see how such a simple suggestion could visibly lift her, even if only temporarily, from the misery that surrounded her.

'May I? Thanks Lou, I'd really love to. We always eat early and I'll get cleared up as quickly as I can.'

'Surely two able-bodied men are capable of washing a few dishes. Tell them you're coming to me so they'll have to clear up for once.'

For a moment, Bella hesitated. After all, who was she to give orders? Then she gave a smile that showed the girl she used to be wasn't far beneath the surface.

'I'll do that.' And so she believed.

Earlier that same afternoon, after Bella left Leo in his work-room, he went back to his drawing board for a few minutes. He, who had done nothing all afternoon except gaze out of the window, had a sudden desire to work. Perhaps he could persuade Eva Johnson to keep his father company, he thought. But when he looked down at the grassy patch they called the garden he saw Harold asleep in a deckchair. So back to his drawing he went. A quarter of an hour later – in fact, before Bella was even aware of her blister – he checked again. The chair was empty. With a sigh he threw down his pencil and went downstairs.

'Dad, how about we go and see how they're getting on harvesting the sweetcorn? Dad?'

With no sign of his father around the house he went on his own to the field of corn. Knowing Harold liked to be with the men, he expected to find him there. But just as had happened on the day he had taken Ali on the walk that had led to her death, so again the men said they'd seen nothing of him. Leo returned to the house before setting out to find where he had wandered, his first thought being that he would have walked down to see Louisa just as he often had with Bella and Ali. For a moment he dropped to sit in the deckchair where Harold had been feigning sleep. Thoughts of Ali filled his mind. Ali, the most wonderful thing that had ever happened to him. He envied Bella her tears – surely tears would release this strange and painful weight of desolation that seemed to bear down on him. Louisa had awakened an emotion in him that he had truly believed was love. Yet, faced with the loss of Ali, it faded into insignificance. And Bella? There had been many times when she had irritated him with what he looked on as her childlike innocence, and yet her love for Ali had been as strong as that of a lioness for her young. In an inexplicable way he felt that in being close to her he stayed nearer to the little girl who had shown him the meaning of pure, unconditional love. Harold was forgotten as he lay back in the deckchair, while in his imagination he felt the soft skin of her face against his and heard the sound of her baby voice. 'Come on, Daddy, up on shoulders, let's see fields.' He couldn't find the release he craved in tears, so the charade must go on. He didn't want the sympathy the ladies of the village gave to Bella, but it hurt that no one considered the loss was his, too.

He heard a car pull up at the head of the track, then a door slam and the car drive off again. The sound brought him to his feet as he remembered his mission to find his father. Perhaps someone had seen him and brought him back home. He started towards the front of the house, and that's when he saw Bella.

'I was glad of a lift home,' she told him, her voice perfectly friendly and yet with no warmth. 'I'd walked a long way and then I met Louisa with the car.'

'So she's gone home now?' he asked urgently.

Bella didn't try to disguise her contempt as she looked at him, although he didn't seem aware of it.

'Dad's gone off somewhere,' he told her.

'Surely you could have looked after him for one afternoon, taken him out for a drive or something. How long has he been missing?'

'How the hell do I know? If I'd seen him go I would have stopped him. Every time I looked out he was asleep in the chair over there.' He saw no reason to tell her that 'every time' was, in fact, just once and that must have been more than an hour ago.

'He can't have gone far. He won't be at Louisa's. If that's where he thought he was going he will have seen that she wasn't at home. When she went out she left the side gate and the garage door open so that she could drive straight in when she got back.'

'Well, he's not with the chaps in the fields. I've asked them and no one has seen him this afternoon. I'd better go down to the lane and see if he's in the village. Everyone knows him; he might have found someone to talk to.' To hear Leo's bright, confident tone, no one would have had the slightest suspicion of the depth of his despair only a few minutes previously.

'If he'd been chattering in the village we should have seen him. Louisa drove up the High Street to get petrol before we came in.'

'Where else could he have got to? The woods, do you think? I can't believe it. Dad. Dad, of all people. Nothing ever threw him off balance, he was – oh, hell, it's not fair. You can't understand – you never knew him before he started to go downhill.' He knew he ought not to have let himself talk about his father; the only way to accept the change in him was to take each day as it came, not look forward and not look back.

So without another word he left Bella and instead of going down the track to the road, turned left at their gate and made to follow where it continued towards the wood. Then, after two or three steps he turned and called to Bella, 'Are you coming with me? It might be a good idea.'

Bella closed her eyes as she shook her head and called, 'No, I have to get some food going,' but closing her eyes didn't shut out the image of Harold wanting them to help look for the ball and Ali lying dead. She turned away and went into the house.

Harold hadn't been aware that Leo had looked down on him sitting with his eyes closed in the deckchair. In fact, he had been aware of only one thing, his plans clear cut in his muddled mind. Fate had played into his hands and with Bella out and Leo shut away in his workroom, he was a free man.

With the car safely put away Louisa automatically closed and locked the garage door then shut the double gate. She heard the clock from the church at the far end of the village chime and strike six, and wondered whether Leo, not Bella, would come after supper. What an odd situation it was that she and Bella, two people so different, should really care about each other even though Bella knew Leo was unfaithful to her and Louisa herself stole the love that he should have given his wife. Or did Bella reject him? She had adored him in the beginning, so how was it he turned to another woman to satisfy him? No one seeing Louisa as she walked towards the house, opening her handbag to take out the key, would have suspected her thoughts were anywhere except on what she did. But the truth was she had a mental picture of how the evening would be if he came. Please make him come, make him need me as much as I need him. She turned the key in the lock of the front door and stepped into the hall. The house felt still and empty and, for a moment, she was certain that this was how it would remain, with her waiting alone in the silence. Giving herself a mental shake, she told herself that she would use the evening wisely; she would start on the work she had collected the previous day from an engineering firm. As if to back up her determination, she went into her workroom, not because she meant to start on it straight away but simply to bring her mind back from where it wanted to stray. That's when she heard a movement behind her that stopped her in her tracks, shock and instant terror driving everything else from her mind.

'Didn't know I was waiting for you, did you? Now I've got you.'

She knew the voice, but there was something about it that made her more frightened that she would have believed possible. Harold Carter was mentally deranged and, more than that, he was strong. But he was a poor, broken man, not an evil one; that's what she had to keep in mind as she faced him. She must keep calm and talk to him in a friendly manner. She even imagined herself lying to him that she was just going to walk up to the farm, so they could go together. All that flashed through her mind in seconds for, although he often came to The Retreat with Bella, she knew from his tone that this was no friendly visit. Something must have happened to trigger memories that upset him. As she turned round to face him he was coming towards her, his mouth open as he gasped for breath as if he'd been running which, of course, she knew he hadn't. Somehow he had got into the house and been lying in wait. She made a supreme effort to bring him back from wherever his troubled mind had taken him.

'No, you usually just come with Bella, but it's nice to see you. Would you like a cup of tea?'

In answer to her effort to give him a friendly welcome the muscles in his right cheek twitched out of control, the expression on his good-looking face being changed into an ugly and angry grimace. With clenched fists he beat the air, while even his feet wouldn't keep still as he seemed to be marching on one spot. Every part of him had lost control as he lurched towards her. She was strong and had seen what was coming, so she held him off with her hands on his shoulders.

'You've got no place here. This is *her* house, hers and mine. How can I find her here if you're here? You drive her car; you pretend you're her. Well, *I* know you're not.' Try as she might to keep him away from her, he loomed closer until his face was only inches from hers. 'You tempt Leo. Get him into your bed, do you? Was that where he was when Ali was lost? Gone, she has, gone.'

'Stop it! Shut up, can't you. Get away from me!'

'You get him here pleasuring you, pretending to be Bella's friend. Glad to get it from any man who'll give it to you, frightened you'll end up a dried-up old maid. We don't want you here, pretending to be my Violet.' As he shouted he dribbled, saliva running down his chin. 'Well, it's too late now. You can burn in hell. You wore her clothes – I've seen you in them. You won't wear them any more.'

'Get out!' Catching him off his guard, she pushed with all her might and he stumbled backwards across the room, hitting the door and just saving himself from falling to the ground. Giving a manic laugh he left her, closing the door behind him. She heard the key turn in the lock, but her feeling was relief and thankfulness that he'd gone. Next time Leo came she would tell him what had happened and surely then he would speak to the doctor about getting the crazy old man put in a home. She heard the front door slam and breathed a sigh of relief. He had gone. The fact that he'd locked the door didn't worry her; she was on the ground floor and could easily get out of the window. So she decided to work for an hour or so, for work must be the best way to silence the echo of his words. He was crazy; he wanted to accuse her simply because he hated to see her here in the house her aunt had left to her. Well, damn him, he needn't think he could frighten her away.

She set out her papers and, determined not to be thrown off course by his accusations, picked up her pen. He must have upset her more than she was prepared to admit, though, for she couldn't concentrate and went to open the window. Someone must have a bonfire – she could smell it and there was a hint of smoke in the air. Gazing down the long strip of well-manicured garden she thought back on what poor, confused Harold had said and, honest to the core, she admitted to herself that his comments had hit home. 'Frightened you'd end a dried-up old maid' . . . 'glad to get it from any man who'll give it to you.' No, that wasn't true – he was a wicked old man. All her thoughts had been focused on Leo; he was the man – the only man – she had wanted. Of course nothing had changed, she told herself. And yet she knew the truth was that nothing was as it had been before Ali was lost to them; then, they had thought just of the moment, caring for nothing more. Now, she knew she could see clearly. Another Road to Damascus moment, perhaps? And was it the same for Leo? Oh yes, Leo had changed even if he hadn't yet faced the truth.

The smell of smoke was getting stronger. It brought her thoughts back from their wanderings. Pushing the window wide open she leant out, stunned by the horror of what she saw. Instinct was her guide as first she grabbed her handbag and then climbed over the sill into the garden. Then reason came to the fore and she ran to the front of the house, groping in her handbag as she went. The telephone was in the sitting room, that's where she must go to send for help.

The fire was on the first floor, the smoke emanating from her bedroom. She remembered him telling her she would burn in hell. How could he have done this to the place where he and Violet had been so happy together? He was wrong; never had she tried to take anything that had been her aunt's. All this time while he had been coming to the house with Bella and Ali, had he been hating her and planning how he would get rid of her?

'Operator,' she said as she picked up the receiver, 'give me nine-nine-nine.'

'Which service do you want, police, fire or ambulance?' came the businesslike reply.

'Fire. Please be quick.'

Then Miss Harding, the ever practical, came to the fore and took the situation in hand. Thankful that the fire was in the upper storey and so far the ground floor was safe, she went back to her workroom and unlocked the door, then into her large briefcase crammed all the papers relating to outstanding work. Next came the bureau for papers that were more personal. Surprising herself, she added all of Violet's snapshots to the pile. It was as she closed the bureau that she became aware of a dull, roaring sound. The smell of smoke was strong and when she went out into the hall she could hardly see up the stairs for it. Fear was her first fierce but brief reaction; common sense told her that she was only yards from the front door and freedom. Without warning the realization of what was happening gripped her. Until that moment she had had thoughts of nothing except what had to be saved from destruction. Only then did it hit her what the fire meant to her. This was her home, the very first home she had actually possessed . . . it was a place filled with memories of Leo and her . . . it had been a house filled with happiness . . . even if the firemen were in time to contain the fire to the first floor nothing could ever be the same. Everything before she came here had faded into the mists of time; everything relevant to her life had been *here*. Leo, Bella and Ali, the transformation of the garden and her real and growing affection for Hamish and his sister, even the movement of the lace curtains opposite: all these had given meaning to her life. And there was something else, something that had given purpose to her days and pride in her success: her steadily growing business, one where she was subservient to no man.

Harold didn't go straight home when he left her. He started up the track until he reached the gate to the field behind The Retreat. It was padlocked, but climbing a five-bar gate proved no problem in his present elated state. Once in the field where through the summer peas had been grown, he half ran and half stumbled over the newly turned earth. This was the place for the best view, he decided. Chuckling excitedly, he rubbed his hands and beat a tattoo with his feet. Then instinct made him realize he would be seen from all directions standing in the middle of the field, so he hurried to the far side, took a surprisingly agile leap across a narrow point in the ditch and sheltered behind a tree at the edge of the wood. 'Look at it burning, that'll teach her. Coming here and living in Violet's house, even wearing her clothes, driving around in her car. And, yes, looking like my Vi used to look. Well, if Vi can't have that house, then neither can anyone else. I did it! Locked her in, too. Don't like that, burning flesh. No, don't like that. I ought to have left it so that she could get out, just as long as she goes away. And that's what she'll do. She shouldn't be there, trying to take Violet's place. I'm glad to see it burn;

now no one can live there. Little Bella, she's a good girl. But *that* one, looking like my precious one, and what is she but a harlot? I could see what she wanted; like a bitch on heat she was, ready to lie on her back for anyone. Well, I hope Leo had a good time with her. I bet a pound to a penny he could see as plain as I could what was up with her. Prim and proper as ever I saw, but hungry for a chance to sample the fleshpots. Gave it to her good and proper, did you, m'lad?' Then, just as his thoughts were racing forward with no conscious effort from him, he changed course at the sight of flames appearing from the roof of the burning house. 'Look at that! That'll do it, Vi. We don't want her there in our house. Remember it, Vi? Remember every hour of it. It was ours, just ours.'

For all his wild ramblings, now that he was satisfied with his work he wanted to get right away from The Retreat. He wasn't in a fit enough state to know exactly why he shouldn't be found near the house, but the wood presented a safe haven. He'd pick his way through the overgrown brambles, ferns and fallen branches in an attempt to reach the more familiar part. So, not turning back to look again at the fire's progress, he stumbled on. Although in the open the light wasn't fading yet, in the wood it was getting dark already. Believing he was heading in the right direction, he moved on. Time lost its meaning, dusk deepened.

'Dad! Dad!' Was he dreaming or could it be Leo calling him? 'Can you hear me, Dad?'

Filling his lungs, he shouted, 'Here! Over here.'

'Just stand still. Stay where you are. I'm coming.'

It was only then that Harold realized just how frightened he was. As long as he walked he'd believed he was making his way home, whereas in truth he was going ever further into the wood. Now he had to stand still, that's what Leo had told him. But if he just stood here quietly with no light to guide the boy, how could they hope to meet? Visions of night-time amongst these eerie trees frightened him. And what was that? Something was falling on the leaves, then on the ground where it could get through. Rain. He'd be here all night if he had to stand still. A few minutes ago his mind had been filled with his success in creating the fire; now all that was forgotten, wiped clean. All he knew was fear. With his arms around an old, long-neglected beech tree he started to cry, thankful to hear the sound of his own sobbing.

'Raining,' he wailed. 'All alone. Just want to die, oh, God, why don't you let me die?' Whether that was a brief flash of clarity or whether it was no more than the fear of the moment no one would ever know, for he alone heard the hysterical outburst. Minutes that seemed like hours went by until he could stand no more. 'I'm going to walk!' he yelled. 'Getting wet. Where the devil are you?'

By that time Leo was near enough to hear his voice if not his words. 'I'm nearly with you. Don't move, Dad. Only a few more minutes.'

And so it turned out. Five minutes later, holding Harold firmly by the arm, Leo steered him in what he guessed to be the direction of the field that divided Ridgeway from The Retreat. It was after eight o'clock and Bella would have had their usual light supper ready for ages. This was certainly not the way he had planned to spend the evening. Now, as they came nearer to the edge of the wood, he frowned, sniffing the air.

'Smells like smoke. Can you smell smoke, Dad?'

Harold didn't answer. His muddled mind was unsure what his reply ought to be. He was aware that Leo was walking faster, having no regard for thorns on the bushes or tree roots that threatened to trip them.

'Christ!' Through a momentary gap between the trees Leo saw the lights of the fire engine. 'Christ!' This time is was hardly more than a whisper.

Harold began to whimper. What was going to happen? Would Leo know about how he had set light to the bedspread and the curtains?

'This way.' Holding tightly to his father's arm, Leo pulled him to the left as they came out of the wood and made towards the stile into the lane. 'We'll take her home with us. There can be no going back into that inferno – not tonight or ever from the look of those flames.'

'Come on, come on, let's go and see.' Harold sounded unnaturally excited, but that didn't make any particular impression on

Leo. 'That's *our* house, Vi's and mine. She had to be got rid of. Don't you see, boy, she spoilt everything. Remember how it used to be. Who does she think she is, coming there, trying to be like Vi?'

'Don't talk rubbish. Come on, we've got to find Louisa.'

Ten

The previous day, when Bella had been walking home with her shopping, she had met elderly Edith Cunningham, whose husband kept the fish and chip shop at the end of High Street. From her first days in Lexleigh she had known that Edith was her friend, even though some of the other village folk had whispered amongst themselves that no nice girl would have been so eager to show off her growing bulge, especially with a wedding ring only recently on her finger. Out of respect for Alice Carter they had only said these things to each other. But Mrs Cunningham had been excited for her and had even knitted a white matinee coat in readiness for the baby's arrival.

When they met by chance that morning, having talked with genuine sadness about Ali's death, Edith Cunningham had said, 'There's going to be talk in the village, wicked talk—'

'How could there be? It was an accident.' Bella had found herself defending Harold.

'No my dear, never about dear little Alicia.' She looked around as if she thought someone might be listening even though the street was empty. 'It's our little Sheila, my grand-daughter. Well, not so little now, she's sixteen and done with schooling. People say it's the goings-on at the youth night in the village hall, but to my mind it never did anyone any harm to have a dance, young or old. Trouble is she's told her mother, my Emmie, that she's two months gone. She'll be a mother before she's seventeen and the lad is only a year older. They haven't told me who he is, only that he's not in the village any longer.'

'Perhaps that's a good thing, Mrs Cunningham. If he still lived here perhaps they would have wanted to get married, and they'd be far too young. Now the baby will belong just to the family. And whether they're planned or slip-ups they bring so much love.'

'That's just what I told my Emmie. But Sheila is little more than a child herself, hasn't had the chance of earning a penny yet, and as if that's not trouble enough, Jack, her dad, lost his job last week. He used to work at Ryders, in town, doing the deliveries, but from out of the blue he fell in a fit – epilepsy, they called it. Never had one before and Emmie blames Sheila for it, says he's worried out of his mind and it's enough to give anyone a fit. Any road, they stopped him from driving so bang went his job. Of course, me and Cliff will help the girl – she's the only grandchild we've got.'

For Bella it had been a moment she knew would stay with her, for with no warning she had known exactly what she must do. More than that, it was a moment when Ali had seemed so close she could almost feel the weight of her in her arms. And Ali had been laughing; Ali had been putting the words in her mouth and telling her that this was the way never to lose her.

'I've always kept everything of Ali's, right from her first vests and her terry towelling nappies to her two-year-old sizes – and her toys, and pram and baby crib. Everything.'

'Very wise of you, child. I know it's hard to imagine now, but you'll have other children and be glad. To see her little things on the tiny body of a brother or sister might ease the hurt.'

'No. I know what I have to do, what I *want* to do. There won't be any more children and I would like to give everything to Sheila. She wouldn't mind – I mean, she wouldn't look on it as a bad omen or anything silly? It's what Ali would want, what Ali *does* want.'

And so it was that on that early evening when the fire at The Retreat started, after Bella had laid the table for a cold meat and salad supper she went up to Ali's room to continue sorting the clothes that she had started earlier. She had made up her mind she would do it while the nearness of Ali was fresh in her mind.

It was getting dark, and she would be late arriving at Louisa's. She had expected Leo to have found his father and brought him home ages ago, for his wanderings usually took him either towards The Retreat or to the edge of the farm by the wood. But Leo must have looked in the usual places and then had to go into the village or even right into the wood. If she had known they would be so long she would have offered to search too, but it was too late now to do anything about it. So, holding close to so many memories as she folded each small garment and added it to the piles in the cot, she pushed the thought of Leo's fruitless search from her mind and concentrated on Ali. It was as she switched on the light and crossed to the window to draw the curtains that she saw the smoke billowing high in the air. Had Louisa gone home and lit a bonfire, then let it get out of hand? With a concerned frown she drew a chair to the window and climbed on to it; from her new vantage point she ought to be able to see exactly where the smoke was coming from. It may not have been from The Retreat at all, but from one of the cottages opposite.

'Oh, no! It can't be.' There was no reason behind her exclamation, for clearly she could see the thick smoke blotting out her vision of the roof of the house. Her one thought was to get to the scene of the fire, to make sure Louisa was safely outside and to bring her home to the farm. The affair between Leo and her didn't even enter Bella's head. She simply wanted to help her friend. Taking a shortcut through the field where the recently turned ground was uneven, she climbed the stile to the road where by that time the original small group had swelled to become a crowd. It was seldom Lexleigh saw such excitement.

There was no sign of Louisa but she caught a brief glimpse of Leo ushering Harold on to the track and back home.

'Is Louisa safe?' she blurted out as soon as she came within earshot of the gathered spectators.

'Yes. She looked right as rain. She'd got her car out and put it up the lane out of the way for safe keeping and was outside here waiting for the firemen,' one of the village women Leo referred to as the Lexleigh Ladies replied.

'Where is she now?'

This time it was the opposite neighbour with a reputation for missing nothing who replied, 'That gardener chap came – not five minutes after the engine arrived he was here. How he heard the good Lord knows, but he was in a right bother. I was just telling your husband, they stood along there talking, then she got into her car and off they went, Miss Harding first and him following in his van. Not a word of explanation to anyone. He'll take her home with him for the night, I wouldn't wonder. He comes sniffing around here often enough.'

'Nothing wrong with Hamish McLaren,' one of the others was quick to his defence. 'A nicer young fellow you wouldn't find.'

'Maybe she thinks so too,' the neighbour who had so much trouble with her net curtains replied, 'or maybe she doesn't. I only know what I happen to see.'

'Well, she can't spend the night here,' Bella said, her authoritative tone surprising her and, no doubt, the rest of the group too. 'I came to tell her there's always a place for her at the farm. But it seems I'm too late.' Then, changing the subject, 'Do you know what happened, how it started?'

'From what we can gather it's mostly the upstairs and the roof space. They'll be here a long time getting it out and damped down. She'd not been home many minutes – well, you know she hadn't. I heard the car and happened to look out as she turned it on to the track, so I saw you'd been having the afternoon together. A funny thing, though, and this is just between ourselves (her glance took in the rest of her cronies). When she came running out and rushed up the road, I suppose to dial for the engine, she was carrying one of those smart cases they keep papers and things in just as if she'd had it waiting handy for when she had to get out.'

Ignoring the innuendo, Bella said to the group at large, 'If she isn't here I'll go home and give the others their supper. I would have expected her to come to us. Anyway, if you just happen to see her come back – although I don't see that Hamish would let her come back to this, but if he does, will you tell her that we are expecting her at the farm and there is a bed waiting for her.'

'I reckon she knows that without having to be told by us.' This was spoken by one of the group with a guffaw that left no one in any doubt of what she was suggesting. Choosing to ignore the remark, Bella made for the track and home.

Sheer chance had brought Hamish through the village, taking a shortcut home from where he had been working. It had taken him no more than a few seconds to take in the situation and know he would offer to take Louisa home with him. Well, before he reached the scene of the fire he recognized her car parked, so he left his van next to it and walked the distance to where she was standing, a little apart from the group.

When he told her he wanted her to come back to the nursery with him, she hesitated.

'I can't just drive away and leave the house like this,' she protested. But neither could she sleep at The Retreat. He spoke to one of the firemen who came from his own village, and after a minute came back to her with the news that the fire wasn't yet under control. As it spread so it burst into fresh life, something they couldn't understand. The roof was in danger of collapsing.

'They'll be there for hours and they won't let anyone inside, not even you. I told him I was trying to persuade you to come home to Mags and me for the night. It's a really bad fire, Lou. Once it's all over there's going to have to be a lot of work done on it before it's habitable. Come to us. We've got plenty of room and you can work from there. What if we go home and have something to eat, then I can leave you with Mags while I come back and see the situation? Tomorrow you can see what the damage is.' Then, with that optimistic smile so much part of his character, 'Tomorrow is another day and nothing looks as bad in the morning light.'

'You're a dear, Hamish, but I can't do that. One night, yes, and I'm grateful, but then I must find somewhere to rent.'

The Retreat had been a symbol of her independence, the end of her days being ruled by the clock: nine in the morning arriving in the office; twelve thirty until one thirty a quick lunch in Millie's Café, then back to the dingy office until six o'clock. Yet, driving towards McLaren's Garden Centre she had the strangest feeling, almost as though she were lifted out of herself and could look down on each section of her life: childhood and working hard at school driven by determination to prove herself; years at the accountancy firm working always with that same determination; a taste of freedom in this most recent chapter – a short span of years in which she had learnt to be at peace with herself. It wasn't simply because she had proved that she could make her own way without the backing of a male-dominated situation; that was but a small part of it. With Leo she had learnt the joy of being a woman. She thought of the expression 'giving herself to a man', and knew she had never 'given herself'. Yes, they had both exalted in wonderful, glorious hours of lovemaking, lovemaking that had made her a whole person, the equal of any woman, married or single. From the start he had said his relationship with her would make no difference to his marriage, and she had determined that that would be the case. It hadn't been a husband she had yearned for; it had been the hunger for something beyond her reach and understanding. With Leo she had found freedom; she had rejoiced in her womanhood and discovered joy beyond belief.

Yet, was she in love with him? Had she ever been in love with him? Driving the few miles to the nursery she dug into her heart honestly. Did she respect and admire him? As a lover, yes. But as a man? As a husband, even if that had been possible? They discussed articles they read in the newspaper, usually sharing the same views but occasionally sharpening their wits on each other when they saw things from different angles. She was never bored in his company. But, if he were free, would she want to spend her life with him? Had she fallen in love with love? And what about Leo? Honesty told her that there had been many women in his life and there would be others. None would make any difference to his marriage, even though what he felt for Bella was no more than affection and appreciation of the security she brought to his life.

Then there was Hamish, her very dear friend. Friendship would endure. Yes, they could grow closer with the years, of that she was sure. Except that marriage surely should be based on something far deeper than the affection she felt for Hamish.

Driving towards the nursery with these thoughts chasing each other through her head, she wondered that while the home she had been so proud of was burning her mind should be set on the future, a future that was a complete blank after the unexpected turn of events. The Retreat had come to her from out of the blue, changing her life; and now surely she had reached another milestone. Once the fire was out and the damage assessed, the work involved to make it habitable would be immense. She had never been an indecisive woman and in that moment she knew without a doubt that her time in Lexleigh was over. In the immediate future she would find somewhere to live while she finished the work she was already involved with. Then there was the question of the house, the insurance claim and a decision whether to sell it or rent it out once it had been restored. All that was for tomorrow; for tonight it was enough to know that ahead of her was another stage, another challenge.

So deep in thought had she been as she drove at a steady pace, not interested in being overtaken, that she was surprised on turning into the car park at the nursery to find Margaret waiting in the open doorway and Hamish coming out to meet her. Perhaps it was the emotion of the evening that had affected her more than she had let herself admit, for she saw them, her dear friends, through a haze of unshed tears.

It was later that evening, while Hamish was making a last check that all was well in the nursery and Margaret was putting out the milk bottles ready for the early morning delivery, that Louisa casually turned the pages of the newspaper. She wasn't concentrating on the columns of news, and yet there was one that caught her eye and held her attention. Surely Fate must have led her to it. She read it twice, knowing immediately that it had come to her notice for a purpose. Her future was suddenly clear.

At Ridgeway Farm Bella was just finishing clearing up after the supper, which had been kept waiting long after its time, when there was a knock at the front door.

'Will you answer it, Dad?' she said, trying to sound friendlier towards him than she felt.

Without a word he went and a minute later she heard the sound of voices in the hall. Perhaps Leo had heard the knock and come down from his workroom where he had retreated as soon as he'd eaten. She opened the kitchen door just enough for her to hear, but she didn't recognize the voice of the visitor.

'I felt I should come. Gossip can be very cruel and certainly not always correct. I'm sure whoever you spoke to, Mr Carter, must have misconstrued your meaning. But there is word going around that you were in some way responsible for the fire in Miss Harding's house.'

'Go back to Bella in the kitchen, Dad. I'll talk to Reverend Gilbert.' Then, impatiently, when Harold made no attempt to move way, 'Go along. Do as I say.'

But Harold was deaf to his orders. 'You won't like it when she's not there waiting for you. I told you, I had to get rid of her, her and the house too. That house belonged to Vi and me, not to *her* with the prim, touch-me-not manner while all the time she was begging for it.'

'Get back in the kitchen and stop talking drivel.'

Bella could stand and listen no longer. 'I'm sorry, Reverend Gilbert.' Coming to join them she spoke with quiet dignity, a far cry from the girl Leo had brought to introduce to his parents not three years earlier. 'Dad gets confused; the last weeks have been very hard on him – very hard on all of us.'

She seemed to have touched the right note.

'My dear Mrs Carter, at a time like this the last thing I want is that unnecessary trouble be brought to your doorstep. That's why I have come to warn you that something he said to one of the ladies of the parish started the gossip and you know how it can snowball. In a quiet village such as Lexleigh everything is magnified in the chatter. They mean no harm, I'm sure, but there are always those who want to add colour to a dreary life. I wanted you to have the opportunity of letting it be known how things are with him and his imagination.'

Before Bella joined them, from her vantage point just inside the slightly opened kitchen door she had seen how, as the vicar had talked, Harold had become more and more agitated. She knew that, although he sometimes spoke wildly and needed constant care and attention, there were times when he was as capable of understanding as the next person. This seemed to be one of those moments.

'Imagination be damned,' he said angrily, glaring at well-meaning Reverend Gilbert. 'You think I'm off my rocker, don't you? Let me tell you, I know what I know. That woman thinks that because she looks like Vi she can queen it there in the house that was ours. Serve her right if she got trapped in it, locked in. Ah, that would be the thing. Locked in that room she likes to call her office. That was Vi's sewing room. Office be damned, yes, be damned to her and all she is. Is? Was? Perhaps she's gone.' He gave a laugh that made Bella shudder. Then, glaring straight at the vicar, he said, 'You and your lot, I expect you think the fire was just breaking her in ready for what was waiting for her.'

Bella could think of no way to interrupt his tirade, but the vicar seemed unperturbed by his ranting. Turning slightly away so that Harold wouldn't see, he mouthed to Leo, 'Phone the doctor.'

Without a word Leo left the room to do the vicar's bidding but was back almost immediately, nodding to indicate everything was under control. Although Dr Saunders used a room adjacent to the butcher's shop on one morning a week to hold a local surgery he lived some four miles away. Leo had phoned his home where Mrs Saunders had informed him that by chance her husband had made a rare evening visit to Lexleigh and she would call him there straight away and explain the urgency. It seemed that Fate had the whole matter in hand, for in less than five minutes the village policeman had shifted the crowd who were waiting expectantly for the roof of The Retreat to cave in, so that the doctor's car could get by and he arrived at Ridgeway.

The vicar took his leave, feeling he had done his best to help the family who surely had seen enough tragedy. Harold's interest in the whole affair had gone, the sight of yet another visitor seemed to him to be making a fuss about nothing. It was over and done with; Louisa Harding would be gone. Smiling to himself, he wandered back into the kitchen without so much as a 'good evening' to the doctor.

'It was the vicar's idea to send for you,' Leo was explaining. 'You and I both know about my father's delicate mental state and, of course, losing Alicia has been a great blow to him. This afternoon he and I went walking, something he always enjoys. We ended up in the lower part of the wood here and that's when we noticed smoke and went to investigate. Louisa Harding is a friend of my wife's and I thought we could bring her back to the farm. You know what people are like if there's a fire – they come out of the woodwork in droves and there was quite a crowd outside the house. Somehow we got separated and I suspect that's when the excitement threw him. It seems he started a rumour that he was responsible for the blaze. Poor Dad. He was always a hero to me and I hate to see this happening to him. I can vouch that he and I were together all the afternoon. Earlier Louisa Harding had been out with Bella, although they were home by that time. She's the only one who will know what caused it. Some materials are dangerously inflammable. I'm told it started in her bedroom, so perhaps she lit a cigarette up there when she was putting her coat away. A match not quite out – it's easily done. But it's Dad we're talking about. The vicar was very concerned because word is spreading that Dad started it. We both know it's a figment of his imagination. In an emotional state, seeing the house destroyed would have unhinged him.'

Bella had been watching Leo. Without a word she turned and left them. How could he lie like that? He knew as well as she did that Harold had been wandering on his own while Louisa was out, and yet he lied, and lied with that same charm that had made her believe herself to be in love with him. And how *could* he imply that Louisa was to blame? Even as the thought came to her, bringing with it contempt and rage such as she had never felt, she surprised herself how defensive she felt on Louisa's account. That her friend and her husband were lovers she had accepted, not with jealousy or anger but with a sense of being a lesser person than either of them. The long shadow of her tolerated but unloved childhood had clung to her.

Harold was busy at the cutlery drawer, making sure that the spoons and forks were in neat piles. It was one of his regular pastimes, and one that irritated her. Every day after she dried the cutlery she would throw the knives into the knife section, the forks into the fork section and so on. He would watch her and then go to the drawer, take them out section by section and replace them neatly stacked.

'Dad,' she made sure her voice sounded interested but not accusing, 'I don't see how you could have got into that house. I have your key for it on my key ring.'

His soft laugh made her blood run cold. 'Silly girl,' he said, turning to her with a smile that held triumph but no humour, 'you think I don't go in there without asking that woman? The door doesn't need a key. You can turn that lock with a sixpence. Vi and I both knew, but she made sure I had a key just the same. Our house, our place. I locked her in, that creature you think so much of. Locked her in Vi's sewing room.'

'You're wicked and you're stupid too. Anyone could climb out of that window.'

At that moment Leo came back from seeing the doctor out. It struck Bella that he looked strained, tense. She knew she ought to care, but all she felt was mild interest, that and dislike for everything about the place. Haunting her as it did a thousand times a day came the acknowledgement that without Ali there was nothing. She no longer cared about anything at Ridgeway.

'It's bedtime, Dad,' Leo said. 'Do you feel like a bath?'

Harold didn't recognize the forced cheerfulness in Leo's voice. Like an obedient child, he let himself be led away.

It was when Leo and Bella were in bed that she learnt the outcome of Dr Saunders' visit. She was on her back, trying to leave a good space between them. Then, in the darkness, she heard a strange, muffled sound.

'Leo?' Her kind nature got the upper hand. 'What's wrong, Leo?'

'Saunders is making arrangements for him to go into a home. Dad . . . in a mental home.' His voice was tight and unfamiliar. Could Leo be crying?

Much of Bella's anger at him evaporated. 'Is he bad enough for that?' She tried to sound encouraging, but her effort failed.

'Damn it, can't you see why he's doing it? Already the village will have made its mind up that Dad started it. The insurers aren't going to pay out without an enquiry. Dad'll be implicated. I'll swear on oath if necessary that he was with me all afternoon.'

'But that's not true. You know very well that he was wandering on his own. The men working here will know it's not true just as well as we do.'

'Do you imagine they'd let him down? Dr Saunders didn't

doubt my word. He's known Dad for years and understands. He's arranging for him to go into a private nursing home for the mentally impaired. He knows as well as I do that if I refuse consent then he will be charged. It must be seen as accidental, although how it could have happened if Louisa was out all the afternoon God knows. You'll have to say you were home earlier than you were if anyone takes seriously the yarn he has been spreading.'

Bella's sympathy vanished. How dare he, how *dare* he try to throw suspicion on Louisa. 'The truth is the truth,' she said, not even trying to keep the anger out of her voice, 'and if you want to lie, then it's for you to sort out your conscience. A fine sort of love you must have for Louisa if you want me to accuse her of something she didn't do just so that you can keep the man who was responsible for our losing Ali safe and comfortable. If Dr Saunders says he should be in a mental home, then that's where he should be.' Disappointment and hurt added a new hardness to her tone.

'He's not *your* father,' Leo pleaded.

'And the man he is today is not *your father* either.'

For a moment he said nothing, then, yet again, 'You really have changed, Bella.'

'Life teaches us lessons.'

Another silence until he broke it in a voice as cold and distant as hers. 'I don't see you've had anything to complain about. You fell on your feet when you came here to a better home than you'd ever had.'

This time the silence lengthened, each pretending to be asleep. Then it was Bella who spoke. She sounded calm. In truth, she felt that all emotion had been drained out of her.

'It's no use, is it, you and me.' It was a statement, not a question.

'We can't pretend our marriage was based on anything but necessity, but I did the right thing by you and, to be fair, you keep house well enough. But never mind all that, what's done is done. It's this business with Dad I can't . . . can't bear it. Saunders says he will arrange for me to take him in tomorrow afternoon. This is his last night here and he doesn't even know what's going to happen to him.'

'I don't expect Louisa is any too happy about her future either,' came Bella's sharp reply.

'Oh, she's hard-nosed. She'll pick herself up all right – her sort always do.'

Bella turned her back on him, plumped her pillows, telling him as clearly as any words that she was not prepared to argue. She longed just to escape into sleep, but it was impossible. She felt him turning her way and prayed with all the fervour she could muster that he would be fooled by her purposely deep breathing and think she was asleep. Surely tonight of all nights he couldn't expect to find exhaustion that way. He turned away and lay with his back to her.

She tried to look into the future, to imagine their life together, but she could see nothing. How wrong she had been in believing he was truly in love with Louisa, but perhaps he wasn't capable of loving any woman for life. Yet he had genuinely loved Ali, of that Bella was certain. If only she hadn't been lost to them perhaps there might have been some hope for their future. But now there was nothing. Ought she to go away, and let him divorce her for deserting him? But still she could see nothing but a thick, dark mist ahead of her, no light and no hope. Louisa had been her first and only real friend, but how could she stay in Lexleigh now that her home had gone? Perhaps she would have repair work done but that would take ages, and if Leo wasn't in love with her why would she want to stay here? There was Hamish McLaren, but Bella was sure Louisa didn't care for him in that way. So Louisa would go. If only Ali were still here – someone to love, someone to want to live for.

In the morning, despite their efforts to persuade her to stay, Louisa bid a grateful farewell to Hamish and Margaret, then drove back to Lexleigh. She knew exactly what she meant to do, but first she must write to Leo. A month ago the idea of such a letter would have been unthinkable, but on that morning she knew in her heart – as perhaps she had always known if she'd had the courage to look for the truth – that she had been no more than a passing fancy until someone else caught his eye. The knowledge didn't grieve her; indeed, it eased her conscience.

The neighbour with so much window trouble 'just happened' to see her arrive.

'Bad job it is, Miss Harding. You missed the real blaze. That came after you'd gone off with the gardener chap,' her neighbour called down to her from the open bedroom window opposite. 'No proper post for you this morning, but I did see young Bella put a note in your box.'

'Thank you, I have the key to the box, I'll get it. I was just going to call at Ridgeway but I'll see what she says first.'

The net curtain must have come off its hooks again, for the window still required attention. Louisa took the note from the box and haggled the envelope open. It was a brief message, but one that cleared her mind of everything but the stark words she read.

'Nothing wrong, is there? She's not been gone two minutes; she cut back over the stile into the field.'

Raising her hand in wordless thanks, Louisa hurried to the stile. Bella was on the far side of the ditch and level with about half the length of the field when she turned into the wood.

'No, Bella!' she spoke aloud to herself. 'Wait for me, Bella.' High heels aren't intended for recently turned soil and after a couple of steps Louisa took her shoes off and ran on her stockinged feet despite the discomfort. Once in the wood she put her shoes on, not caring that they would be ruined. Glancing at her watch, she saw it was twenty-five to eleven, which meant there was only five minutes before the express train would rush through Lexleigh Halt. As she ran, repeatedly her skirt was caught on sharp twigs and each time she tore herself free with no thought of anything but that she *must* reach Bella before the train came. The centre of the overgrown wood was dark in comparison with the autumn morning, but with relief she saw the first glimmer of a bright sky as the trees towards the edge thinned. In the distance she heard the whistle of the train as it approached and then, oh, thank God, there was Bella. She must reach her, she must!

There was a steep slope down to the railway track and Bella knew she had to time it just right; too soon and on the long, straight track the driver would see her and stop before he reached her; too late and she wouldn't be in front of it before it reached her. In a normal mental state she would have heard Louisa blundering through the bracken on the edge of the wood, but neither her night nor her morning had been normal. As she closed her eyes and lurched forward, ready to hurl herself down the slope, she felt strong arms around her.

'No!' she screamed, fighting to get free. 'Let me go, let me go!' But she knew it was too late; the express was leaving them in a cloud of sooty smoke.

'No, Bella, dear Bella.' It was not at all the way Louisa usually spoke, but the words came naturally as she held the younger woman.

'Why did you stop me?' Bella sobbed. 'Just want to die. I can't go on, Lou. I would have found Ali, I know I would.'

'And Leo? Do you think he doesn't feel the same? Share your grief with him, Bella.'

'Can't.' Bella was shaking from head to foot and crying so that it was hard to understand her words. 'Don't love him. Thought I did. We never laugh. No, I don't love him. He doesn't love me. I thought he was in love with you. Ought to have minded but I didn't. Proves I never loved him. Just want to die.' As her garbled words poured out amidst snorts and sobs, with Louisa still keeping a firm hold on her they sunk to the ground where they sat with Bella leaning against her as if for support.

'Did you leave a letter for Leo?'

Bella nodded, still struggling with sentences. 'I told him I was leaving him. There's nothing without Ali. He's taken Dad out. Last time he can take him from home. He's taking him to a mental nursing home this afternoon. Dr Saunders said so.' It was hard to understand all she said. Her short, half-formed sentences tumbled out, almost lost in the crying she couldn't control. 'I don't care. Not about any of it. Not any more. Is that wicked? Oh, Lou, why didn't you let me go? I was screwed up ready. By now it could have been over.' But her crying was getting quieter and she leant back against Louisa, clearly finding comfort in her nearness.

They stayed like that for some time, not even noticing that after rain in the night the ground was damp. Hysteria gave way to quiet misery; misery gave way to acceptance. Bella's strength seemed to come from Louisa, even though she could see no shape to the future.

There on the far side of the wood they felt cut off from all humanity. When Louisa saw that Bella's swollen eyelids had closed she still held her, her own thoughts going on a far off journey of their own. So they sat for perhaps half an hour or longer, until Bella woke with some of her hopeless misery overtaken by thankfulness that she was alive.

'Is it a sin to feel sort of hopeful?' she murmured. 'I'm walking out on Leo, I don't know what sort of a job I can get, and yet I feel – I feel *safe*. Is that wicked?'

Louisa laughed, looking down at her snagged skirt and broken shoes. 'It's a very promising start. And despite my tatty appearance, that's how I feel, too. You know the best medicine in the world? An adventure. And that's what we're going to have. But first I must brush my hair, repair my face and then buy something to wear. This is all I have. And while Leo is seeing Mr Carter settled in his new surroundings you must go back to Ridgeway and fill a case with clothes. I look like a tramp; I'm ashamed even to go into a shop in this state. Collect a hair brush when you get your things.'

Bella turned her head and gave a weak smile, but at least there was the light of hope in her eyes. 'This really is a new start – for both of us.' But she had no idea in what direction the new start was to take them.

Nothing could happen overnight but when, driving to town in the afternoon, Louisa talked to her about a plan to start a new life in Australia, Bella felt like a person rescued from the hangman's noose. She listened as Louisa told her what she had read in the newspaper about the Australian government wanting immigrants from Britain.

'But I'm not clever like you,' she said, frightened to let herself believe what she was hearing. 'I can't see that they'd want *me*. And I couldn't afford the fare to Australia.'

'But you could, Bella, It's subsidized. It will cost us nine pounds. How's that? The paper gave a whole list of people they want and we both fit the bill,' Louisa reassured her. 'I am an accountant and you, from today onwards, are my secretary.

How's that? We'll go to Perth, I'll start my own business. It was successful in Lexleigh and so it will be there. But there are things we have to clear up first: the house, your marriage, my outstanding work, and there will be medicals, I expect, and masses of forms.' Then, with a teasing smile, 'My new secretary is going to have a busy time. You do type?'

'I was taught in the orphanage.'

It was January when they left the lodgings they had found in town and returned to Lexleigh to spend their last night with Hamish and Margaret. In the afternoon, while Louisa was with the solicitor signing papers to give him Power of Attorney over all her affairs, Bella took a bunch of early snowdrops to put on Ali's grave. For a long time she knelt on the winter-cold earth, imagining the sleeping child only feet below the newly erected headstone. How could she go to the other side of the world and leave her? Never to come here and know that she was close . . . She put out her hand, rested it on the marble Leo had chosen and was shocked by the coldness even on her own chilly hand. Ali had been warm; her soft, baby-chubby flesh had smelt as fresh as a spring morning. Closing her eyes, Bella folded her arms as though she were holding her, and surely those little arms were around her neck. She moved her face in the emptiness of the cold air, and yet she knew the sweet softness of Ali's cheeks and heard her chuckle in the cold January air.

'You'll be with me, Ali, my blessed darling. Wherever I go you'll always be with me and I'll always be with you.'

Even though she knew the truth of what she said, walking away was hard. She knew that something of her would remain by that tiny grave no matter where she went or however long she lived.

The next day a 'Closed for One Day' sign was nailed to the locked gate of the nursery so that Hamish and Margaret could drive them to Southampton.

'The best is yet to come,' Louisa said as, with the ship's sirens sounding, the liner slowly pulled away from the dockside. Around them some people were keyed up and excited; others were weeping. Louisa was neither. She was confident that whatever they found on the other side of the world they would make a good life out of it. Gone was the austere, unbending woman cut out for spinsterhood. What she had become was due to Leo. He had made her whole; her confidence was no longer a façade. It was as genuine as the certainty that, just like Jessica, she and Bella were following the path of Destiny.

In the throng of people on the quay she couldn't be sure which were Hamish and Margaret but she gave a last wave anyway. Turning to speak to Bella, she was surprised to see she had her eyes closed and her arms loosely folded in front of her, while on her lovely face was the hint of a smile.

'Yes,' Bella said, opening her eyes. 'The best is yet to come. And we'll see to it that it's a really good best.'